DANIEL EVAN WEISS

THE ROACHES HAVE NO KING

LONDON / NEW YORK

JOB hous13$$26 PKA—PostScript

11-07-96 17:11:15

First published under the title *Unnatural Selection*
in the United Kingdom, Australia and New Zealand in 1990
by Black Swan Books of Transworld Publishers Ltd.

This edition first published in the United States in 1994
by High Risk Books/Serpent's Tail
180 Varick Street, New York, NY 10014
and in the United Kindom in 1996 by
High Risk Books/Serpent's Tail
4 Blackstock Mews, London N4 2BT

Reprinted 1996

Library of Congress Catalog Card Number: 94–2085

A catalogue record for this book can be obtained from
the British Library on request

Cover and book design by Rex Ray
Typeset by Loos Amalgam
Printed in Finland by Werner Söderström Oy

For John Speicher

Many-legged thanks to Pati Cockram

The locusts have no king, yet they go forth all of them by bands.

—Proverbs

Prologue

1

WHAT DOES IT MATTER when you lose a lover? At the top of the animal kingdom the answer is easy—not at all. Coitus is a great experience, right up there with excretion and gluttony. But all things end, especially good things, and the lover fades, looking again just like all the others.

Never for long. Unlike humans, who rightly worry if they will commingle again, we never do. When pheromones are calm we are sexually indifferent. When pheromones storm, these miraculous chemicals always bring us an ideally suited lover, each the equal of the last. At floor level there is no unrequited love.

As for offspring, we have a policy adopted only by certain cagey urban humans—no one knows the identity of his father. One sperm injection can fertilize a female's lifetime production of eggs—but it might not. After each go-round you can never know if the next brood is your doing or that of one of your predecessors. But after all, who would want to know a thing like that?

This is not braggadocio. When I was released into the intimidating world of *Homo sapiens*, it was their reactions to separation from their lovers that offered me first comfort. I would soon realize that man is only an eerie visitor to our ecosphere, like a jack-o'-lantern on a windy night, frightening, but already flickering and certain to go out. The reason is simple: humans cannot adapt because they are not rewarded for diversifying their gene pool. Separation engenders not a sense of satisfaction at a job well done nor a heart-pounding anticipation of the next opportunity, but instead a black, debilitating insecurity. In fact, separation ignites human passions unmatched by those occasioned by consummation.

During my first days, the Bible assaulted me with illustrations of this trait, but I refused to believe it. Later corroboration by the *Iliad*, however, made me concede its possibility. As told by Homer, the *Iliad* is the story of a man who led his countrymen to bloody death on foreign shores because his lady-friend found greener grass. I would soon learn the full account, passed down from an ancestor who was there—the word of a sober witness with compound eyes, not the drunken crowings of a blind man.

Helen was not abducted. Menelaus' garlic breath left her frigid, and she was chronically diarrheic from olive oil in her diet (and raw from wiping with grape leaves). One day Aphrotella—my ancestor, and the real heroine of this tale—heard Helen conspiring with her handmaiden to leave. Aphrotella was torn. Greece had its advantages—a family of forty could easily live off the food matted in the beard of one man, who made access easy by drinking himself to sleep after dinner every night. But even Aphrotella was disgusted by the sanitary conditions. And she had always wanted to see Troy.

While Helen toppled the furniture in her chamber, simulating her abduction by Paris, Aphrotella's pheromones drew the avid attentions of a passing stud. That evening she and Helen left for Troy. The gates opened for Helen's chariot, but it was a moment later, when Aphrotella followed, that Troy was properly conquered. Her first brood was soon born, and our new colony flourished.

Then the Greek fleet came. The foolish young men of the Greek and Trojan nations turned each other into crab chum on the gray sands of Troy. No *Homo sapiens* protested this absurd tragedy. No, it was thought the height of manliness to fight and die because a woman you'd never even met was copulating with another man.

It took the Greeks ten years, thousands of cadavers, and a huge horse to pass through the gates of Troy. Our conquest was made by one demure female in a trail of horse piss. Menelaus again had his fair Helen but, in fact, Aphrotella reported that her mistress spent most of her time alone with a plaster of Paris. And then the Greeks torched the city, killing not only most of the Trojans, but also most of Aphrotella's descendants, who by then outnumbered the Trojans by a factor of twelve thousand. Some of the survivors went back with the fleet for moussaka; others went on to do what the Greeks could not—conquer Asia and the New World.

The two versions of this tale agree: when humans are separated, or even threatened with separation, from their lovers, their behavior knows no bounds, no matter how dry or futile the romance has become. I do not gloat over this ugly knowledge. But when humans thrust the fight upon me, three thousand years after the fall of Troy, I chose to stand and face them, as anyone would, on the treacherous field of romantic distress.

Genesis

4

MY MOTHER NEVER trusted the kitchen cabinets. Since the founding of the colony it had been a tradition to unload *oothecae*—egg sacs—in the cabinets so the younglings would be near the principal food stocks. But, bloated with her brood of thirty-eight, my wonderful mother dragged all the way to the hallway so we would debut at the base of the bookcase.

She never wanted us to read. Had she ever suspected what the books would do to her babies, she would have killed us all first. She intended only that we suckle; the sweet, creamy library paste that bound the books was our mother's milk.

The moment she dropped the *ootheca* there was a stampede to get out. Churning legs pounded my head and blurred my eyes. I emerged and stumbled across the shelf to a volume with a calm earthy smell, which suggested that the book had seen a lot of use, but not for a long time. I could not make out the gold-plate stamping on the blue cover. But with the unflinching certainty of youth I climbed to the top of the spine and began to eat my way through.

I flinched many times during those months. Every page was filled with betrayal, murder, lust, vengeance, delusion, genocide, treachery, incest, or some other unspeakable vice. Why had someone chosen to disseminate these chronicles, when they should have been dumped into a pit and covered with rocks? I desperately crawled over the top of the impervious divider and into the little second section of the book. It was even worse. Now, no matter how grim the crime and hardened the criminal, everything was forgiven! As if it had never happened! I knew then that I wanted nothing to do with humans. If man did have dominion over every creeping thing that creepeth upon the earth, I would hide here and suffer only the written record of his perversions.

Alas, my mother was right; this book was a growing experience. I molted twice. The space became suffocatingly tight. It was daytime when my head squeezed from between the pages. I looked over the top of the spine. The gold letters were now sharp: I was a Bible baby.

Twenty or thirty of my kind were scavenging casually in the expansive hallway down below. I saw no murders, betrayals, or cruelty—nothing to forgive. But I already knew too much to want to live on the outside.

I jumped onto the top of the neighboring volume—an oft-thumbed paperback—and burrowed in. The stories of the *Iliad* were as unaccountable as the ones in the Bible. But for me they were fateful. I was infected with curiosity. Like an anthropologist, I had to see for myself whether these common accounts of human savagery had any merit. Luring me from my Trojan sanctuary was humanity's first triumph over my good sense.

When I reached the shelf I saw two of my siblings. Though we had quadrupled in size since we last met, I knew them immediately. "You remember Phil," said one, pointing to the other. "And I'm Columbo."

We had had no use for names in the sac. "Numbers," I said. It was all I could think of.

Phil continued with the conversation. "The more mature a language is, the more specific its sounds are. In ancient Egypt, the sound *ab* meant: to dance; heart; wall; proceed; demand; left hand; and figure. All of those. Can you imagine?"

I said, "No wonder the Lord led the Chosen from the land of Pharaoh."

"The same sound meant both 'weak' and 'strong,' another meant both 'toward' and 'away from,'" said Phil. "These early humans couldn't conceive an idea without its antithesis."

Miller came up the shelf from behind me. "Poor fucking savage. Gets set up on a blind date, and what does he know? The chick's going to be foxy or a dog, tall or squat, sharp or stupid. After they eat, or they don't, the savage gets a virgin or a whore, so he might or might not poke a pussy that's rank or sweet."

Columbo said, "No wonder they reproduced so slowly."

"They were not fruitful," I said. Only then did I realize the air was filled with the smells of exotic foods.

Columbo said, "What do you make of a sound that means all this: a small fish of the carp family; a seam of coal; a variety of Portland stone; a cut in a square sail; to clip a horse's mane; and the butt of a marijuana cigarette?"

Phil shook his head. "Extremely primitive."

"One more clue," said Columbo. "It also means one hell of a handsome insect." He waved his antennae in wide circles.

Phil laughed. "'Roach' means all that? And such an ugly sound. I'd rather be called 'ab'."

Columbo said, "Here's one from Latin: in 1758 a chap named Carolus Linnaeus decided to tidy the living world. From the word *Blatta*, which means 'shunning light,' he stamped out this classification: suborder *Blattaria*, superfamily *Blaberoidea*, family *Blattellidae*, subfamily *Blattellinae*, genus *Blattella*."

"The primitive light-shunner," said Phil. "The ostrich? The vole? The worm?"

"The rapist," said Miller.

"Satan!" I said.

Columbo said, "They are we."

"Light-shunners?" said Miller. "I was just going to catch some rays."

Columbo said, "And the species name is. . . No, you try to guess."

Miller punched the Tropics. "Light-shunning blind daters?"

"Blind daters don't shun light," said Phil.

"They should."

I said, "How about light-shunning King of Kings?"

Columbo said, "Your scientific name is. . .*Blattella germanica.*"

"But we're American!" said Phil.

Columbo said, "Yes, but if you want to talk roots, we're African. The west German humans call us the French roach, the eastern Germans call us the Russian roach, and the southern and northern Germans name us after each other. We have an image problem. But let's not forget who made up the name—the animal who calls itself '*Homo sapiens.*'"

"Latin for 'thinking faggot,'" said Miller.

Columbo said, "Humans trace *homo* to the Indo-European *dhghom-on*, meaning 'earthling.' But it's African, savannah dialect. When the hairy runt first fell out of the tree, we cried, 'Hoho!' The name stuck."

I learned that Phil had taken his name from *Classical Philology*, his first home. It was a fine choice, an old volume slathered with vintage paste, a well-worn college text now likely to remain untouched in perpetuity. Columbo had come of age in the formidable *Columbia Encyclopedia.*

EVEN IRA'S CHEAPEST BOOKS were printed in indelible ink: we never forgot our early lessons. Most of us knew and remembered them as curiosities. Only when we were under great stress could book dogma menace us by seeming real. Even then it could be suppressed. On this first day out, my mind swirled with characters from my Book. I knew they could never get the better of me.

But some citizens were affected profoundly, tragically. Many books had been opened so few times that air never permeated the pages. Infants who chose these books were destroyed. We held an annual commemoration for the many lost in *Gravity's Rainbow* and *Finnegan's Wake.* Others, like the philosophers, labored through oxygen-poor atmospheres that stripped their natural immunities to book toxins. These poor souls were the true imprinted. Words deprived them of the 350 million years of *Blattella* wisdom in their genes.

I soon found that one bit of written rot had had a persistent effect on the colony—the *germanica* in our classification. The idea held the colony like a long fad. Two generations before mine the apartment was overrun with Heidis and Siegfrieds, and my generation was not much better.

I wouldn't have thought much about it except for this: we light-shunning Germans lived under the aegis of Ira Fishblatt, a candle-lighting Jew. From this day on I was wary not only of his Old Testament excesses, but also of his modern ethnic vengeance. I awoke many mornings expecting cataclysm. When it came, I felt like an unhappy prophet.

But I only had these thoughts when I let the written word get the better of me. The war was not religious at all. It was biological, caused by a population crisis. Our finely balanced ecosphere would tip when Ira overloaded it with *Homo yidus.*

THAT DIDN'T HAPPEN for some time. I was born during a time of great prosperity. In fact, I came out to a ceremony that would have done justice to a bumper harvest.

Ira was living in the intermittent company of a self-styled Gypsy woman, whom I soon came to adore. She described the timing of significant events like traffic accidents. The night Mercury crossed into Taurus, say. The night I first met her, dinner crossed into wall.

After speaking with the citizens of the bookshelf my first day out, I was drawn toward the source of the thickening aromas. It was the Gypsy, preparing one of her Eastern European specialties, her root cuisine.

Ira, whom I had been hearing about for several hours, came home at what I would soon recognize as his regular time. He was as unprepossessing a foe as a roach could hope for. He picked the lid off the pot. Steam fogged his glasses. "Mmm. What's that, goulash?"

"You're not sure?"

He dipped in a wooden spoon. "Tastes good. A little heavy on the paprika."

She pushed him to the side and took a taste. "It's perfect." She slapped the cover down. "What would you know about Hungarian cooking, you and your pot roasts and chicken soup. You call that cooking?"

Ira shrugged. "You're the expert."

"I put in exactly a palmful, as usual."

"These potatoes must be smaller. That's it." He started to leave the kitchen.

She challenged him. "You make dinner next time."

"I work during the day."

And then came my first experience of human fury in the flesh. She turned pink, her brow furrowed, lips trembling and nostrils flaring. "You rub that in my face every day."

"I'm not rubbing anything in your face."

"Maybe the martinis at your three-hour working lunch numbed your taste buds."

"I never drink at lunch."

"Neither do I."

Pause. "I have to go change."

"Don't you dare walk out that door."

"I'll be right back."

"Don't you leave me here with all this terrible goulash."

"Oh, it's fine. That's not what I said." He shook his head and walked into the dining room.

She looked at the pot the way I knew Moses looked at the Golden Calf. "Try it one more time." She walked to the doorway and hurled the pot. It slammed against the wall beside him, spraying his suit with flaming red sauce, and sending great gobbets all over the room.

Ira was immobilized, speechless.

"I'm not taking any more of your superior shit," she said, and walked out the front door.

Soon he was in pursuit. Legions I hadn't seen suddenly swept down from hiding places to plunder. Meat and potatoes and vegetables disappeared into their ravenous mouths, their faces and limbs dripping with mammalian blood. Only the paprika was spared. It was thrilling to eat my first meal beside virile *Blattellae* twenty times my size, to march en masse through thickening sauce, to attack as the Book said men did thousands of years ago.

At the same time I was uneasy. Plenty like this was usually visited with punishment. In the Book it is not considered plenty when insects eat well. It's called plague. But how could we be punished when we are the punishment?

I toasted the resolution of my first moral crisis with a juicy globule of fat, lukewarm and with the first hint of a skin, the way I have liked it best since.

"There'll be plenty more. She'll be back. They have a scene every week or two," said an adult named Bismarck.

THOUGH THE GOULASH hurling was an exceptional event, the Gypsy was truly hot-blooded, aggressive, and insistent—a natural ally for us. Her sexual ruthlessness gave us many hours of safe time to scout and harvest. She had no regard for Ira's household rules and regimens; she exercised power over him by defying them. In the kitchen she was munificent. If a recipe called for two tablespoons, at least one more would find the countertop. A cup of wine? She'd pour us one, too. Ingredients spilled and flowed over every surface, into cracks, behind cabinets. She never picked up her droppings—after all, she had already made the floor filthy, so what was the use of retrieving something too dirty to eat?

When I was born, the colony was based in the back of the kitchen cabinets, as it had been for seventy-five years. We never had to forage. We traveled only for treats the Gypsy left, and only in the safest circumstances.

One day I descended to the counter to a pool of potato leek soup.

Bismarck was already eating. "I wish she'd go easy with the paprika." Crusting soup made him look like an albino. He looked at me and belched. "Our human population is generous. But when it changes I'll yearn for the days when I had food like this to complain about."

Still new to this life, and quickly growing accustomed to its riches, I was alarmed by the suggestion that it could end.

Bismarck preened his mouthparts. "The others don't want to hear it either. But don't worry. We'll get by. We always do."

That evening, I joined him on reconnaissance and began my lifelong study of the contemporary human. It wasn't a pretty picture. I knew biblical hygiene: pick your nose and your ass often enough to keep them open, and change your rags when they start to fester. The gray funk on your skin protects it against insects and infections, but fall into the water once a season anyway, just to impress the ladies. However, Ira, the modern man, scoured himself and changed his designer rags daily. His orifices were dredged like inlets, left ripe for infection. Though he brushed his teeth relentlessly, they were loaded with fillings.

His treatment of the apartment was just as obsessive and irrational. By ritual dousings of toxic solvents, he not only regularly thwarted the Gypsy's efforts (on those surfaces he could see), but went so far as to eliminate dirt insufficient to support the tiniest, hardiest life. I didn't understand why.

Bismarck said, "Class *Mammalia* has this thing about show. They bang antlers, beat chests, work out on Nautilus machines. Ira scrubs."

Today's lunch was burgers. Bismarck wiped red from his antennae and jumped.

"Just ketchup," I said.

"Thanks. . . She messes; that's her show. That's why they're doomed. By cleaning after her instead of beating her, Ira is being civilized. But she hates him for it."

Reud was eating with us today. Another native of the bookshelves, his first home had been *Civilization and Its Discontents*, an environment so horrifying that he ran out before he could consume the *F* from the author's name. Now he said, "A very free interpretation."

Bismarck said, "I don't care about the theory. I'm telling you, she's going to leave, and when she does Ira is going to turn on us like you've never seen. Have you heard about the Great Depression?"

I wasn't sure I wanted to.

"There was a fumigation twelve years ago. The colony had to flee over exposed hallways and treacherous streets and sidewalks. Most who ended up in public projects wished they had stayed to die in the gas. You baby boomers don't know how bad things can get."

"Where should we go?" I said.

"There is no place to go," said Bismarck.

"Then shouldn't we start storing food somewhere?"

"Ants do that. They're so obsessed with protecting themselves against a bad day that they never have a good one." Bismarck spat. "That's not living."

"Then what do we do?"

Bismarck did not answer.

Reud smiled at me avuncularly. "Eat, bubbala, fortify yourself."

A fine idea. And so resolved, I dipped my head back to the puddle of hamburger grease, only to find that they had finished it.

The Gypsy returned to the apartment late one night, after several nights away. She didn't stop to take off her coat, not even to make us a snack, but went right to the bedroom and snapped on the light. "Let's have this out once and for all. Oh God, Ira, how can I even talk to you in those pajamas. What are you, a grandfather?" Several of us ran down the hall to watch. I was breathless with fear. "You wore me down. The mind of a lawyer, Ira, for God's sake. Who could stand it?"

He sat up and felt for his glasses on the night table. "Did you just get here?"

"Don't cross-examine me. That's just what I mean."

"Are you suggesting that I misled you about being an attorney?"

"Oh, Ira, you jerk, don't you see? You always play by the rules, Ira. Rules don't make my pussy wet." Ira started. She laughed nastily. "Women want excitement, passion, hard cocks. I'm a free spirit. You're suffocating me."

"Suffocating you? Suffocating you? I hardly see you. . ."

As he sputtered, she thrust a carpet bag into his hands. "Hold this." She picked up pieces of rumpled clothing from the floor and bureau top and threw them in. She pulled him to the bathroom and continued.

He held the bag open while he implored. "I love you. I treat you well. We make love all the time. I don't know what you're talking about. Where have you been all these nights? That's what we should be discussing."

She stopped and looked at him. She was a small, dark, exotically beautiful woman. But now I saw the strain in the lines of her face. Her eyes darted. Her mouth was shriveled with tension from a conflict that had nothing to do with the man in the blue pajamas. Bismarck was right. Ira could never handle her.

She sighed. "Maybe it's not you, Ira. Maybe I just can't make it with a nice guy. Don't think I regret it. It was a worthwhile experience." She took the bag and snapped it closed.

"An experience? I love you. That's not just an experience."

"Oh, Ira, let's leave love out of it." She walked to the living room, and he donned his bathrobe and went after her. We raced after his flip-flops, two big tongues clicking with rude sarcasm. At the front door she reached into her bag and said, "I won't need these anymore." His eyes had not adjusted to the low light, and he was no athlete anyway. The keys struck his face. His glasses crashed to the floor a second before the door slammed.

The bells on the Gypsy's boots, which had become the masters of my salivary glands, faded down the stairs. The second greatest woman I would ever know walked out of my life.

"*Finis,*" said Bismarck. "She's never taken it this far before."

THE CHANGE in Ira showed immediately. He was desperate, scared, whiny. The next day he began to make long, morbid telephone calls to his cousin Howie. Soon Howie stopped picking up, and Ira was forced to make shorter calls to Howie's answering machine.

Ira walked the apartment mournfully. I was sure he was searching for a pair of the soiled panties or one of the dog-eared volumes of poetry that the Gypsy had used to stake her claim to the apartment; if he found one, the claim still stood. It would be a pretext to call her. But for once she had been thorough.

His clothing soon began to replace hers over the chair backs and between the sofa cushions. He grew more careless in his hygiene. A bacterial odor began to precede him.

Though Bismarck's famine failed to materialize, there were disturbing signs in Ira's behavior. Already halfway through possible reproductive life, he lost a mate. Any other organism would seek another immediately. What would it take for a skinny, liberal, Jewish lawyer, forty years old, single, solvent, and without children? Wasn't he the archetypal catch for a generation of modern women who'd neglected to pull their diaphragms until their time had just about passed?

He was struck down by what I now recognize as Romantic Mourning Syndrome. A perversion sanctified in human song and verse, RMS plunges its victims into self-pity, debilitation, and sometimes self-destruction. It nullifies those qualities, such as dignity and self-possession, needed for the only cure: replacement of the lost love. It also renders the victim immune to the restorative knowledge that usually he is far better off without the lost love.

"How did human genes come this far?" I asked Reud.

"The mystery of love," he said. "I think."

Shelley went on and on about love's chemistry, but life's chemistry depends on the continuous purging of a body's antigens. Ira did not seem to know this. Adam hadn't, either.

But I had no complaint; Ira's RMS served us well.

"The shikse finally takes her schmutz someplace else—thank God—and what do you do, Ira? You work overtime to make up for her," said Faith Fishblatt, his mother.

"It's not healthy to be obsessive about cleaning," he said. A Gypsy line. He had truly fallen.

"Healthy? Aunt Jemima couldn't make this place healthy if she worked time and a half." Faith piled cleaning implements—a mop and pail, broom and dustpan, even the vacuum cleaner—in the living room.

Ira sat. "Stop it, Mother. If your doctor saw you he'd have you put away."

She peeled off her bandana and primped her hair. "All right, suffer. Live like a swine. Let that Bohemian go on tormenting you. Who am I to interfere."

The utensils sat in the middle of the room for a week like a great trophy, swords of surrender to us.

Ira cooked less now, but for the first time he started to eat in front of the TV, greatly enlarging the area of food fall. Dishes piled up in the sink. Long escape lines had always made this an unpopular feeding ground, but now the magnificent booty justified the risk.

Cuisinart stuck a human eyelash to his clypeus with saliva, twisted it into a handlebar mustache, and greeted citizens as they arrived at the rim of the sink. "*Monsieurs, mesdames*, good evening, *bon soir. Enchanté.* For this evening might I recommend albacore, from the Pacific Ocean, aged six days, with a side of smartly turning mayonnaise, and ah! *monsieurs et mesdames*, she is bursting with gas like a fine sparkling Burgundy. *Bon appetit!*"

His antennae and all six legs bound with alfalfa sprouts, Houdini instructed that he be dumped into a rank mush of horseradish and gefilte fish. Fifteen minutes later his head broke the surface all legs freed to an antenna-storm of applause.

Bismarck was now taking ridicule for his dire prediction. "What do you think, Numbers? Am I a fool?"

I shrugged as I worked on a grain of brown rice sticking to the television channel selector.

He said, "An animal cannot live forever on the brink. It either dies or recovers. I'm afraid Ira will not die." He put a leg on my carapace. "I have seen the future of this apartment. . . Interested?"

I pointed to the dining room with my left antenna. "Prosperity is just around the corner?"

"Grubstein."

Maybe they were right; maybe he was a fool. I could not believe our future was large-footed, thick-ankled, big-bottomed, plump-bellied, pendulous-breasted, wide-lipped, narrow-eyed, half again as wide as the Gypsy and several inches shorter. Ruth Grubstein was a friend of Ira's cousin Howie and an occasional visitor with him to the apartment. Ira had proven to me that males of this unsightly species will endure unnatural sacrifices to attain females marginally less unsightly. Blight though he was, I could not see him at peace with this woman's appearance.

But there was something about Bismarck's confidence that continued to make me doubt. I sat in the molding above Ruth, Ira, and Howie the following week. Ira was polite but still preoccupied. Howie made gentle fun of him. Ruth had a calming influence on the affair that I didn't quite understand. But Ira showed no appreciation of it nor interest in her.

Ruth kept returning. In the succeeding weeks she gently directed conversations so Ira could relate them to legal aid for the wretched, the one topic he still spoke about with enthusiasm.

One afternoon she took from the shelf and opened a book entitled *The Conquest of New Spain.* "Is this a college text? I took a course on Mexican culture when I was in school. I'll never forget an illustration, an etching I think, of the Aztecs tearing the hearts out of the conquistadores while they were still alive." She snapped the book closed. Two baby *Blattella* Cortezes screamed.

Ira told her the little he remembered of Montezuma's tragic character. Howie told a story of Montezuma's revenge, in which Howie had been the tragic character. Ruth laughed. "I kind of had a crush on Montezuma—the vulnerable prince. I'm amazed I remember anything after all this time. Probably because I never had to take the final. We boycotted that year—the war, racism in America, the university's expansion into the community. It seems so long ago now. What's happened to idealism?" Ira's eyes were alert. She was awakening him.

One day the following week, as she was making cappuccino, she started on the pots and dishes in the sink. She continued to reduce the pile at every opportunity, and vanquished it a month later. When in the living room, she would rise and slyly pick up one of the strewn articles of clothing and deposit it in the hamper in the bathroom. "Does she have a bladder infection?" Ira asked Howie after her fourth sortie in one afternoon. Soon her tidiness grew infectious.

"Getting the idea?" said Bismarck.

"She's still just a visitor," I said. "She has many trials ahead."

At her first meeting with Ruth, Faith Fishblatt unleashed a peroration on the decay of values in her son's generation, the choice of quick cheap sex over enduring commitment, and the damned shame that people didn't know how to make each other happy anymore.

Ira rolled his eyes.

"What do you think, honey?" she said to Ruth. Her red eyebrows rose in challenge.

Ruth smiled and said, "I think you're right."

Later that afternoon Ruth took down recipes that Faith swore were worth their weight in gold.

But Ruth's primary adversary was the Gypsy. One night behind the leek soup in the cabinet, Sufur said, "The Gypsy show up, she beat Ruth big ass without touchin' it or sayin' nothin'. Chubby never show her face again."

"Hah!" said Reud. "Compared to Ruth, she's built like a boy. That's the problem with this species, core gender confusion."

"Ruth wouldn't even ask Ira. She'd recognize the mandate of the people and leave," said Rosa Luxemburg. I wasn't sure I believed her, but I certainly did like the way she smelled as she said it.

"What makes you think she feels she's facing superior pheromones?" said Bismarck.

Rosa smiled. "What do humans care for pheromones? It's exploitational material, like the cover of *Vogue*, that matters to them."

Reud said, "Ruth is the real female here."

Bismarck agreed. "Don't underestimate her."

"I don't," said Rosa. "It's Ira I'm forced to underestimate. Men." I nodded and moved closer to her. Something was trying to happen in my little body.

Perhaps retrospection is foolish, but I think it was our colony's greatest tragedy that the Gypsy did not immediately return in the flesh. At her leisure Ruth could vanquish her image inside Ira's febrile mind. Her tactics were ingenious; she gently picked at his scabs until he hemorrhaged the Gypsy all over her. After the first opening, it took little to initiate hours of puling about the baffling and tragic separation. Long after Ira's emetic confessions had driven Howie and the rest of us away, Ruth sat beside him on the living room sofa with sympathetic ear and soothing tongue. Ira treated her like a selfless confidante, heedless of her womanly pride. Ruth bore it well. This troubled me, until Rosa pointed out that this was a temporary exercise; Ruth had no intention of being a permanent emotional slop bucket. While I was more comfortable thinking of Ruth as selfish and ambitious—and therefore natural—at the same time I feared a natural Ruth as a more formidable barrier to the return of my beloved Gypsy.

Soon Ruth was in complete command. Ira was reviving. I could feel the great dead weight of his dependence shift from the Gypsy to the woman who had chosen to hear about her. Still, three months later, he made none of the embarrassing gestures of human sentiment. He showed no sexual interest. I clung to my hopes for the Gypsy.

One night, as several of us chipped at a blackened plaque of tomato sauce on the stove—so quickly was our easy food dwindling—I said, "Explain this to me. Did you ever hear of two animals of late reproductive age consorting for months without copulating?"

Columbo said, "Let me see. Yes, there is a subspecies of barnacle that will hold off reproduction for weeks in the presence of high concentrations of raw sewage."

"That's it?" I said.

"The only one. And of course nuns and priests."

Bismarck said, "I know Ruth is a functioning female. After that talk yesterday about the ACLU, I got caught in the wake of her skirt. It reeked of hormones. I think Ira is gland-dead."

Rosa grimaced. "If only. I was in the bedroom the other night and he hit me with a tissue loaded with seed. Ugh. At least it was neatly folded." The image of her at impact sped my heart.

Clausewitz spat out a mouthful of carbon. "It's her looks. He'll never accept them."

Reud said, "Humans like the way humans look. They even take pictures."

"And slugs like the way slugs look," said Columbo. "But then, they don't see very well."

"Now *that's* natural selection," said Bismarck.

He and Sufur slapped antennae.

The following weeks were harrowing; every innocent gesture set me on edge. Then, at eleven thirty-five on a Monday night, the phone rang. At eleven o'clock Ira had made a final round of the apartment, hung up his clothes, treed his shoes, and showered. At eleven-twenty he had peeled back the covers of his crisply made bed and gotten in. This recently restored routine never varied by more than a few minutes.

He answered sleepily. "Hello. Ruth?. . . Huh?. . . Start again. . . You lost your keys?. . . In a cab?. . . What was his name?. . . How about earlier in the day?. . . Did you look. . . How did you get in?. . . Was the super still up?. . . Oh boy, you're going to hear about that at Christmas."

I climbed the night table so I could hear Ruth's voice. "I keep walking around, looking for a sign that someone's been here. I'll die if he went through my things."

She was speaking with more animation and at a higher pitch than I had ever heard her. But was she upset enough?

"I'm sorry for carrying on like this, Ira. I'm just real nervous. Do you want to go back to sleep?"

I thought it would be better for everyone if he did. I looked for something on the night table to push over onto his head.

"Don't be silly," said Ira. "What are you going to do now?"

"I want to stay here but I know I wouldn't sleep."

"Don't you have any Valium?"

"I don't want to be sedated. What would happen if someone came in, a psychopath or a rapist—I don't know, Ira, I'm upset."

Ira reached for his glasses and looked at the clock. He said, "Don't you have anyone you could stay with, just for tonight? You can get the lock changed in the morning."

"No, not really. I couldn't call anyone now, it's so late. I'm sorry I called you so late, Ira. If I wasn't so scared I wouldn't have. Every noise makes me jump."

Bismarck walked onto the night table.

Ira rose on one elbow. "Tell me your address. I'll be right there."

Ruth hesitated, then said, "That's really sweet of you, but I can't stay here any longer. I've got to get out."

"But where to?"

"I don't know. . .just out. . ."

In a moment she had her invitation. Bismarck dropped his head. He knew better than to gloat; he was going to suffer with the rest of us.

Ruth must have been talking from a phone extension by the door, coat and bag at her feet, because she was over in astonishing time. Ira had barely finished brushing his teeth again when the buzzer sounded. She dropped her bag miserably. If it wasn't a ring of keys I heard, she had brought along her scrap iron collection. She buried her head tearfully in to his chest, locking her arms around him. Her massive bosom pushed into his stomach. Perfume rose to his nostrils.

Three weeks later she moved in. "I hope you're satisfied," Julia Child said to Bismarck.

The Terror

TWO WEEKS AFTER Ruth had moved in, Bismarck and I spent an afternoon scouting the bookcase. Though there had been no radical change in our food supply, we were planning for the day we might have to harvest the rest of the library paste. We were shocked to find that there had been severe overgrazing by our swelling population. In fact the entire library had been devalued—many of Ira's old volumes had been replaced by Ruth's newer ones, bound with inedible, space-age adhesive.

"Let's do this some other time," I said.

As we descended from the shelf, Reud squeezed out of the spine of *Beyond the Pleasure Principle*, tergites and sternites cracking against the book's brittle headband. "Thanatos!" he exclaimed. The day Ruth had moved in, he returned to the bookcase, desperate for more understanding. Though I resented my biblical burden, his was a more terrible knowledge to carry around.

Bismarck and I exchanged annoyed glances; we were not in the mood for his intricate pardons of human behavior.

Reud jumped to the shelf and intercepted us. "The death wish. It's true! And it gave me such heartburn when I was young."

"It's a death wish to stand on this shelf in the light," I said.

Reud's eyes were aflame. "That human, the female. Have you watched her? Resourceful, intelligent, a superb manipulator. And have you seen those huge glands? Hubba hubba! If I were a few years younger. . ."

"You're only six months old," Bismarck interrupted.

Reud continued. "What does she know about her chosen mate? That his last choice had the instincts of a black widow spider. That in times of crisis he weakens and becomes easy prey for disease. If she mixes genes with him, she will doom her fine lineage. Why is she doing it? Freud saw the death wish in the individual. I think it runs throughout the species."

Bismarck nodded. "I've always thought so. Psychiatrists, neonatologists, transplant surgeons, social workers, Democrats—these humans are esteemed for maximizing the reproductive success of those who minimize the chance of survival of the species."

"So it must be the ineptitude of these professionals that guards the species," I said.

"Yes, that's it," said Reud, descending over the spine of Malinowski to a lower shelf. "Thanatos has to be inept, yes, or it couldn't be at all. . ."

This conversation stuck in my mind long after I returned to the kitchen. I carefully watched Ruth come in. When she took off her suit jacket, the straight skirt clearly showed that her hips were wide, perfect for bearing egg sacs, and her legs were thick and sturdy. Her fat, spread all over her body, even in her knees and her neck, guaranteed survival through short famines and cold spells. And yet she was considered an unattractive woman.

The cabinet doors yowled as she started to make dinner. "Ira, this kitchen is shot. The cabinets don't really close anymore. The countertop is cracked. Why don't you get it redone?"

"The landlord would raise the rent by a lot more than the job would be worth," said Ira.

"Then we should do it. I always wanted to plan a kitchen."

"I don't know," he said.

"With these doors you'll get bugs."

"I know how to keep them under control."

Hundreds of citizens gorging in the cabinet hooted.

Later in the week, Ira tore off a corner of the wallpaper, making a frightening, brittle noise. "This is as old as I can remember. And you can't even make out the pattern in the flooring. Can you see the little horsies?"

Ruth said, "What are you doing?"

"The stuff is linoleum. They don't even make linoleum any more. I got some of these appliances from my mother on her thirtieth anniversary, when she got new ones. Even then they were old."

He paused. I didn't like his smile. Then he said, "It's all arranged. The whole thing's being remodeled. Welcome home."

She clapped. "Really?" They kissed.

Later on in the cabinet Bismarck said, "Doom. I never thought she'd strike so hard so fast."

"The end of an era," said Kotex wistfully.

Clausewitz barked, "What is this talk? We will anticipate the enemy's next move, establish new lines, maintain pressure."

Snot said, "We took these cabinets, and we'll take the new ones."

"Ruth made him do it," I said. "We have to get rid of her."

"No, no," said Reud. "It's the Gypsy. Her droppings are all over the kitchen, and Ruth is cleansing the apartment of her. It's ritual murder. After this she'll stop."

Bismarck said, "Once she does this, who cares if she stops?"

Where was the food going to come from? There just wasn't enough outside the cabinets to support a colony of this size.

Sufur strutted in under the cabinet door. "Yo, man, you rappin' came clear down the other end of the room. What you tryin' to do, get gassed?"

"Did you hear the news?" Rosa said.

"Yeah, ain't that too fine?" He looked around the cabinet. "What's wrong with you? They gonna be tearin' up the wall. We gonna be gettin' back to the wall cavity, and then we slide in the cabinets any time, easy, from behind. Never walk the floor again. Great big space, warm all year round. Paradise! You oughtta get out there and kiss that bitch's big butt."

The cabinet was silent. No one had thought of that. We, history's optimists, assumed change would be for the worse. Was this clever psychology by Ira, or were we already losing our nerve?

After he and Ruth went to sleep, a hundred citizens scouted the apartment's woodwork, and in the dining room discovered the baseboard that became our home. We began moving food from the cabinets to the baseboard. Neither Bismarck nor I felt the ignominy of acting like an ant.

When, two nights later, Ira left his plans on the counter, we learned about the cabinets, the flooring, and the appliance models that would be serving up food for our future generations. Sufur was right; the drawings were certainly promising.

We transported food every night until Ira and Ruth moved the remaining stocks from the cabinets into boxes in the pantry. Ira laid a breastwork of boric acid around the boxes—a strange gesture for a man who knew his bugs were under control.

The next evening, Ruth stood on a chair and put her head into the cabinet. "What are all these little dots?" she said, spotting generations of our feces. With a sponge she wiped them out, along with the remaining food and the mementoes we hadn't had time to move.

She took one final look, then reached to the back. "What's this?" she said, yanking out some rolled-up bills.

"The money? Just a little safe-keeping. I like to have cash around, in case of emergency," said Ira.

"Safe-keeping? There are hundreds of dollars here. They should be earning interest. Don't you believe in cash machines?"

"My grandmother used to tell me an old Jewish saying: 'Keep a third of your wealth in cash, in case you have to run away in a hurry, a third in gold, in case the goyim won't take your cash, and a third in real estate, in case the goyim won't sell you land.'"

Ruth laughed. "So you've got your lease, a few gold fillings, and some dirty money stuck in your cabinets. That's very traditional, Ira."

He took the bills from her. "It can't hurt. You never know."

When the buzzer sounded at eight o'clock the next morning, the entire colony was lined up in the hall molding to greet our savior. In shuffled a stooped, middle-aged Asian man.

Ira brought him into the kitchen and showed him the plans. "The new refrigerator will open the other way," said Ira.

The Asian narrowed his eyes.

"The refrigerator will open the other way," Ira said, slower and louder. Like all humans, he refused to accept that his world was not the only world.

The Asian compressed his face, and deep weathered lines formed.

Ira returned to the plan, pointing to each symbol and then to the corresponding object in the room. Now the Asian smiled and nodded.

After Ira and Ruth left, the Asian spent hours poring over the plan. He walked to the threshold and looked back into the room. He held the spot, eerily, for thirty minutes. Suddenly he leapt across the room with an agility I had never seen in a human. When he reached the window he froze again and studied the plan. Then, to our amazement, he left without touching the kitchen. We were left uneasy.

That night I made a point of sharing biscuit crumbs with Rosa. As we ate, one of her antennae crossed mine, and the perfume she delivered electrified me. I had grown quickly. Before, she had frustrated and paralyzed me, but today I suddenly knew all the answers.

I dropped a crumb; I wanted only her. I turned to take her right there, beside the dining room table. But then I remembered the moment of this night, and in a rare instance of *Blattella* sentimentality, I throttled my biology and led her into the kitchen and up the wall to the cabinet above the sink. Here is where I had fantasized I would first exchange chemicals with her, among the colanders, spare pot holders and candlesticks, now packed away in the pantry. We slipped under the door, which was cracked promiscuously open. I savored the faint moistness, the smell of decay of the oak surface and of the food once kept here. There was even something sensuous about walking over the gently warped wood. Piles of boric acid, long since hardened and benign, still lined the perimeter like park benches. The fragrance of the cabinet blended magically with Rosa's chemistry, and the urgency of my initiation, and of our one last chance in this doomed romantic setting, drove us to rut extravagantly, like young humans, until the early morning.

Ajax, Ivory, Hefty, Windex, Spic 'n' Span, and the Raid orphans were among those who returned for a last night in the cabinet below the sink. Bismarck and Barbarossa went too, having grown up in a box of steel wool. Melancholy filled the molding when we met in the morning.

At eight o'clock the Asian reappeared, carrying a satchel. After Ira and Ruth left, the Asian meticulously inspected the cabinet edges along the walls. I wondered how he could perpetrate the expected violation with ancient hand tools. He undid screws and bolts, poked at the plaster, and then, poised like a martial arts master, sprang at the cabinets, pulling them out quickly, almost silently. The plaster crumbled in one place; the rest of the wall was intact.

We looked at Sufur.

"No sweat," he said. "When he be puttin' them back up, the plaster all gonna go."

That night we took a closer look, and found that the walls were in better shape—that is, more flawed—than we thought. Many little chunks of plaster had fallen out, leaving holes large enough for us but so small that the Asian wouldn't bother with them.

The following day the Asian did not appear. Three loud white men with mustaches and large bellies stripped and replaced the old floor. The new refrigerator arrived in the afternoon. It opened the other way.

The holes in the plaster beckoned. "Colonize the cavity now, while we still have a chance," said Clausewitz. "Never depend on the grace of enemy."

"Now?" I said. "But what if we get trapped in there?"

"Be cool, no hurry," said Sufur.

"He couldn't seal all those holes," said Rosa. "Not if he's working for profit."

Poe had decided. "At length I would be avenged," he said, picking up a body-length of spaghettini. "This is a point definitely settled." He disappeared through a hole in the wall. I could not answer my fears, and for all his iron, neither could Clausewitz. In fact, the rest of the colony stayed outside to wait and see.

My misgivings about the Asian were soon borne out. With a little bowl of putty and a spatula, he spent a week filling the innumerable cracks and irregularities that had been our hope. As the light changed during the day, he used shadows to expose minuscule imperfections.

"My, he is thorough," said Ruth.

"He's an old-world artisan," said Ira, proudly.

"Can you introduce him to the concept of 'finish this year'?"

But the old-world workmanship was an inadequate explanation for this man's efforts. By finishing surfaces that would not show, he did nothing but threaten to wall our colony from the Promised Land and leave us in a vinyl desert. Man has been a destroyer since Genesis, but unlike his predecessors, the Asian destroyed without passion or self-righteousness.

Columbo said, "In the western world, he's happy to find someone shorter than he is to beat on."

"I'm not sure he is after us," Rosa said. "He might want to stretch out his employment, to bleed Ira, a capitalist oppressor."

Two days later the Asian held up his little arms to indicate a sheet of plasterboard. He pointed to the one sizable hole in the wall and made a face of dismay. Ira shook his head and said, "No, the cabinet will cover it." The Asian repeated his gestures. "No. We'll leave it. Too much money. Too. . .much. . . money," Ira repeated slowly. Surely that was universally intelligible.

Later that week the wallpaper was hung, an impervious plastic of pinkish pastel. It did not cover the hole, which would end up behind the cabinets. Still, I felt foolish for having taken for granted the black-eyed susans, designer camouflage, that dotted the old paper. The new stuff might as well have been covered with cross-hairs.

The cabinets arrived. "Factory-built for easy installation," said Ira. "Get this done quickly." He pointed to his watch. The Asian looked at his own watch.

The Asian spent three days carving the edges of the cabinets to conform to the gentle irregularities of the wall. Dissatisfied with the holes already drilled through the back, he drilled two of his own.

Ira lost patience. He stood over the cabinets, still piled on the floor, and said, "No plasterboard, no shaving. You put up now. Remember deal; you do job quick, I help with Immigration." The last word jerked the Asian's eyes wide open.

Bismarck said, "There's the answer. The longer he dawdles, the longer he stays."

"You don't think this Jewish defender of the oppressed would let this tired, poor, huddled man be deported, do you?" I said.

"No, but he wouldn't be above letting him fear it to get the kitchen done," said Bismarck.

The cabinets went up the next day, and that night the colony blanketed them. The man was a fine artisan. Everything was level, all joints snug. The doors' thick flanges fit tightly into the frames. Ira had bought well. As I walked the perimeter of the door above the sink I discovered the most fantastic thing—I could not get in. A roach could not get into a cabinet.

Rosa and I had been planning an initiation for these cabinets. Now fear made me indifferent to her. There was one large hole in the wall. If I couldn't get to it through the cabinet, I'd go over the top and get to it behind the cabinet. But the craftsmanship was too good; the cabinet fitted the wall perfectly. I began scratching desperately at the wallpaper.

Rosa tried to restrain me.

My mind was racing. "I'll tell you what's going to happen. This wood is not dry. It's going to shrink. And then there's going to be a gap so big that we're going to walk through it, side by side, and right into that wall."

"Sounds good," said Rosa soothingly.

Bismarck appeared. "When the cans and bottles go in, the cabinets are going to pull away at the top."

That night I kept thinking: why should the cabinets pull away? The old ones didn't. The wood probably was dry; and even if it wasn't, it shrank slowly. What could we do until then?

The Assassination of Rosa Luxemburg

"DON'T PUT THAT THERE."

"Why not?"

"Vegetable soup goes to the right of tomato soup. It's alphabetical."

"I see."

"Don't put that there."

"Cream of mushroom comes before lentil in my dictionary."

"But it's mushroom, cream of. It wouldn't make sense to have all the cream soups together."

"Yes, of course. I should have thought of that."

The night following our discovery of the Asian's treachery, Ira and Ruth flaunted their wealth of food as they moved it from the boxes into the impregnable cabinets.

Ira stopped and looked at her. "Now what?" she said.

"You can't put matzoh meal next to matzoh ball soup."

"OK, Mr. Alphabet. What goes in between?"

"Boxes in the left cabinets, cans in the right. *B* before *C*. It's all alphabetical."

FOR THE FIRST time in my young life I witnessed signs of resignation in the colony, which I instinctively knew was out of our character and boded ill. Clausewitz, who until now had gone so far as to avoid even passive sentence structures, said, "We're going to have to wait for him to make a mistake. But when he does. . ."

The entire colony retired early to the dining room baseboard.

The next night I returned to the kitchen with Rosa. Kotex, her sister, was already there. She was pushing her head into a tumbleweed of hair and dust that had been formed and blown across the floor by the refrigerator fan.

Rosa started toward her, legs laboring on the new vinyl. "Don't eat that! Where's your dignity?"

The dust roll disintegrated, covering Kotex with grime. She found no food. I had no idea what she was thinking.

"There are important things to do," Rosa said to her. "Why don't you go on reconnaissance?"

"Why bother."

"Why bother?" Rosa exploded. "Give me that." She reached for a small clump of dust.

Kotex pulled it away, then crashed it over Rosa's head, where it stuck like an oversized crown of thorns. It slowly fell to her sides in pieces. She and her sister looked identical in their filth.

"I won't allow it!" Rosa said, and ran from the room.

I did not see her the following day. That evening I decided to go alone to find food.

It was hard work crossing the floor. The factory coating on the vinyl pulled at my legs, and the pits in the texture of it wrenched my joints. Pits might help hide dirt in a normal kitchen; they would be wasted here.

I reached the base cabinet. Polyurethane made it easy to grip, but not so easy to release. I struggled to the counter and descended into the bottom of the sink, an area uncomfortably far from safety.

After taking a drink I looked up. I realized that I didn't have a reasonable plan. Why was I intent on scaling the towering wall cabinets? I not only doubted I would find food, I had no reason to think I could get in at all. I decided to come back another night, better rested and with help.

The fear of the black unknown down the drain drove me out of the sink. I didn't want to return to the morbid baseboard. I chose to take a modest climb, up the peg board beside the stove, where the pots and pans hung.

I was thrilled to find a rare patch of crusted egg on the lip of the frying pan. It was my first food in days. Soon, contented, I fell asleep.

I was awakened by sounds of brushing and flushing. I had slept right through the dawn. The percussion of wingtips approached. Stupid! How could I have ended up in the frying pan at breakfast time!

I looked out. I had seconds to make my move. I couldn't race the shoes across the floor; I would lose. But I couldn't stay here. The small saucepan beside me? No, it could be used to boil eggs. The larger one hanging below? It might cook oatmeal. The steps were upon me. I had to choose. I raced to the small saucepan, praying today was one of Ira's cholesterol-free days.

Terror winded me. I peaked out. Ira was reaching for a bowl and spoon. That could mean anything—except fried eggs. I should have stayed put.

Now I could only wait. I thought I saw something move beside the edge of the cabinet door. I stared through the low light. But for what? No one had gotten into the new cabinets yet. Still the image was real: I could make out the tips of two antennae. A head soon appeared. The figure squirmed, thrashing the wood with antennae and front legs. Slowly, painfully, it emerged, one segment at a time. A small puff rose from the back. The second pair of legs pulled free just as I received the first wind. It was Rosa.

Why in God's name was she coming out now? In half an hour she could promenade down the door in safety. Now Ira had only to turn his head and he would permanently putty the door with her.

She finally pulled free and started to run across the cabinets. Ira got out a glass and then the orange juice carton, which he set beside the bowl and spoon. He even folded the napkin. He was giving her every chance to get down and out of the room.

But she refused. From the cabinet above the refrigerator she made a spectacular leap to the cereal box, ran over the tab, and disappeared through the slot.

Ira still hadn't declared today's menu. Raisin bran, boiled eggs, or oatmeal? I now ruled out oatmeal, because he didn't cook it alone, and there was no sign of Ruth.

Raisin bran or boiled eggs. Then I understood his diabolical plan: It was Rosa or me—she in the cereal box and me in the pan—in a grisly game of breakfast roulette.

It was Nature's shame that one like him could menace one like her. Poor Rosa, light of my young life.

Then Ira turned toward me. I assumed he would take the cereal. Now I could only think of the yards of shit that I hoped were insistently backed up in his colon this morning. He walked to the sink, within an arm's length of me. Would he reach up for my saucepan? Could he stomach watching me tread water, softening, then melting over his eggs? Bran was so much better for him.

I heard him wash his hands. My heaving chitin grated as I flattened against the pan. But then I heard wingtip patters. He was turning back toward the refrigerator.

I peeked out. He seized the cereal box. Poor Rosa. He flipped tab from slot and tipped box to bowl, pouring out brown flakes and body-sized raisins. There wasn't much left in the box when he was done.

Was my Rosa in the bowl? I couldn't see her, but then I knew she wouldn't lie on the surface. I didn't want to call out and distract her. But the uncertainty was maddening. I shuddered as the freezing vitamin-A-and-D-fortified-pasteurized-homogenized-99%-fat-free milk rose in the bowl. She couldn't withstand it for long. Nor could she allow herself to float and be exposed. She might be clinging to one of the flakes projecting from the milk. But those would be the first to be spooned up.

Ira turned the box around and read the quiz, answering aloud. "Thomas Jefferson. . .the Liberty Bell. . .Philadelphia. . . shit, New York, I meant New York. . ."

If she was in the bowl, milk was starting to choke her. If the worst happened and he saw her, would she break across the counter? His little breakfast napkin was so flimsy that he would have to go for a paper towel to strike her; that might give her time to reach the edge of the counter.

But even if she did, what chance did she have on that slick, rutted floor against his manly wingtips? Maybe she'd stay on the counter and make a dash up his sleeve, taking the fight to him.

The volume in the bowl was decreasing quickly. Ira's incisors shone with milk as he tore at the flakes, pushing them back in his mouth for annihilation by his gold-capped grindstones. His tongue shot from its lair every few strokes to swab the teeth, hesitating as if to draw a breath before it retreated. Bits of flake flew from his mouth, most landing back in the bowl, only to be spooned in again. I hoped that if Rosa had to die it would be just once.

As he was finishing his meal Ira read the ingredient list on the side of the box, making faces as he stumbled over the names of the chemicals. He looked at his watch and stood up.

He put away the milk carton, tucked tab in slot, and put the cereal box back on the refrigerator. I hoped he would leave me the bowl with the last inch of milk, cool and sweet from the sugar crusting the raisins. But, at the sink, he tipped the bowl to his mouth and swallowed. His mother would have been pleased.

He paused. His tongue was working, chasing an elusive last chew. A raisin twig? One last flake? Blinking his eyes with satisfaction, he pushed it forward and closed his incisors. From the cavern came a thin snapping, and a muffled howl: "Imperialist!"

Noble Rosa! Submerged in the cold milk to avoid the adult, she now fell prey to his training as a child. When he opened his mouth wide, I saw my indomitable lover. "Take that!" she cried, kicking her back legs against his eye tooth. Her front legs were broken, limp. His jaws still drifted as he felt for the last material, the upper incisors rising and lowering like the blade of a busy guillotine.

Rosa had never learned the virtue of silence. She thrashed until the tongue finally found her and swept her to the front, pushed her head on the block, and the ivory blade came down swift and sure, cutting her in two. She snapped like celery, with a scream that echoed around my pan.

Ira dug a pinky into his ear, then sniffed at the wax that came out.

Rosa still hadn't found her peace. Her severed head, stuck to the front of his incisor, appeared when his lips parted. She stared at me, and I knew she was going to speak. My legs wanted to run, but the weight in my gut held me still.

Without her body her voice was weak and diffuse. I stared at her mouth, and made out her charge: "Numbers! Numbers! Why have you forsaken me?"

I was relieved when the tongue returned and claimed her. I even waited to be sure that when the lips reopened the incisor was blank. Ira whistled as he washed his bowl. A moment later he left.

I stood on the peg board. I was confused. I could not understand why Rosa would be so cruel as to try to knit the responsibility for her death into the woof of my primitive biblical mind. I had to remember that she spoke under the ultimate duress. It was Ira's doing, Ira's responsibility.

How could I live with an animal who would starve my colony, slaughter my love, and still go off to work right on schedule?

"ROSA LUXEMBURG has been assassinated," I said. Most of the citizens in the baseboard ignored me.

"How did she buy it?" said Sufur.

"Ira ate her."

"He ate her?" Barbarossa said. "He doesn't even eat his own girlfriend."

"Maybe we can save her. Like Jonah," I said.

Julia Child laughed. "You get toilet duty."

Bismarck said, "Even if you could find her, she'd be a constipated pebble at the bottom of the bowl."

"She gave great pheromone," I said. "The best."

"Oh?" said Kotex.

"Some of the best," said Bismarck. "But that's in the past."

The morning went, then the afternoon. No one spoke. We were dispirited.

Ira and Ruth returned from work and prepared dinner. Only then did it occur to me to ask what Rosa had been doing in the kitchen the night before.

Bismarck shrugged. "I thought you knew."

"Why would she stay in a cabinet until morning? She must have found something. We have to go find out. Citizens?"

Six hours later, when Ira and Ruth were asleep, I scaled the face of the wall cabinet alone. The opening where I had first spotted Rosa was dusted with her chitin, shaved by the sharp edge. I climbed through carefully and it extacted a painful contribution from my shell.

The food smells in the cabinet were overwhelmed by the stench of wood finish. Here were the ordered edibles, from apricots to ziti. But the neat lines resembled a cemetery more than a garden of earthly delights. Sure, now we could find anything, but to what use? The bottles and cans were impregnable. The cardboard boxes could be mined, but each would take days of boring and digging. If we lived here or in the wall we could do it. But never with a single, treacherous line to safety.

In the old kitchen we had feasted on the boxes and packages. The Gypsy tore them open freestyle and replaced them gaping, covered with thick fingerprints of grease and debris. Even Ira believed that if he meticulously rolled down the inner bag, he could then simply Tuck Tab in Slot. This rare tactical lapse had allowed us to bathe in food.

Today I didn't see any open boxes. When I climbed to the next shelf I found out why: Ruth was on to the tab technique. She had introduced to our turf one of *Blattella*'s mortal enemies—Tupperware. I walked across the cover of a lentil sarcophagus. It was maddening to see those poor dead beans just below me, forever out of my reach, knowing the life I could breathe into them. Pasta, raisins, oatmeal—coffin after coffin. Had Ruth chosen translucent covers just to taunt us?

As I walked along the back shelf, I began to feel uneasy, as if I was no longer alone. I stopped and looked around. What could be in the back cabinet with me? The thing Rosa had run from?

I continued on and still I felt the eyes. I sprang onto the oatmeal coffin and whirled. Then I saw them, peering through spectacles from a convex head lying on its side.

They were Ben Franklin's eyes. These were the same rolled-up bills that Ira had stuck in the old cabinet, the third of his wealth for running away with. No one had told me that he had put them in the new cabinet.

I walked up to the soiled, silky paper. I liked Ben's pleasingly ugly, earthy look, the warm ruts of his forgiving face. He always looked as if he knew something. I suspected that he knew all about Rosa's fatal delay.

Following his eyes I walked across the shelf. On the other side I found a hole drilled through the back of the cabinet, but it was pressed flush against the wall. I could never get through. But why was it there?

Then I remembered: the Asian had drilled his own two holes through the back. Where was the other one? I guessed that this most symmetrical of men would place his holes symmetrically. I counted my steps as I walked back across the cabinet. By my calculation the other hole, which would lead through the gap and back into the wall, our only chance of surviving in this forbidding new kitchen, was right behind Ben Franklin. Was that why he was smiling at me?

I asked Ben to move. When he refused I pushed my head as far behind the bills as I could. Ira had lodged them very securely, as if he were afraid they would run away on their own.

"This won't hurt a bit," I said, as I slid an antenna up the crack behind them. I detected the scent of freshly drilled wood. I felt the slight swelling in the board. The hole was there. This was what Rosa had found, and what had cost her her life.

White Night

"YOU DON'T SEEM to understand," I said. "If we can move that money, it'll be as good as the old days. Better, because it's safer."

"So go move it," said Julia Child.

We were in the baseboard, sharing a miserable meal of dried oats.

Columbo said, "He's got credit cards, checks, a cash machine down the block. What is this money for?"

"It's his Jewish paranoia stash," said Kotex.

I felt a stirring in my primitive mind. "If we swarmed over him like locusts, maybe he'd leave."

Kotex patted me on the head. "Yes, dear. He'd pack up his matzoh and go."

"He's never going to budge that money. It's like a mezuzah fixed in his cabinet," said Clausewitz.

Bismarck, who had been eating, now said, "He uses it. I've seen him." We listened. "The last time was during the early days with the Gypsy. She called him on the phone and he grabbed the money and ran out the door. I never found out why. The time before that, with his girlfriend Esther, was also on impulse. My guess is that when Ira feels spontaneously, regressively irresponsible, he likes fast cash. There's something too grown up about credit cards."

"So it's up to Ruth to strike the mood," said Kotex.

"He's already got that bitch," said Sufur. "No way he spend cash on her. That for new pussy."

Kotex struck him across the forelegs. "Pig. Where did you get that?"

Bismarck said, "It's probably too late. Now he's comfortable with her. And I'm not sure Ruth ever lit him up the way the other two did."

"I heard that Esther has three kids," I said. "Are you saying that our only chance is for the Gypsy to show up again?"

"Or anyone else who can make him crazy that way."

I SET OUT to find the one quirk that would bring Ira's spending under our control. Since this quirk had eluded the colony through the years, I had no idea what it might look like.

One evening the following week, Ira and Ruth dined out with their neighbors, the Wainscotts. I was waiting in the hallway molding when they returned.

As Ira held the door, Ruth slid past him. Oliver Wainscott III appeared in the doorway. The threshold cracked under the tall, obese man, whose shoes could flatten a *Blattella* battalion in a single step. He said, "I don't see how you can defend these people when you obviously don't understand them."

Ira said, "I understand that most people do bad things because circumstances force them to."

"Oh, piddle. Is that your Legal Aid Pledge?"

Ira took off his coat and draped it over his arm. Ruth hung hers in the closet. Elizabeth Wainscott, tall, thin, blond, pretty, stood silently at her husband's side.

"You'll never believe this, Oliver, but bankruptcy is not the worst thing in the world," said Ira. "Moral bankruptcy is. And people know that."

Oliver formed a cross with his two pointer fingers and held them as if to fend off Ira's words.

Elizabeth shifted on her high heels and said softly, "Ollie, I'm very tired."

Oliver said, "If you handed a ticket to heaven to your clients, I bet every last one of them would redeem it for cash."

"Good night," said Ira. "See you Friday." He shook Oliver's hand and accepted a kiss on the cheek from Elizabeth. Ira closed and locked the door. "He never stops. What a routine."

"She's an angel to put up with it," said Ruth.

"I don't know how she does it. That's quite an outfit she was wearing, don't you think?"

"Yes, it was." She headed for the bathroom. I got Kotex, who was grazing, to join me in her pursuit.

By the time we arrived, Ruth had locked the door. "Something to hide," I said. "A good sign."

"But she's wise enough to hide it," said Kotex.

We climbed up the outside of the door so we didn't have to cross the gleaming ceramic floor tiles. We made full use of the little teals that covered the wallpaper. When we saw Ruth's eyeglasses on the sink we knew we were safe. We climbed to the top of the medicine cabinet.

Ruth was standing several feet from the mirror, with a straighter posture than usual, looking at herself with a critical expression. "That's right, Elizabeth. I was once a dancer. You probably don't think of me that way." She shook her head.

"I don't think of her that way," said Kotex.

"You know, Elizabeth, under this corporate lard lie the thin bones of a dancer." Ruth made a raspberry at the mirror. She rotated her head slowly, full left profile to full right, pupils locked forward like a compass magnet. Then she worked the other axis. She started well with one chin pointing straight ahead and nose foreshortened but ended with two chins pointing down her nose at full staff. She frowned.

Ruth stepped up to the mirror and tipped forward, her stomach resting on the sink. Her nose streaked oil on the glass. Muted scents of day-old moisturizer, makeup, and hair rinse rose to us. She ran her fingertips over her entire face, then laid the two longest fingers around the outer vertex of each eye, and pulled smooth the lined skin. When she let go, the wrinkles sprang back.

"Poor Ruth," said Kotex. "She lives in a world of men insensitive to fifty points in a woman's IQ, but alert to a hundredth of an inch in her nose or her cheeks. And if one of them shaved his head or put on forty pounds, it really wouldn't matter to his wife. How can men care so much about features that aren't at all sexual? It's perverse."

"If anything, human IQ is a sexual inhibitor." It was hard to muster sympathy for Ruth, mother of Tupperware. But Kotex was right about appearance. Thinking back over the females I had inseminated, I couldn't recall anything about their looks, except for the antenna that Legs had lost to a splinter and Ivory's stump. I looked at Kotex. Did she have a higher epicranium than Rosa? Bigger palps than Julia? Tighter sternites than Peach Pit? Nothing matters in females but chemicals and genitals. What could a face possibly have to do with fucking?

Kotex seemed to be identifying with Ruth. Stroking Kotex's foreleg I said, "I've never told you this but I've always liked the line of your clypeus, the fine gleaming mandibles, and your dark brown kitchen eyes, all two hundred of them."

She pushed me away, then tossed me a tiny dose of pheromones. The huge erection it aroused made me lose my balance and nearly fall down the face of the mirror. She laughed. "That's all you understand. Sometimes I wonder if we're any better than humans." Immediately I was back on six legs. It was the first time a female had ever said something repugnant enough to quell my excitation.

Ruth stepped back from the mirror, hands on ample hips. She rotated at the waist and said, "You know, Elizabeth, I used to be a dancer until I was cursed with these large breasts." She smiled.

This was a false pride. Breasts were treacherous organs, designed to sustain young when the good of the species depends on the young being able to make it on their own. In use for no more than a few months, maybe a year or two in a woman's life, the sacs of fat then begin a long, irreversible descent that causes her great torment, until eventually they hang as useless and forlorn as a pair of abandoned orioles' nests.

But what did the truth matter? I had only to look at Ruth's smile as she swished back and forth to be reminded that human males, like big babies, love tits. In most places, in most times, Ruth's formidable pair would have drawn her all the male attention she would ever want. But I knew from the magazines on the coffee table that in this society, at this time, they were too big, fit only to be dieted or jogged away, or perhaps surgically reconfigured. I had to admire her indifference, however fleeting, to the dictates of fashion. She clasped her hands and locked her elbows, squeezing her breasts out with her upper arms.

"Wow!" said Kotex.

Ruth leaned forward and scratched something on her face. Again she frowned. "What's wrong with her?" said Kotex. "She's not like this. Do you think something happened at dinner?"

Ruth's face revealed nothing, because it showed everything. As she soaped up, her contorted features conveyed briefly every mental state from bliss to despondency to insanity. After rinsing, she scooped up some thick cream and rubbed it into her face until the white disappeared and just the grease remained. It gave her a well-basted look.

"Those poor pores. Just watching makes my spiracles ache," said Kotex.

As Ruth brushed her teeth, Kotex and I started down the wall. When Ruth turned to raise her skirt we raced to the inside rim of the toilet bowl, just beneath the seat. This was our chance to get at the facts of the evening.

Her bottom lowered toward us, accelerating and expanding with astonishing speed. A primitive panic seized me. Was getting sat on such an ancient danger? As the buttocks eclipsed the room light, I cowered beside Kotex. The speeding bottom darkened, and then it hit. The toilet shook like Golgotha. Black, silent, still. I was dead.

Then I heard a little *pfft!* Methane. Could the afterlife have farts?

The earth had trembled, and now cracked open, just as the Book said. But when light poured in, I knew that this was no cataclysm. I was still in the toilet, and the light was streaming through a wedge between Ruth's thighs, like a slice from an adipose pie.

An extraordinary change had occurred. Impact with the toilet seat had transformed the pitted glob of flesh into a tighter, neater shape, veined gently like a young casaba melon. The pits disappeared. "And Jesus put forth his hand, and touched her, saying be thou clean. And immediately her leprosy was clean," I said.

"Spare me."

Ruth's crack, largely obscured by her cheeks when she stood, was now exposed. A line of fine black hair led from the back to front, like the tail of a little gerbil.

"What's going to happen?" I said. "I'm nervous."

"Ruth is steady. Her delivery is good, and her parcels are even and firm and dark, almost as regular as ours."

She didn't look so steady tonight. She shifted her buttocks from side to side. Her anus strained. I felt uncomfortable.

"Don't worry," said Kotex.

I could see Ruth's bowed head through the gap between her slowly waving thighs. Her breathing was shallow and loud. She grunted. Was she davening?

"Is this Friday night?" I asked.

Her bottom became prickly and flushed. Her legs bounced. I lowered my antennae for protection.

"Here it comes," Kotex said. The brown bud threw open its petals. I stepped back. Gas hissed through, and it closed.

Ruth groaned. "Oh God!"

Several minutes later the bud again stretched and quivered. But the payload was not at all what Kotex had led me to expect. There was nothing smooth, no neat, elegant parcels, no *Blattella*-brown. Instead a sour-smelling, green-speckled colloid shot out. After impact, its ghost slid unevenly down the porcelain walls toward the water, where a slick had already formed.

I pulled Kotex back. Though Ruth couldn't hit us with a direct shot, I feared upsplash. After five bursts, she hissed like a dry well.

Acrid urine crackled against the front of the bowl, clearing away a little parabola of scum.

"I've never seen her like this. Something's definitely up," said Kotex.

As Ruth reached for the toilet paper, I remembered a conversation between Ira and her on the subject:

"It's not neat crumpled," he said.

"It's more absorbent crumpled," she said.

"It's more hygienic folded."

She said, "I don't believe that. But remember it is more expensive folded."

He laughed. "My treat." After thinking for a moment he added, "You know, I bet it's not cheaper crumpled, because the breakthrough threat means you have to make more passes."

"Oh, Ira, I've been practicing for thirty-five years. I hate to brag, but I'm good. I'm real good."

Her volume on the philosophy of vaginal care, *Candida*, which she kept on the window ledge, said that orifices should be wiped independently. At least wipe front to back, to keep those nether bacteria from the fertile vaginal earth. To silence Ira, Ruth had become a folding front-to-backer. But tonight she tore off a scroll-length of paper, crumpled it, and wiped randomly.

We backed under the seat as Ruth rose. The miracle expired—the pits and ridges instantly reformed on her behind. Taupe flotsam remained after the first flush, so she flushed again. She washed her hands and left.

Before we could get out of the bathroom Ira came in. We decided to get his view of the evening as well.

As soon as he took off his glasses we climbed back to the top of the medicine cabinet. His self-examination was not aesthetic but medical. He sprouted periodic pimples, which he refused to squeeze or lance because, as he once told the Gypsy, bacteria would then storm his brain the way the Nazis took Poland. His weapon was the washcloth, his strategy that bacteria would sooner move elsewhere than endure relentless antisepsis.

He scrubbed his face, then brushed his teeth. While he sang through mouthwash, we returned to the toilet.

A cool veteran now, I watched the descent of Ira's little dimpled ass in very handsome detail, the black curly hairs, the shining pimples, the sag lines, the patches of pink chafing.

Even when he sat, his bony thighs allowed sheets of light into the bowl. Now another extraordinary thing happened: though the displacement of Ira's ass was a fraction of Ruth's, though his was eroded and slipping while hers was pitted and swollen, though his had the silhouette of a diseased tree trunk while hers that of a manta hung by its tail, stretched across the toilet seat they looked virtually the same.

"A hundred times I've heard Ira insist that all men are created equal," I said, "and until this moment I never knew what he meant."

"I wonder how Jefferson found out," said Kotex.

The one obvious difference between the two behinds was Ira's baby boa. A skilled handler, Ira grabbed it safely behind the mouth. It spit a furious stream, which he directed around the bowl until it echoed with manly resonance. Though I did not think splashing was a danger to Kotex and me, Ira suddenly shook it viciously, as if he were trying to throttle it. Salvos of golden venom rang against the porcelain beside us. We backed further under the seat; Ira had taken our Ophelia to a watery grave just this way the previous month.

Though it was obvious that Ira did not get any regular exercise, he was a toilet athlete. He worked out nightly, but successfully defecated no more than once or twice a week, no matter how much raisin bran he ate. Flexing and unflexing his gluteus, he rose and relaxed in the seat as regularly as if he were under the spell of Jane Fonda's simpered commands on Ruth's tape.

"This is obscene," said Kotex.

Ira did a set of twenty-five. Though not a hint of feces had appeared, not even a leak of gas, he leaned forward and drew neatly folded toilet paper across his anus. As the wad floated to the water, he folded and applied another. The black perianal hairs, now charged with electricity, stood up and fanned apart, an antipodal plume. Whistling, Ira flushed, washed his hands, and left.

"If something's wrong, he doesn't know about it," I said. "I trust Ruth. Let's stay with her a while longer."

We walked inside the bedroom molding until we were above the headboard. Ruth lay under the covers, watching Ira undress. He was about to put suit in the closet when he began to sniff. Then he buried his nose in the fabric.

"Oliver said the perfume was cheap. He said it didn't last," said Ira triumphantly. "But it's what, six hours? Smell."

Ruth took a perfunctory whiff. "Yes, you gave Elizabeth a lovely gift. Do we have to go through this again? How did you get it on your suit?"

"At dinner. She was sitting right next to me. How else?"

"I don't know, Ira. You're an unusual guy. I don't know many men who know brands of perfume, or who have suits that absorb them. I don't know many men who would sniff their own armpits when there was a naked woman right there." She sat upright and dropped her covers, challenging him with the huge appendages mounted on her chest, two torpedoes on a sexual bomb rack.

Ira stared at her, suit still at his nose.

"This is embarrassing," said Kotex. "Maybe we shouldn't be here."

Ruth grabbed him by the waist and pulled him into bed on top of her. He managed to lay the suit down flat before she rolled over on top of him. She removed his glasses and pulled his face into hers. Their noses butted. "Ouch!" said Ira. She slapped his hand away. Air fluttered through the stalactites of goo in his nose.

"Think how less vile human kissing would be if they breathed through their backs," Kotex said. "And Ruth would look great with spiracles."

Ira pulled away and gasped. In a second her mouth was back over his. A small trickle, a fifth column, of saliva ran down his cheek and into his ear.

Kotex said, "That does it. Let's go. I don't want to see any more."

But now I wanted to stay. There was a truth lurking below the surface of this repellent demonstration, and I needed to learn it.

I had an idea. "Zoology! Just like under the toilet." Ruth's tongue, tracing across the inside of his cheek, peeked out from between the lips to an impassioned moan. "This isn't human at all. It's the mating dance of slugs."

Ruth pulled his loosened shirt, then his undershirt, over his head and threw them against the wall. Her mouth found his Adam's apple. This provoked some powerful childhood anxiety in me.

She moved quickly to the nipples. Kotex took exception. "Numbers, she knows they don't work. What is she doing?" She tried to cover her huge compound eyes with her antennae.

I was just now beginning to see that Ruth knew exactly what she was doing. She sucked and chewed until the roles reversed; he cooed as if he were the one at the teat. Then she descended to his navel.

"She wouldn't!" said Kotex. She would. We cringed as Ruth plunged her tongue into the fetid cavity, recalling his natal eviction, a helpless, puling pull-toy—which was pretty much what she was making of him now. She yanked off his briefs, and his penis swung up and oscillated to a halt, like a sand-bottomed beach toy. Ira lay motionless, eyes closed, fingers outstretched, hyperventilating.

As a human being he had been taken all the way back. But I couldn't help suspecting the story was far older than the species.

I said, "Now look at that thing. No hair, no spinal column, no lungs. The penis is a mollusk. The Portuguese man-of-war is not one organism, but a colony of different ones that grow together. The same is true of man and penis—mammal and mollusk."

Kotex said, "What's that growing on Ruth, barnacles?"

Ruth's tongue danced around Ira's member, mollusk courting mollusk. Suddenly she engulfed him.

"Maybe she's a praying mantis," Kotex said. "But she was supposed to wait for the sperm before she ate him."

The penis popped out, tied by an umbilicus of saliva to Ruth's mouth. "Don't stop," Ira said.

Ruth pushed herself up on her elbows. Her breasts, which had pooled over his thighs, resumed their explosive shape.

"What?" Ira said desperately.

"I'm feeling separate and terribly unequal." She crawled forward, then shifted her hips. Her vulva, a shiny pink ellipsoid with short radiating tentacles, looked like a sea anemone that someone had stepped on.

"Ah, justice!" she sighed as she inserted his penis into her vagina, his mollusk into her coelenterate. Sex between species—unnatural and abhorrent.

Ruth began wildly pumping her chubby but lithe hips, her breasts flapping wetly against her chest. Ira looked up at her, then let his head fall back against his pillow, eyes tightly shut. "Oh, my knees," she soon said, and straightened them, flattening against him. She grabbed him around the waist and rolled, pulling him on top.

Ira inhaled through clenched teeth. When his hollow chest landed on Ruth's wet tits, pockets of air collapsed with wet blasts. Ruth began to cry, "Ooh, ooh, ooh." Ira grunted as she dug her fingers into his behind, like spurs.

Ruth farted. "Oh, Ira, I'm sorry." In an instant she was again lost in sensation.

"Quite a lovely serenade," said Kotex.

"Aren't you glad we stayed?" I said.

"No! No! No!" cried Ruth. Miller had taught me that by this human females usually mean yes, yes, yes. But this time Ruth did mean no. She reached down. The little critter had slipped out. It was so well marinated that she was having trouble corralling it.

Funk from her cavity quickly rose to the molding. "I know that smell," said Kotex.

Ira collapsed after several more minutes. Chin on her shoulder, he kept pumping. There were no words now, not even groans or moans. Primitive diphthongs churned in the back of their throats, primeval Semitic relics of the struggle with the arid heat of the Levant.

"What are they saying?" I asked Kotex.

She was humming loudly to drown them out.

I had to know. I vaulted over the lip of the molding and started down the wall. Halfway to the bed I noticed that the light from Ira's bedside lamp was casting a shadow many times my size, with Ruth-sized rear flanks covered with formidable spikes.

"Holy shit!" yelled Ira. *Blattella* was one of the few forms he could distinguish without his glasses.

"Yes, you animal!" cried Ruth.

He rose on his hands. "Look at that damned thing."

"What thing?"

"A bug. Right behind your head."

"Don't you stop moving."

I retreated quickly. From my first day in Eden I had known better than to depend on the power of human love.

"It's getting away."

She grabbed him by the shoulders and locked her ankles around his back.

"Let go," he said. "I have to kill it."

"I need you right where you are." She wrapped her arms around his neck and kissed him passionately.

Ira pulled his head loose so he could watch me hurdle the molding. He fell back on his lover and said, "It's revolting. Right in the bedroom."

Kotex stopped humming. "That's exactly what I said."

"Oh dear," said Ruth softly. "I'm not through with you, little one."

As Kotex and I started to leave the room, she said, "Ruth completely controls him. It's kind of pathetic."

It was far worse than pathetic. I was already worried that my beloved Gypsy would not come back to us after all this time. Now Ruth, who apparently lacked the power to inspire Ira to use his secret money, seemed to have attained such sexual power over him that she might be able to repel the Gypsy anyway.

"I'm not sure I understand," I said. "Is it possible to control someone without 'lighting him up?'"

"Just concentrate on the sensation, honey," Ruth whispered.

Kotex drew her antenna across mine like a foil. The nerves in my back exploded as her pheromones stormed me. I lost interest in Ruth, in reclaiming the apartment, in everything but Kotex. "Do I light you up, baby?" she laughed.

I backed under her, and she slid over me like perfumed silk. I barely felt her on my back, though an equal weight of anything else would have been an intolerable burden.

My eyes focused on the tangled hairy limbs of Ruth and Ira. She was still trying to revive him. What did their charade have to do with sex? Who cared about his money anyway?

My wings had parted, and Kotex was feasting on my fount of pheromones. I could feel her heart pounding against my back. Soon we were perfectly aligned and balanced. I reached up into her snug genital chamber with my phallomere, my erotic grappling hook, which ensured that what happened in the lower orders didn't happen here. Slipping out! What could be a more malign omen for the destiny of *Homo sapiens*?

Hooked at the genitals, Kotex and I rotated so that we faced in opposite directions. I would not allow my face to distract her from her pleasure, and I insisted on being left to mine. Air from our unimpeded spiracles fed our fire.

Ira and Ruth were fading. "I've got it, Ruth. Oh, God."

If Kotex and I were face to face, could we have sounded like that?

My steel phallus shot into Kotex's womb, solid, secure. Teleology. I couldn't put it any other way.

There is no greater anticipation than sitting absolutely still, knowing that your chemistry is working omnipotently for your ultimate pleasure. With a beatific tremor, I released my spermatophore, a tidy capsule of DNA, into Kotex's womb. The heat rose from me. I was at peace.

"That was wonderful," said Ruth in a soothing voice. "But we have to figure out how to stay together at the end. It's so messy."

How liberating not to have to talk now, when desire was gone. No lies, no exaggerations, no promises. "Why do humans try so damned hard?" I said. "Because they are so sexually inept? Or is their coda the real romance?"

Ruth lay on top of Ira, stroking his thinning hair.

Kotex said, "It's the lack of pheromones. How could any species choose, court, or mate intelligently without it's basic chemicals? What is there to rely on? It's chaos. Imagine how pheromones would change Ruth's life."

I could imagine. The chemicals would induce Ira to alter his lifelong ways and propose marriage, within the hour. He would grovel to be her faithful, grateful everything. However, when alone he would still tell himself that their bond, caused by his addiction to her secretions, was instead cultural and spiritual.

But why bother with him? She could stroll around the block and, like the Pied Piper, lead back a pack of hungry suitors. She would hump the ones she wanted and discard the rest, confident that she could find others equally pleasing to her at any time. Ira would shrink in the competition. She would be too secure, too happy.

"I SUPPOSE SHE could make him take his little stash and put it in the bank," I said.

"Or roll up the bills and stick them in his nose. Lady's choice. Who knows what naughty tastes lie suppressed inside the homely girl."

I waved my antennae. "We shouldn't be talking this way. I might as well hope Ben Franklin pops out of the cabinet and goes jogging." Postejaculatory blues were coming over me. "Be serious now. What woman is going to light up that little coward?"

I reviewed the meager list: Ruth, no; the Gypsy, no; Faith, no. That covered my lifetime.

The toilet flushed, and Ruth returned to bed. She said, "Now, do you have anything more to say about Elizabeth's perfume?"

Every eye in Kotex's head looked as if it would pop right out. Elizabeth! Blonde and unhad. Of course!

All that remained was letting Ira and her in on the romance.

A Lock Is Picked

KOTEX AND I walked toward the dining room. The cold wood held a dim, flat light that seemed to come from below, as if up through ice.

We reached our new home, a section of the baseboard, which was no warmer. The single opening was provided by a rift in the layers of wall paint that had accumulated over eighty years. The subtle crack was inconspicuous to the human eye, and I often wished I had never seen it either. We used to own the night, when our patrols commanded the far reaches of the apartment. Now the citizens sat hugging the walls and base of the cavity as far as I could see. It was too easy to act demoralized here.

As we entered, Kotex and I had nowhere to step but on the heads. "Sorry, sorry, sorry..." she said as they cracked against the wood. Harris Tweed suddenly butted us out of his way and jumped out of the opening, immediately letting off a blast of flatus worthy of a horse. It was considerate of him to go outside.

Kotex and I located the group we had spoken with the previous day. I told them about the events of the evening and offered my conclusion: "Elizabeth is the key to moving the money. She can light him up."

"She's light, that's true," said Reud. "The two women he adored were dark. Like Ira's mother before she became a redhead."

Kotex said, "This one's prettier. And she's a shikse."

Reud shook his head. "Do you think Oedipus would have rather had a shikse?"

"Whatever," said Bismarck. "You just said that even the Gypsy might be unable to dethrone Ruth. Why would faithful, unemotional Elizabeth do any better? Why would she even try?"

Kotex paused. She didn't know the answer.

I said, "The sexual taste of an animal with pheromones can be defined within a few atoms. Ira, who has no chemical guidance, is indiscriminate. His taste can be molded."

"Still," said Barbarossa. "What makes you think Elizabeth can do things the Gypsy can't?"

"Elizabeth is tall and blonde and thin and pretty. Forbidden to him by marriage and by religion she is even more desirable—and unlike the Gypsy she is unconquered and she is right next door."

Bismarck said, "Even if all this is true, how are you going to get them together? The rules of society are all against it, and these are civilized people."

Goethe said, "If you can't convince them directly, get their mates to help you."

It was a brilliant suggestion. But when I asked for volunteers for the campaign, no one offered. Goethe said, "This is between you and Ira."

"You gave me the idea. It's for all of us," I said.

Bismarck said, with an antenna salute, "As soon as anyone believes it's in his interest to do as you do I'm sure he will." The *Blattella* way.

I left them. It was all between Ira and me—no advice could change that disturbing fact. Could I convince him of anything? I had only to look around the dark, crowded baseboard to see I was dealing with an animal lacking not only normal passions, but also reason and honor. A liberal committed to eradicating discrimination and the wretchedness of the crumbling city cores, Ira had forced us to live in this most straitened of ghettos, where he treated us with starvation, intimidation, and random murder. I wondered if he would ignore or scorn my gentle *Blattella* ways, if he would show compassion only if I became as savage as a human.

A BIT FARTHER into the baseboard our little ones—nymphs—were playing Bats, a game they invented in the weeks since we had moved there. Thirty of them hung from the wood at the top of the cavity by their back legs, their other legs and stubby antennae swinging free. The object of the game was to outlast the others, to be the only one up—the Mammal.

Touching was officially forbidden, but antennae soon whistled like bolas as the nymphs cut each other down. Adults asleep in the cavity swore at the nymphs landing on them.

The line of bodies was made more and more uneven by the loss of the fallen. As I stared at it the shape became more abstract, and then I had a vision—I thought I saw the edge of a key!

"I'm sick of it," said Julia Child when she absorbed her third fallen contestant. She delivered to the first hanging nymph a fearful blow that brought them all down like a line of suspended dominoes. The small space soon got very loud. I slept outside.

Blattellae grow discretely. With each of our eight molts we jump from one size to the next. An instar is what we call a nymph, or youth, who has undergone a particular molt.

Early the next morning I returned to the scene of the Bats game to find a complete set of instars, one of each size. After seeing them under fire I knew which ones I wanted to help me begin the liberation of the kitchen.

I picked my group, then spoke to them in general terms. How much could they understand about life outside the baseboard? They didn't even have names.

But right away they knew exactly what I was up to. The seventh instar said, "Like, it's a plan. Why do we need a plan?"

"Yeah, who are you, anyway?" said the fifth.

Skepticism is healthy, I told myself. Grating adolescent whining, too. I said, "Food is dwindling. Something's got to be done."

They looked dubious.

I said to the fifth instar, "Are you molting on schedule?"

"Maybe a couple of weeks behind. No sweat."

I flicked the back of her carapace with my antenna. "Sounds a little hollow to me." To the newborn I said, "By the time you're her age you'll be months behind. You're looking at life as a runt."

"Don't sell me," she said in her tiny soprano. "Go for it."

"I mean, it's never going to work," said the seventh. "Humans can't be that dumb."

The fourth instar spoke for the first time. "Getting food is not all that matters. This plan is imperialistic. We must accord humans the dignity we expect in return."

Insidious Ira had reached this generation. Perhaps his shrill voice had penetrated the baseboard.

"Starvation is the dignity I expect in return," said the newborn to her brother.

The fourth said, "That's why we're always at war. We've been selfish and shortsighted."

His words alerted me to the fact that by trying to manipulate the nymphs with words, I too was acting human. In order to get, I had to give.

"Come with me," I said. The instars followed me out of the baseboard. From behind a radiator leg I pulled out a coveted *Blattella* delicacy, a Cheerio. "This is mine. I brought it from the old kitchen. Here's the deal: if you agree to help me we'll eat now. But I need you all; it's everybody or nobody. Talk it over."

The redolent Cheerio soon decided it. We surrounded it and began to bore through its loud, crunchy volume. Having the biggest mouth, I was first to break through to the central core. The others appeared around me in age order. For one horrible second I pictured us as stuffed heads mounted on a Cheerio-colored den wall. I was roused when the last little plug of cereal fell and the newborn pushed into the cavity yelling, "Go power!"

We backed out carefully so our wing tips would not catch on the rough Cheerio surface. Then I led the nymphs across the dining room floor. They marveled at the dimensions of the room that had housed them their entire lives, but that they were now properly seeing for the first time. They shrank from their first experience of the midday sun. *Blatta.* Light-shunners.

We walked down the hall and climbed over the threshold and into the closet. My heart pounded at the assortment of carefully paired boots and shoes. I knew that unworn they posed no danger. But I couldn't help thinking of them as the arsenal of my mortal enemy. Not only could I smell rubber and hide, but the powdered chitin and crusted *Blattella* blood on the soles.

I steadied myself, then motioned to the nymphs, who had frozen just inside the threshold; fear of footwear had made it into our genes. I led them between a pair of galoshes to the back of the closet. I never would have anticipated their response.

"There it is!" screamed the seventh instar. He ran for the door.

I caught up and grabbed him. "There's no danger," I said. "It's dead, like the shoes."

He struggled. The others slunk back under the shoes. My nightmare.

"Watch this." I released the nymph and walked to the vacuum cleaner. I stepped into the metal sleeve, then went up the hose and inside.

"He's dead."

"Good riddance."

"Let's get out of here."

I reappeared.

"He fucking came out!" said the seventh. "I can't believe it."

I said, "The tail is rolled up inside. The humans pull it out and stick it into a hole in the wall. When it isn't in there the vacuum cleaner is harmless."

The fourth said, "You insult us."

Electricity is hard to believe. I walked to the end of the hose. "Let's not go near the mouth, just in case. Let's go into the asshole." I showed them the hole where the cord passed into the cylinder.

"What's to stop it from licking us out of there?" said the fourth. "All animals can do that."

Except for *Homo sapiens*, he was right. I said, "Look at that little anus. Now look at the size of the mouth." I pointed to the large sleeve and hose. "It could never get us."

"It could shit us out," said the seventh instar. "What a trip that would be."

Just as exasperation set in, I got some unexpected help. "Go power!" said the newborn. She raced up the cord and disappeared into the hole. A moment later she peeked out. "Piece of cake!" I think it was shame, not honor, that forced the others inside. They soon became comfortable exploring the cylinder and were captivated by the potpourri of odors.

Ira was terrified of electrocution, and replaced cords and fixtures at the first sign of wear. ("He doesn't want to risk becoming a lampshade at this point," Oliver once said.) A length of the cord which passed into the motor of the vacuum cleaner was the only exposed wire I knew of in the entire apartment.

I made the initial bend in the fine copper strand which had unwound from the others. I positioned the four larger instars to run a relay race, bending the end of the wire back and forth as they ran. The nymphs began to lick their legs as the strand heated up. Soon it broke off.

Looking up at the swollen dust bag, I shuddered at the tortures this appliance had seen. "Come on, come on, move it. We have a long way to go." We carried the wire strand down the cord and through the hole.

We went the length of the hall and under the front door of the apartment. Harsh fluorescent light from a naked fixture in the outside hall stung our eyes. A fourth-floor door slammed. A crosswind rippled our antennae. These were unsettling new stimuli for the young ones.

"Look at this," I said. A gray strand of fetid cloth lay on the floor. "The mopping has been done today. The super won't be back to bother us." Still the nymphs slunk down the edges of the tiles.

It wasn't far to the Wainscotts' door. The three largest instars and I carried the wire up to the handle and rested it on the lip of the lock.

"Yale?" the seventh instar said hesitantly, dragging his foreleg around the incised trademark.

"Don't worry. Getting in is a lot easier than you think."

The seventh instar took the end of the wire and stood at the keyhole. "This is really dumb." I kicked him, and he climbed in. He didn't get far before he stopped and squeezed back out. "There. Satisfied?" He preened a little graphite from his legs. The sixth instar went into the keyhole, moving the wire a little deeper. When she came out the fifth took his turn. About ten minutes later the first instar proudly announced that he had left the wire just outside the first tumbler.

"You remember where to lodge it?" I said to the newborn. "If you get it right, the lock won't turn." But I was anxious about sending her in; she had grown on me.

"Piece of cake," she said, and disappeared into the hole.

Though I knew the route was long and paved with slick graphite, she still seemed to be gone a long time. I would have to rescue her. For the first time during this long, hazardous day I thought about the *Blattella* breakaway principle: we have fourteen points, two on each leg and one on each antenna, where we easily break; in danger's grasp, we can escape and leave the limb behind. But where the newborn was going, into the lock tumbler, one of her breakable parts might be all a rescuer could reach. We can regenerate lost limbs when we molt, but we could never regenerate this precious nymph from her leg.

I called into the keyhole, but I got no response. Smaller heads than mine did no better. What was it with humans, that even something as benign as a door lock had to be designed as a mortal peril?

Now who would come first, Elizabeth or the newborn? The agonizing wait began.

Some time later I heard adolescent voices downstairs.

"I'm dying. He made us do twenty sets of 220 sprints."

"Why do you do that shit? Why don't you quit?"

"I don't know. What would I do after school?"

"Maybe you could get laid. . . On second thought, you better stay on the team." They laughed. School was out. It was late in the afternoon.

I had to limit our losses. "Citizens, we're going back."

All of them were willing—almost too willing—except the fourth instar. "What about her? You sent her in. You're not going to just leave her there."

"There's nothing we can do. She'll make it."

"No," he said. "She's going to come out filthy and exhausted. She'll need our help."

"You don't risk nine lives for one," I said. I heard that from one of our pragmatists, whom the colony treated as borderline brain-damaged.

The nymph said, "We'll risk your life for hers. We'll go back. You stay."

"Go, get away from me." They soon disappeared under Ira's door.

The shadow from the lock plate was too small to hide me, and the door was industrial green. I felt naked.

The downstairs door opened again, and the wind brought the scent of garlic and onions. I knew this would be Hector Tambellini, the postal inspector who lived down the hall. I didn't bother to hide. He trudged past the door looking so distracted that he wouldn't have noticed me if I were an orangutan.

I kept calling into the lock. I had visions of Elizabeth's blonde head rising into my view, one step at a time, I heard the delicate tapping of her high heels on the tile floor, I smelled her perfume, I saw her reach for the handle. . . What was I doing here? I was going to get killed!

I raced down the door. As a reached the floor I heard a wee voice. "Where is everybody?"

I ran back up. The nymph sat on the lip of the lock, a graphite blob with legs. I scraped her back to ease her breathing. "Where have you been? I've been calling you for hours," I said. I was glad her vision was blurred; my face burned with cowardice.

"In there. I didn't hear you."

"Did you set the wire? Is the lock jammed?"

She wiped her head, and her antennae sprang up in a victory *V*.

I walked her back to our apartment. Then I returned to the hallway and climbed to the ceiling.

OF THE FOUR who lived in apartments 3A and 3B, Ira was almost always home first. Today was no exception. Puffing from the climb up the stairs, he put down his vinyl briefcase beside the door. After inserting his key, he looked back at the stairway, and then at his watch. Why? Because Elizabeth Wainscott usually arrived second. He could have gone home, disencumbered, and then come to visit. But he never did. Why? An evening visit, just the two of them, was too close. Making their meeting seem coincidental buffered him from his desire for her.

He waited, and soon she came up the stairs. "Hello, neighbor," he said, smiling.

"Hi, Ira."

"The trains are really getting bad."

"Yeah. The platform was packed tonight. If they can put a man on the moon, I don't see why they can't make the trains run on time."

"The media should report that the Russians run their trains on time," said Ira. "Then you'd see some results."

"Do you think that would work?"

"Oh, I don't know. I was kidding really."

She opened her bag and fished for her keys. Ira was still looking at her. "Is that a new coat?" he said.

She twirled. "Do you like it?"

"Smashing." His bald spot flushed.

"I'll tell Ollie. He doesn't like it." She put her key into the lock.

"He's blind." With a pleased smile Ira entered his apartment. A moment later he was back. She was still at the door. "Won't open?"

She pulled the key out, held it up to the light, and put it back in. "I can't seem to get it. Funny, I've never had any trouble before."

Ira moved closer, into the sphere of her perfume. He made two aborted gestures in her direction, as if embroiled in a conflict between his chivalrous instinct, which wanted to come to her aid, and his feminism, which told him he shouldn't assume he was any better than a woman at achieving anything other than feats of brute strength. As Elizabeth struggled, her expression invited his help. Finally she asked for it.

Ira tried the key gently, then forcefully, then violently, one way then the other, ignoring her suggestions that counter-clockwise had always worked. His sweat soon covered the key.

Elizabeth put her hands on his. "Let's get some help."

"Maybe it's just gummed up with pollution."

She gently moved between him and the key. Ira would not quit. He wrapped his arms around her from behind so all four hands were on the key. "We can get it. One hard tug. When I say three. . ."

Though I was relying on the principles of human courtship and vanity, now I got plain lucky. I heard heavy lumbering steps on the stairs. Oliver, usually the third to appear in the evening, now did.

Elizabeth and Ira were so intent that they did not hear him. He cleared his throat loudly. "Oh, have you two met?"

They leaped apart. Simultaneously they began explanations, then stopped to defer to each other, then began again. They sounded flustered and guilty.

Oliver held up his hand. "May I?" He stepped between them to the door. He tried the key, removed it and handed it to her, then tried his own. "This lock is broken. Ira, it was white of you to help us determine that. Good night."

"Good night." Ira retreated to his apartment.

Oliver said, "I'll get the super. This is exactly why I bribe him every Christmas."

Elizabeth waited in the hall. Soon she began to shift her weight from foot to foot, and roll up on her toes. She could not sit down next door; she was already going to pay for her indiscretion.

It must have been twenty minutes before Oliver returned with the super, a burly West Indian in his fifties, who exhaled spices from dinner. I liked this man because he shared my respect for forces beyond man's comprehension.

The super wore at his side scores of keys on a ring that looked like a knocker on a mansion door. When he pulled it out the cable zipped. He tried a key, then another, and a third, and the cable zipped back in. "I don't know, mun. Maybe is cursed."

"No, James. This is America. In America things get busted," said Oliver.

"The keys say hello, but no answer inside." James shook his head.

"My friend, we must get in our home. Can you help us?"

James pondered. "I feel bad for you and your pretty, pretty wife, Mr. Wainscott." His face brightened. "You and Mrs. Wainscott, you come and spend the night with us. My wife be so proud."

"That's very good of you, James. But we must get into our home." Oliver pulled out his wallet. "We want that very much."

James smiled. He picked out another key on his ring. "Perhaps this get the spirit inside." He went up the stairs.

Oliver and Elizabeth waited in the hall. He refused to talk.

"Why are you standing out here?" said Ruth, who soon arrived. "Are you locked out? Isn't Ira home yet?"

"James is about to save us via the fire escape," said Oliver. "I have to hold the cash here so he can follow the scent."

"Why don't you come in and sit down. You both look so tired."

"Thank you, Ruth, but we'll wait here."

It probably startled Ruth to hear Oliver turn down an opportunity that could be converted into a free meal. "Let us know if we can help," she said, and let herself in.

I could smell Oliver's fury in his sweat. "How damned long does it take to shuffle down a fire escape?"

There was a soft tinkle from inside the apartment like porcelain breaking on carpet, then a loud crash. Oliver grabbed the door handle and yelled, "What the hell is going on in there, a demolition derby?"

Finally the door opened and James's face appeared glowing from the dark. "Very, very black inside."

"Yes," Oliver said, and handed a dollar to James, who held it up to the light to examine. Elizabeth and I followed Oliver into the apartment.

Without taking off his coat, Oliver fixed himself a martini and slumped into the living room chair. Elizabeth rushed to the vase fragments beside the window. Making little *tsk* sounds, she fit several pieces together. "I think it can be fixed."

He didn't look at her as she walked past him and into the kitchen. Some time later she called, "It's ready." He removed his coat and joined her.

She watched him anxiously as he ate. He would not return the look, nor would he speak.

Finally she said, "I think the vase can be fixed." He nodded, and continued to eat. "You never liked it anyway. You said it was fussy." He wouldn't respond. She could not eat. "What is it? The dollar?" She went for her purse and placed a bill in front of him on the table. He put it in his wallet.

He soon finished enough food to sustain the colony for months. With a deep belch, he returned to the living room. Elizabeth threw her fork into the salad bowl. She put away the food, and washed the pots and dishes. Then she stood at the kitchen doorway, staring at her husband, who was still drinking and reading the paper.

Finally he spoke. "I object to my wife in public display with my Semitic neighbor."

"Oliver, for God's sake, what are you talking about? We were trying to open the door."

"You are a liberated woman, and far be it from me to tell you how to live. All I ask is a tad of decorum. Take the man inside at least."

"How can you say that about me, or Ira, your friend. You should be ashamed."

"I have nothing more to say," he said, and raised his head papally.

She walked into the bedroom. After a while he followed. By the time I got there the lights were out and both were in bed, Elizabeth in fetal position, facing away from Oliver, who lay on his back, his butt buried in the mattress, his eyes open.

What was it, Oliver? Lying there behind that adorable woman, in the halo of her perfume, was your determination being undercut by your lust? Take her, man; it's your right. But no. It wouldn't do to give her the satisfaction of knowing you want her, not after she betrayed you, in public yet. She'll have to do without you tonight.

Elizabeth soon fell asleep. Oliver heard her regular breathing and looked over at her. He sighed loudly and gave the blanket a tug. He flopped over onto his side, but even the seismic movements of the mattress couldn't rouse her.

I was quite sure just now Elizabeth had no intention of betraying her husband. That didn't matter. If I created steady friction between them Oliver would magnify whatever germ of affection she held for Ira into such an intention. Abuse would drive her toward a kinder, gentler man—Ira—and perhaps Ira toward his money.

I was so pleased with the night's results that I decided to try the same technique next door. I wondered if Ruth would cooperate and imagine that Elizabeth's comely face lay behind my deeds.

I picked one of Elizabeth's loose hairs from her pillow and returned to my apartment.

A Watermelon on the Ground Too Long

AS IRA PUT HIS key in the door he looked furtively over his shoulder, but entered the apartment without delay. He sat down at the kitchen counter with his mail. The pile of heart-tugging, open-palmed tales spoke not only of diseased and deprived humans, but also of the plight of big, gaudy birds and mammals—all of them maladapted, marked for extinction. These pleas had come to the right address.

The doorbell rang. Ira straightened his tie and went to answer.

"What you smilin' at?" said the gravelly ghetto voice. It was Rufus.

"Oh, come in. This is a surprise." Rufus always came on Friday night; it was Wednesday.

Rufus was a tall anemic man of indeterminate middle age, wearing a full-length black leather coat and matching applejack, black leather pants, and exotically scaled boots. He always exuded the smell of cure.

"A walking morgue," said Bismarck. He had gotten bored in the baseboard and was again doing his rounds.

Rufus said, "Had to come by today, whitey. Trouble with my wheels. Some punk come by and rip off my brand new Seville and leave me some '64 boat, rusty piece of shit I be embarrass' drivin' to the junkyard."

"He stole your Cadillac and left you another one?"

Rufus stared at him. "Otherwise it ain't ethical. Lawyer suppose' to know that."

Ira shook his head. "All these years and I never heard that one."

"Friday I go shoppin'."

There was a tap on the door. Ira opened it. "Hi, Ira. Hi, Rufus," said Elizabeth. "Just wanted to let you know the lock is fixed." She showed Ira her shiny new key.

"That's great. Well, bye."

"Well, good night."

Ira locked the door. In the living room Rufus brushed off a small area of the coffee table, and, once seated, gently lowered his boots there. Elbows propped against the sofa back, he stretched his fingers and mated their pink tips.

Ira hated shoes on his table. But he said only, "What are those boots made of?"

"Somethin' dumb enough to get caught. Soft, though. Don't hurt my corns."

It was time for the ritual cocaine purchase. Because he was caught by surprise, I hoped that Ira might be short of cash and need the stash in the cabinet. But he opened his wallet and counted out the money on the table with the demonstrable honesty of a casino dealer. Rufus removed a small white pouch from inside the sweatband of his hat.

As they made the exchange, Rufus said, "This chump-change don't make no sense. A smart Jew like you know cost go down when volume go up. Today I got factory fresh material at big savin'."

When he specified the quantity and price, Ira started. "I don't have that kind of money for recreation." He walked to the mantel and tapped a piece on the chessboard. He seemed confused, apologetic. Rufus let the silence hang.

"This is uncomfortable," said Bismarck. "Rufus is good."

Finally Rufus said, "Make me wonder. Why you have me comin' round so much when it cost extra green? Ain't right for a Jew like you. Like the prestige of a real live nigger in you' house?"

Rufus rose and faced Ira from the other end of the chessboard. On it was the current position of a game Ira was conducting by mail with a refusenik in the Soviet Union. It represented a spiritual bond with his captive brethren, and Ira guarded the board fiercely.

Knowing this well, Rufus picked up the white queen and turned it upside down, as if to look up her dress. Rufus said, "You grow up in the 'burbs? Big house with the lantern boy, little nigger on the lawn?"

Rufus put the piece down. While Ira returned it to its proper square, Rufus seized the other inviolable object on the mantel, the menorah. He balanced as if in midstep, right leg up, holding the menorah in front of him, grinning with oily deference. "Like this? Rain or shine, ole Rufus light de way."

"I'm a Legal Aid lawyer," Ira whined. "Why are you talking to me like I'm some kind of ignorant bigot."

Rufus laughed. The fillings in his teeth matched the gold bracelets around his wrists. His wide nose lay flat on his face, a sensible flap, not a pup tent like Ira's.

"Why are you laughing?"

"It's nothin', Slim, don't worry 'bout it." He wiped his eyes. "Hey, this thing use' nine candle every time you light up. No wonder you short on cash. No, wait, ain't this the special Jew light that tell God to keep the frog and locust and shit out you' house?"

"Something like that."

Rufus looked around the room and smiled. "No frog. No locust. Work pretty good. I got to get me one. They come in gold?"

He brushed off the sofa and sat back down. Ira joined him. There was a small gift-wrapped box on one of the chairs. "For me?" said Rufus. "How nice."

"It's for Elizabeth. It's a scarf. Her birthday is next week." He had the voice of a man just reprieved.

"Why you leavin' it out? You' old lady gonna see it."

"Of course she's going to see it. She bought it."

"She lettin' you wipe you boot in her face?"

"I beg your pardon?"

Rufus pointed at the menorah. "That mean you follow the commandments. But you live with a bitch and fornicate."

"The Bible was written thousands of years ago," Ira said. "Life has changed. I obey it in spirit."

Rufus laughed. "I like that. 'That right, officer, I be buyin' a kilo off this nigger, but it be legal—in spirit.'"

"Look, when I work on the Sabbath it's for a client. I don't kill; I prevent my clients from being killed, and protect them from false witness. I don't commit adultery—that's right, neither of us is married. I don't steal. And everybody knows I honor my mother."

"How about an eye for an eye, a tooth for a tooth, life for life?"

I would have loved to hear a straight answer to that, after Rosa and all the others. But he ducked it. "That's not a commandment. Anyway, it's misunderstood. When it was written it was intended to check barbarism—you could lose your life for stealing a chicken back then." He finally stopped talking, but then said, "How do you know so much about the Bible?"

"Sunday school. My momma made me go ten year. But answer me this: how about diggin', I mean covetin', you' neighbor wife? That be a commandment."

"What about it?"

"Who you kiddin'? The bitch come by and you be smilin' at her like Howdy Doody."

"Elizabeth?" Ira shrugged. "Sure, she's an attractive woman. I'm not an Arab. I don't have to avert my eyes."

"Shit, ain't them raghead somethin', coverin' up the only thing on the big green earth worth lookin' at." He rolled his eyes to the ceiling and shook his head. "But I got to tell you, whitey, who doin' all the powder if you ain't primin' the blonde? No way you up with the Pillsbury dough boy 'cept to poke his old lady."

Ira jumped up. "They're my friends. Is this what they taught you at Sunday school?"

Rufus cracked his knuckles. "Make me wonder why you Jews go to the expensive university, come out not knowin' shit stink." He opened his coat. The collar of his black silk shirt was embroidered with his name in metallic thread.

Bismarck said, "That's the shirt. Right after my brother was born he climbed up and read the damned collar from the inside: 'Sufur'."

Rufus pulled a silver flask from his coat pocket and took a draft. "Want to lose money buyin' chicken-bag, cool. Want to settle with one bitch all the time—nice bitch, but she wearin' too much flesh—and leave go that foxy blonde pussy, cool. I don't believe it.

"If I was you, shit, I know my bitch ain't goin' nowhere, right? Who she goin' to get better than me? And I know that blond old man, tub of guts ain't goin' nowhere, so I ain't goin' to have no divorced blonde bitch botherin' me, right? So I got no trouble. I got mine and I got his. I got me a big stash of powder to work the blonde, and I got all the opportunity I need. And this plantation nigger don't need no law degree to spread the bitch's legs like fried chicken, and pop that pussy like a watermelon on the ground too long.

"Fact, even if I was just some ghetto-nigger pusher, I stuff the beefaroni into the bitch. I seen her lookin' my way. . ." It was masterful.

"Stop!" Ira's hands were clenched.

Again Rufus laughed. "Take it easy, slim. I just sayin' if it was me, I buy the goods and play both way. You do what you want." He stood up and buttoned his jacket. "But the discount price don't last long."

He walked toward the door, shoulders rolling and arms pumping in urban strut. He had learned to use his forward appendages in locomotion, like the higher orders, while Ira lurched peg-leggedly. As Rufus opened the front door Ruth arrived at the landing. "How's everythin'?" he said. Without waiting for an answer he passed her and went down the stairs.

She kissed Ira on the cheek. "Why is he here today? Is something wrong?"

"Sometimes I wonder."

Ruth gingerly drew off her shoes and put her feet up on the living room table.

"Please don't," Ira said.

"Sorry. So what did Rufus have to say?"

Ira sat down. "He's offering me quantity. His car was stolen and he needs to raise cash."

Ruth laughed. "You must be kidding. I've never seen him wearing less than a car's worth of jewelry and clothing."

"That doesn't mean anything. Every day at work I see guys who dress like him and are over their heads in debt, being evicted from their apartment, having their furniture repossessed. They feel they've got to show. Ostentation turns them into criminals."

Ruth rubbed the dark red marks on the outsides of her feet. "I can't see how it's your problem if Rufus decides to buy jewelry instead of pay his bills."

He wasn't asking for a handout. He was making me an offer. Why are you assuming he's trying to screw me?"

"Isn't it enough that your risk you health and endanger your career to give him fabulous amounts of money? Do you owe him more because he's a prisoner of ostentation?"

He walked back to the mantel. "It's a victimless non-crime, like pornography and prostitution. Politicians play on it for reelection while poverty and discrimination ravage the country. These laws are garbage."

Ruth softened her voice. "Whatever merit they have, or lack, you have sworn to uphold them. If you want to change them, go into politics." She leaned over and reached for him. "But please don't. I don't want to live with a politician."

"When I give Rufus money, it goes back into the black subeconomy. That's as it should be."

Ruth shook her head. "What is? His apprenticeship program for prostitutes and dealers, or his entitlements, to the Cadillac and cocaine salesmen? When you buy drugs, you're just making new victims."

"She's wonderful," said Bismarck.

"Would you be so insulting if he weren't black?" Ira asked.

Ruth laughed. "How could you ever imagine Rufus not being black."

"Oh?" he said bitterly. "This drugmonger, pimp, and car fiend could only be black?"

Ruth tried to turn his shoulders toward her. "What's wrong, honey?"

Ira was silent. I hoped that the primary irritant was the image Rufus had left him with: Elizabeth lying smiling on the warm soil, dress pulled up, legs obscenely splayed, her dark pink pussy yielding to his big black member. If it was, Ruth wasn't doing herself any favors by being maternal.

Bismarck disagreed. "It's the drug thing. He knows better than to defend Rufus. It's guilt speaking, and I'll tell you why.

"I was there the day Gypsy first introduced cocaine into Ira's life. It was long before you were born.

"She didn't identify it by name. 'It's an elixir from the old country, which sharpens the senses and heightens the urge for love,' she said. What a woman.

"Ira said, 'You don't believe in aphrodisiacs?'

"'Oh, yes, my pet. I've tried this one, and it works.' She showed him a little glass vial.

"'Thanks for telling me.' He held it up to the light and said, 'I was expecting something earthy, like a root.' His face discolored. 'That's not *cocaine*, is it?' He whispered the word. Still an associate with a corporate firm, he hadn't had exposure to criminal evidence.

"She touched his cheek. 'Partner material, I'm sure of it.'

"Ira yelled, 'I can't believe this. Don't you know that possession of that. . . material. . . is a felony?'

"The Gypsy shrugged. 'Who cares? It's my business.'

"'Who cares? Who cares?' he said, louder and redder. 'I care. I'm an attorney-at-law, remember?'

"The debate started to mirror the one you just heard, with him arguing the other side. He said, 'I have sworn to uphold the law, all law. You can't just pick and choose the ones you like.'

"The Gypsy led him to the bedroom. With her free hand she unbuttoned her blouse and unfastened her skirt. 'Ira, if there was a law against scratching, would you enforce it?'

"'That's ridiculous,' he said. But there was uneasiness in his voice.

"'I want to know, lover.' She stripped naked and lay down. 'What if the government passed a law against scratching? And then what if I really needed you to scratch me, right here. What would you do, lover? Would you help me out?"

I said, "And so much for his oath. Human males are so easy. When Ruth tucks him in tonight, he'll forget again." Ruth had already calmed him. They were preparing dinner. Elizabeth was never mentioned.

Bismarck said, "But Ira didn't scratch the Gypsy. He stood there and said, 'You're testing my loyalties.'

"Through her vulva she ran a finger, which she licked. 'Yes I am.'

"Still he resisted. His eyelids fluttered as he anticipated her explosion. But she surprised us both by demurely covering herself with a robe. 'We should obey the law. Thank you, Ira. I should have done this long ago.' She sat down at the phone. Ira watched her apprehensively. I had no idea what she was about to do. At first I thought she was bluffing because she didn't dial seven numbers. Then I realized it was 911.

"She said, 'I want to report a crime. . .in the home of a friend. . .'

"Ira waved at her, mouthing, *No!*

"'Yes, the accomplice is here, Ira Fishblatt.' He put his hand over the mouthpiece, but she tore the receiver away. 'We want to surrender to the police.'

"'What are you doing?' Ira said in furious whisper."

I said, "Why didn't he just hang up?"

Bismarck said, "Hell, I don't know. Maybe he didn't want to violate her First Amendment rights."

"She was near tears. 'I'm so ashamed. Sodomy. At least a hundred counts. Yes, oral-genital intercourse. . .'

"'Oh God!' Ira cried, and pulled the phone line clean out of the wall.

"Ten minutes later, his legal principles refined, Ira was in bed, drugged and scratching."

TONIGHT'S RARE conversation had to be exploited. I descended to the floor and trotted to the hallway corner where I had left the hair I'd brought from Elizabeth's pillow.

Ira and Ruth were seated at the dining table. Embers of conflict were glowing again. She said, "But he doesn't come here from love."

"I think he likes us."

"I think he likes our money more."

"You make him sound evil."

"That's not evil," said Ruth. "Everybody likes money. But he's immoral in pursuing it. And he's making you feel bad to get more."

I started up the back of Ira's chair with the hair. I called up to Bismarck, who was still on the ceiling. "Where is she looking?"

"Right into his eyes."

"Look at it this way," she said. "When Rufus visits he is always offered good food and good conversation, and he leaves wealthier than he comes. If only you and I had friends like that."

I climbed onto the back of his navy wool jacket. The footing was treacherous. "Still clear?"

"Do it now," said Bismarck. "I think she's getting disgusted."

I raced up his back and draped the hair over his shoulder onto the front of the jacket. The glossy gold leapt from the navy matte.

"It's not charity," insisted Ira. "I'm paying him for goods and services."

She leaned across and kissed him on the cheek. I was already back on the floor. "You sure can twang the heart-strings of a capitalist," she said. As she leaned back she saw the hair and brushed it from his jacket. "That's as blonde as Elizabeth's."

Ira doubled his chin as he scanned his lap. "Why do you say that? It's probably from work."

"No, dear. It doesn't have a black root."

He found it and held it out to her. "So send it to forensics."

"What's wrong with you ?"

"What is this today, an Inquisition?" He walked from the room. Ruth followed.

I rejoined Bismarck on the ceiling. "I doubted you, but I see it now," he said. "You, Ruth and, Oliver will get the romance started if it kills all of you."

"And Rufus."

The argument continued in the living room. I wondered how blind Ira would be to the pits in her behind tonight. "It's just a matter of time," I said.

There was a chitinous report directly below us. David Copperfield came through the baseboard opening massaging his head. "I am a lone lorn creetur and everythink goes contrairy with me."

Cicero came after him, yelling back down, "How long, Catiline, will you abuse our patience?"

Bismarck and I raced down the wall. Perhaps we were overestimating the matter of the time we had.

Julia Child's Hottest Recipe

SNOT RAN UP to meet us four feet above the baseboard opening. "It's Julia Child. You're never going to believe this," he said excitedly. "It's safer from here. Watch now. Right at the crack."

A small puff rose above the baseboard before quickly dissipating. I said, "Has she set the place on fire?"

As Ira and Ruth returned to the dining room, we ran up the wall to the molding. Ruth said, "Next time he gets to you, tell me, honey. Don't let it churn inside." She shuttled the dirty dishes into the kitchen.

Ira said, "I suppose you're right." He wiped crumbs off the table. The tension was gone. I would have to give them another dose.

Meanwhile clouds continued to issue from the baseboard. Snot said, "Julia has gone berserk."

"Why don't you stop her?" said Bismarck.

"You can't get near her."

Ira sprayed the table with furniture wax from a can that looked like a can of poison. Artificial lemon stung our spiracles. Just as he turned toward the wall, on his way out and to bed, a huge burst erupted from the baseboard. Ira looked down.

"There, that's what I was waiting for," said Bismarck. "Kiss them all goodbye."

Ira made no immediate move. The fleeting datum had not registered in his mind. Inhibited by man's pride—the oversized brain—his thoughts were scattered, the pathways between them rutted by conditioning. Just as he was more alert to movement in the kitchen, he saw intelligence only in the behavior of his own species. My grand strategy depended on this deficit.

But Ira bent over to the debris that had precipitated from the baseboard onto the floor.

"Wotan, keep her still," murmured Bismarck.

Without a moment of wonder, Ira wiped it up, turned off the light, and left. We ran down the wall, keeping clear of the opening. Kotex and Peach Pit, Julia Child's sisters, were on the floor.

Now I saw what had been erupting—finely-chopped bits of our scant remaining food. Since the previous renovation we had been living on subsistence rations. I could only guess how many hundreds of meals Ira had just thrown away.

"I think she dragged through the boric acid without realizing it," said Kotex. "She's poisoned."

Bismarck and I climbed back up the wall and looked into the baseboard. Julia was sitting in a pile of food up to the first joint of her legs; since it had been stored at the far ends of the baseboard, she must have been quite determined to collect it here. Her head was down as she sifted and sorted.

Suddenly she shrieked, "Let them reach room temperature!" Two missiles shot from the opening. I ducked one, but the other struck and lodged in one of Bismarck's eyes.

He swore in German as I carefully extracted the projectile. I had assumed there was some method to Julia's activity. Now I saw that she was not grading stocks; she was indiscriminately eliminating them.

The toast crumb soaked with Bismarck's tears and blood should have sickened me. But after months of hunger, I devoured it.

Barbarossa, an animal large beyond his chromosomes, yelled in his commanding basso, "Julia, I am calling for a ceasefire. Should you refuse, we will come for you."

The room was suddenly quiet. Barbarossa started up the wall.

Antennae tips appeared from the opening. "Hold on," Kotex said. "She's coming out."

The antennae grew. But it was not Julia. It was Sufur. He ran up the wall. "Ceasefire, shit!" he rubbed his rectum. "She try to serve me up dinner backward."

I couldn't understand this. To her sisters I said, "I never thought Julia was imprinted. Was she?"

"The Gypsy dropped some paprikash between the pages and Julia went in," said Kotex. "I guess the Gypsy didn't use the book much."

"Why is she acting up now, after all this time?"

"Just a pinch!" came a shriek, and we were lucky that's all that flew out this round. Barbarossa growled.

Peach Pit said, "She wasn't out of the book more than a week when she decided everything was too bland. She insisted on spices. Salt and sugar were obvious poisons. But chips of paint, which she ground with her mandibles, look just as good, and I must admit, they do taste better. I only tried them once. They're a staple for her."

A moth alights on an off-white wall, the apartment's closest approximation of a flower. It eats. Within days it will sizzle itself on an incandescent bulb or flutter against the ceiling until it is killed. Ghetto babies snack on paint chips, which look like the potato chips their mothers feed them. When they get older they alight on gaudy enticements, such as drugs and guns, and are destroyed. Julia, first imprinted, then poisoned with lead, was now starving. What chance did she have?

"Stir!" A steady motion began inside the baseboard. Julia was lying on the center of the food pile, while her legs, antennae, and palps whirled through it, raising two rows of formidable vortices.

Bismarck said, "If she goes much faster it will all fly out the top."

"We have to stop her," said Kotex. "And make her promise not to do it again."

"Whip!" cried Julia. The piles were approaching the top of the baseboard cavity.

Bismarck said, "And if she doesn't?"

"Then we'll throw her out," said Peach Pit.

"And she'll march right back," said Barbarossa.

"Break the bitch's legs. That keep her away," said Sufur.

Peach Pit struck him across the wings.

Bismarck said, "She'd molt and return on new legs."

I said "If Ira didn't find her first. . ."

For 350 million years our guiding instinct had been a simple self-reliance. But today Julia presented too great a common danger: we could not wait for natural forces to determine her fate. It was a prodigious leap for the colony, discussed and decided almost matter-of-factly.

Peach Pit said, "The important thing is that we don't hurt her. She hasn't hurt anyone."

"Go take an enema from the bitch and tell me it don't hurt," said Sufur.

I said to Kotex, "What about your sixteen other sisters, and your hundred twenty-four half-sisters? Julia is putting them all at risk. Only someone like Ira would defend her actions."

"At least humans punish a crime," she said bitterly. "What do you know, Numbers? She could stop any second, and tomorrow find it was all just bad tofu, with nobody the worse. But you're ready to go after her now. Maybe you, the Prophet, are the imprinted one."

"If she weren't your sister you'd be demanding her blood," I said. But she had me wondering.

"What are we waiting for?" said Barbarossa.

"I thought you were better than that, Numbers," said Kotex. "You're not going to stain me with my sister's blood." She and Peach Pit ran back up the wall. Snot, who had been so shrill, hesitated, then ran after them. Once again, Julia was ejecting food that I had labored to carry from the kitchen. The pile grew, dangerously, on the floor.

Without another word, Bismarck, Barbarossa, Sufur, and I crept toward the opening, pressed so hard that our sternites, our ventral plates, flipped like playing cards over the bumps in the wall. It filled me with dread that this female, once my intimate, had turned alien.

On Bismarck's signal we rushed in. Julia shrieked and fired, hitting all of us several times, but no one seriously. We scattered down the baseboard cavity. I looked into the darkness but couldn't see anyone.

"It's over, Julia," I called.

"Frappé!" The mounds swirled like angry bees around their queen.

Bismarck, who was on the far side of Julia, inched toward her. She swung around, springing her labial palps like cobras. Sufur and I moved up. When she turned back toward us, Bismarck and Barbarossa closed. I felt weak.

But when Bismarck cried, "Now!" we charged.

I managed only one step before the cry from hell: "Liquefy!" Julia surpassed the critical speed, and the food exploded. Mad but calculating, she had hoarded large, honed missiles that now struck and gaffed us. Large sectors of my vision shut off as pain radiated from one eye to the next. When the end of my right antenna was lopped off, terror sped me away.

The pain slowly subsided. I saw that I was near the end of the baseboard; I had made good time blind. I knocked myself against the wood to loosen the shards. Pocked with clotting blood, my cuticle burned. I was trapped, scared. I no longer cared that Julia was a victim of hunger; she had made me her victim.

What delicate shadings of the mind force it to see a different reality? What, for example, pushes aside a vivid dream in favor of a drab morning? I don't know. But just then Julia pushed me into a new reality. As my instincts failed me, Exodus reclaimed me.

"And all the people saw the thunderings, and the lightnings, and the mountain smoking: and when the people saw it, they removed, and stood afar off."

Yes, so true. But what to do.

"An altar of earth thou shalt make unto me, and shalt sacrifice thereon thy burnt offerings and thy peace offerings, thy sheep, and thine oxen: I will come unto thee, and I will bless thee."

It would be so.

During the next few hours I acted in the interest of the colony. Did it matter that I was motivated by fables I had engorged by chance as a baby? Without them I might have died instinctively at the end of the baseboard.

We again moved up to the perimeter of Julia's chaos. At Bismarck's call we plunged in. This time we angled our assault to deflect her shot.

We each went for a leg. The rear left pounded my head again and again, then slipped away into the black vortex. I was willing to accept the punishment; the end was preordained. When one of my stabs finally caught it, I held on tight. She shook the four of us like maracas.

Our weight slowed her and the cloud of food began to precipitate. Soon I could see my peers, in a thickening camouflage of bran, wheat germ, pepper, rice, and pasta, each clutching a leg with all six of his own, just as I was. I opened my mouth and harvested a few falling grains.

Julia Child finally settled us into the soft pile. She was still for a minute, then started kicking her middle legs. Pinned at the corners, she couldn't do much harm.

Her eyes still raged. "Don't let go, not for a moment," I said.

"Muthafucka, the bitch done scratch up my new duds. Shit," said Sufur. He looked as if he had slid down a cheese grater.

Bismarck said, "Let's lock her."

We turned her over and folded her legs across her body, securing them by interlocking the spikes and bristles. Breaking this hold, while not impossible, was painful and noisy enough to forewarn us.

Warily, one at a time, we let go of her. She howled and strained, but the lock held. For the first time since we arrived, citizens began to appear from the far reaches of the baseboard.

"What are you going to do with her?" said Navel Lint.

"What are you going to do, honey? I'll tell you," cackled Julia. The newcomers backed away. "You'll chop, and then you'll whip, and you'll mix, and you'll grate. . ."

The matter was decided; I would not allow another discussion. I indicated to the other three to help me pick her up. Freed from responsibility, they were happy to comply. We turned her upright and carried her through the opening. I brushed debris off her back.

As soon as we left the baseboard Julia stopped struggling. Divested of the hostage food that had given her power, she knew her reign was over. "Agitate slowly," she said softly.

"What's your plan?" said Bismarck.

They were shocked when I told them.

"Hypocrites," I said. "This is just what you've been suggesting. Here. She's yours."

In a minute she was my charge. Julia listened without struggle or protest, which I interpreted as proof of the divine justice of my plan. In retrospect I think she simply went into shock.

We carried her up to the stove top. This was the single most lethal area of the apartment because of the slick enamel that highlighted us and then deprived us of the footing to escape. We slid Julia on her back across the surface; for once Ira's fastidiousness aided us. We lowered her under the front burner. I felt a little safer here, beneath the cover of the black steel arms. The pilot light, the eternal flame of the wrought earth altar, warmed us.

Julia had gone limp. I began to unlock her. Bismarck seized me. "What are you doing?"

I said, from deep within, "Fear not, for God is come to prove to you that ye sin not."

Sufur said to Bismarck, "My feet don't like the sound of that."

I freed her legs, certain she would not try to escape. I motioned to the others to take hold of them, but now they seemed as apprehensive of me as of her.

Bismarck said, "Why are you doing this?"

I wanted to convince him that this was what he would do if he were thinking clearly. But my serenity bade me say only, "Thou shalt not suffer a witch to live."

There was a long silence. For the first time I was frightened—that they would leave, and I would be unable to finish. I didn't care about their approval.

Bismarck, my true friend, said, "I don't understand you, Numbers. But I'm getting old and I have little to lose. This is my first act of faith. Don't make me regret it."

He took the forelegs and I the rear, and we carried her back under the stovetop. Then the word was done, justice was served, the common good was protected. We had held her over the pilot light for only a few seconds when the flame split and grew up both sides, turning from cold blue to a strangely warm and reassuring orange. Her chitin hissed and spit. Soon we were covered with the stench of burning protein—which should have frightened me but didn't, because I associated it not with death but with the Gypsy's cooking.

Julia accepted it fatalistically. Her body jerked from the heat, but it was reflex, not resistance. Her last words were a calm instruction: "Flame broil two minutes on each side."

After two minutes we turned her. Her back was charred. The spitting and popping resumed, and the stench intensified, but it was needless. She was already dead.

"I hope we can live with this," Bismarck said. "I really do." As we lowered her beside the flame, one of Julia's brittle legs broke off in his grasp. He stared at it. The other two flinched and backed away.

"Go," I said.

After they left the kitchen, I picked up the body. My moment of queasiness had passed; this was charcoal now, much blacker and much lighter than Julia had been. It smelled like carbon, not pheromones. She had been polished, but this thing was greasy to the touch.

I climbed up the back of the stove and squeezed her between the angled slats of the ventilator. I laid her down inside the duct. There was a resigned look on her black, disfigured face. That was fine; I didn't expect to be thanked in this lifetime.

I knew I hadn't chosen the most dignified resting place; I never did get to the verse about that. It was enough to know that here, Ira would not be able to sweep her up or vacuum her away as just so much garbage. If he turned his technology on her again, he would only make her fly, and ride with the angels.

American Legions

"SHE WOULD HAVE doomed us by sunset," I said.

"I know," said Bismarck.

"I had no choice."

"I know."

Still, today I felt sticky with her blood. "What's the use? By the time I get Ira and the blonde together we'll all be either mad or dead."

Bismarck said, "That's part of the challenge. You have to keep everyone alive long enough to save them."

The signs looked a lot worse than they had a day ago. Julia's disintegration had provoked thorough regressions in me and many book carriers. Why hadn't it inspired heroic acts of self-defense? If hunger had eroded us more than we suspected, what would be the effect of last night's disposal of our stocks through the baseboard hole?

Bismarck was probably right: the only possible moral and physical restorative for the colony, and the one way for me to regain their faith, was immediate food.

I could think of just one place I might find some—down the hall. Though I wasn't sure I could succeed alone, after the stove episode I knew no one would come with me.

EVEN IF JULIA had lanced every eye in my head, I could have found the Tambellinis' apartment with ease. The aroma of olive oil, tomatoes, garlic, onions, cheese, and pepperoni billowing from under their door made our pickled herring and horseradish seem as appetizing as rubber gloves. This, the prized apartment in the building, was for generations the site of a huge *Blattella germanica* colony. Ten years ago *Periplaneta americanae*, mutant roaches many times our size, took it in a bloody four-month war. We knew little about what had happened here since. I walked under the door, wondering if I would find a fat happy colony, or nasty giants who still bore my species a grudge.

I was surprised that the door was not guarded. I walked into the apartment. From the bedroom doorway I could see ghoulish television light dancing over garish wallpaper—hell in the modern Catholic household.

Hector Tambellini, somewhere on the bed, said, "Look at Johnny. His ex-wife taking him up the wazoo. Never worked a day in her life. You leave me, you know what you get, Vi? This. . ." *Smack!*

There was laughter from the TV. I walked past the doorway.

"How could any woman leave a gentleman like you?"

I stepped over the kitchen threshold, tensed for confrontation. The room was empty. I was relieved, but at the same time annoyed that *Periplanetae* could be so blasé about their riches while my colony languished.

I suddenly felt chastising eyes on my back, as if I had been heard thinking aloud. But I couldn't see them. I took a few slow steps forward, then back, and the eyes followed me. I jumped into a crack in the old linoleum.

Nothing moved. It could only be a *Periplaneta americana* somewhere in the shadows, engaging in high-minded entertainment. There was no sense pretending to be hidden.

Soon after I left the crack, I realized I was wrong. These eyes didn't have *Periplaneta* motion; they were stationary. Fixed, in fact, on a redwood plaque. They were not compound eyes, not simple human ones—they were quattrocento human eyes, belonging to none other than my childhood chum the Madonna. She hung flattened on the wall two feet above the sugar bowl. Her son, laminated in her arms, did not look at all well. Never had I imagined this scene illustrated so gruesomely. And though I had acted by biblical fiat the previous night, I didn't believe I would be capable of making much of a plea for mercy from someone who did this to me.

Mercy was not to be the theme of the evening. I descended from the chair leg to face a *Periplaneta americana* nymph. Nymph? This second instar was already twice my size. As she started to scream I stuffed dust into her mouth. But we were soon surrounded by her Watusi brethren.

I was amazed by the size of these animals. Ira bowed and scraped before basketball players, people a hundred pounds heavier and a foot taller than he. These *Periplaneta* monsters stood about four times my height and displaced thirty times my weight; I was not only an unworthy adversary, I was an inadequate footstool. I wondered how Ira would plead to a black mugger the size of a bus.

A playful tap from the nymph dropped me to the floor. Someone very strong hoisted me above his head, so I could see all the surface he might smear with me. "We don't like Huns," he said.

He launched me across the room. My flight ended when my abdomen scraped along the dirty floor. I burned to a stop in front of a toothpick sticking up from the exposed floorboards. A decaying *Blattella* head sat pierced on its point.

A human totem. Why, in this prosperity, had the *americanae* become so cruel and let their culture fall so low.

"Let's get that other toothpick," said one of the monsters.

"We can shove this one's head down over the other one. Make them into an hors d'oeuvre."

I was quickly running out of time. I said, "I came here depending on your honor as roaches."

"Honor? You Hun bastards fought us like lice," said a grizzled *americana* who looked old enough to have participated in the war. He was probably right.

"That was years before I was born," I said.

"Listen to that voice. Is it really male? Vi'd call him a countertenor." They laughed, and I hated them.

"It's prudent to have allies in another apartment," I said in my deepest tones.

The grizzled one tore the toothpick out of the floor and menaced me; it was as awesome as if Ira had extirpated an oak. The *Blattela* head nodded at me. Not yet, I thought. The grizzled one said, "We don't need you for anything, and never will. What do you want from us? Ask me. No, beg me."

The crowd around us thickened. One female showered us with pheromones which, to me, were sickly and coarse. Sexual allure does not cross species lines, and even if it did, hers was eclipsed by toxic levels of garlic.

The other males didn't seem to feel that way; their albatross wings began to beat. Their wind suddenly swept me across the floor. Trying to plant my legs I took a splinter that felt like a javelin. When I tried to tend it I smacked into the wall.

Each time I stepped away from the wall I was blown right back against it. I balanced on my rear end, legs free. "All right, Goliath, listen good. The way you're living, the dagos could take you out with one jar of boric acid. I'm literate; that means I can read. I can tell you things, warn you. In return I want one of your used skins. That's all."

The beasts laughed, filling the air with Italian halitosis. The grizzled one said, "What's the kicker? You want it stuffed with ricotta cheese or sweet sausage?

"Just the shell."

There was a buzz of disappointment; my request was a penny, too modest to refuse. Molted shells are important components of many insect diets. But because they were not quite al dente, here they just littered the room.

One ugly *Periplaneta* with a deep scar across its head pushed between the others. "It don't mean nothing to us, but he could plant it. Set us up. Look in his eyes; he hates our guts."

He was right. But the others turned away. When the breeze dropped so did I.

I looked up to see the perfect *Periplaneta* specimen, huge and sleek, with thighs like polished obsidian. Her expression was alluring but malevolent. I was in trouble.

"I understand you've come for a piece of our lives," she said. She led me to a pile of carcasses.

"Just a discarded one, that is, of course, if you don't mind."

"I am American Woman, queen of the bodies. Our culture is based on the exchange of goods and services." She rocked a carapace with her midleg. "We are not a charity."

The others were gathering around again. "My colony is so poor that I cannot offer you anything you don't already have," I said.

She reached down and patted me, which felt like blows from a sledge. "There, there. If you want the shell badly enough I'm sure you'll think of something." I looked for the fire door. "We are not heartless. I'll give you the goods, if you service me good."

The crowd cheered.

"I'm flattered," I said. "But what good could I do a gorgeous hunk like you, surrounded by these virile bulls?"

Males applauded. Females hooted. She said, "They bore me, the awkward puppies. All the same moves, one, two, three. They don't understand my needs."

She stepped toward me. I tried to back away, but I was blocked by the crowd.

"Don't you desire me?" She sprayed me wantonly, like a cosmetics salesgirl.

My pulse sped and my wings quivered. This was not possible. "I'm just a little Hun who doesn't want to disappoint you."

Her second blast of pheromones cramped my legs and blinded me. Her antennae honed on mine, knives on a steel. I knew who was to be the turkey.

My insides were oiled and moving. When my wings spread, common sense flew from me; I thought not of my pain, the deviance of my captor, or even the perversion of this scene. I thought only that sex was possible. Stranger things had happened—Ira and the Gypsy, Sodom and Gomorrah.

Then I delivered one of my life's most regrettable lines: "OK, American Woman, go for it."

I awaited the touch of her mouth on my gland. As my eyes cleared I saw a lowering crane. I crouched against the floor. But she was tender. The power of my chemicals would equalize us; if anything, she'd soon be in my thrall. I'd bring her back to Ira's, and she'd tear Ben Franklin out of my cabinet like a little scab. We could bag this human romance plan altogether. And then, who knew? A family?

American Woman suddenly ripped me into the air. I thought my gland would tear off in her mouth. I couldn't help churning my legs as I swung high above the hardwoods, and this brought the monsters' laughter to a new pitch. The searing pain in my gland pulsed—American Woman was laughing, too.

"You've got a hot one this time," said the grizzled one.

She spit me out. When I hit the floor my wings could not completely close over the swollen gland.

"You know the puddle in the soap dish?" she said, laughing and spitting. "That's what he tastes like."

While they carried on, I slipped between some legs. Even if I didn't reach the door, I might find a crack in the woodwork where I could wait them out. They had had their fun; they would soon tire of me.

I didn't get far before I heard American Woman. "Where are you going, my prince? You told me to go for it, and your word is my law."

She stepped in front of me and stood imperiously still. I backed under her; it might as well have been into a barn. I didn't know how I was going to reach.

"American Woman," I said. "Where I grew up they say, 'She stoops to conquer.'"

"But when in Rome, *amore,* do as the Tambellinis do."

The Tambellinis would have lowered a boot on the lot of them.

I used American Woman's shadow to line up my genitals with where I assumed hers would be. My phallomere, my hook, had never been fully extended; it had never been necessary. But this seemed an awfully long way.

"Come down here a bit, or let's just forget it," I said.

She looked down; the play in her face was gone. I took aim. My phallomere soon elevated a record distance. I could feel muscles flexing for the first time. When I began to ache, I felt for her opening, but I couldn't find it. The *Periplaneta* savages taunted me. I looked back: I was no more than halfway to American Woman's body. My proud phallomere wavered, a piece of lint beside her gleaming limbs.

"Careful, he'll tear you up with that monster," said the scarred one.

The bitch would not move. I shunted blood to my rearquarters. But I was just not constructed to prevent this humiliation.

"Timber!"

The natives whistled the sound of a dropping bomb. Now American Woman lowered herself onto me. As soon as I felt her weight, I gave my phallomere a flex and drove it up into her. Her mocking laughter stopped. But her hole was so huge and its lining so thick that I couldn't hook on. My phallomere circled the crater twice but then, exhausted and cramping, flopped out.

"She stoops to conquer," American Woman whispered. "You were right, it's a wonderful idea." She dropped her entire weight on my back.

My legs sprang straight out, like a crab's. I was pinned to the floor, the pressure beyond anything I had ever felt. American Woman adjusted her position to seal more of my spiracles. Soon I could barely breathe. What was she after? There were simpler ways to kill me.

"Easy on her, stud," the scarred one said. "No rough stuff."

It took all my strength just to support her weight. The noise was swelling. Soon there was a wild cheer. The *Periplanetae* leaped around the floor like simians. I had never seen such a display from a higher life form.

"A bull! A pile driver! She'll be deformed for life."

I hadn't any idea what they were on about, and I saw no need for them to be so rude as to collect behind me. Everything in my hindquarters seemed as it should be. I tensed the muscles to be sure.

And then I knew. The unthinkable had happened. The combined pressure of American Woman and my effort to support her had squeezed out my phallus like a line of toothpaste on the floor, where I was quite sure it lay, flaccid and useless.

I was powerless to prevent the ultimate degradation.

"Mayday! Mayday! German nukes at six o'clock!"

And so my precious spermatophore, my genetic guarantor of the future of my species, a commodity bid for many a sexy *Blattella* female, now ignominiously plopped onto the Tambellini's dirty floor. The crowd climaxed.

American Woman got up. The relief from her weight was greater than any sexual release I'd ever known. She rolled onto her back and pedaled her legs, moaning. "Oh, baby, it's never been like that before."

At that moment I would have been glad if Hec and Vi had taken us all out with the spray. As the crowd clustered like brutish children around my spermatophore, I picked up a shell of an earlier version of American Woman and carried it off. I had earned it.

Down the hall I dragged the shell. It was thicker and heavier than I would have ever guessed.

Vi said, "My sweet Hec." There were little slaps on loose flesh. "You're not enough of an asshole to get Letterman's job. Stay at the post office. Maybe stamps will go up."

"Oh, Vi, you Magdalene!"

The TV snapped off. There was loud kissing, and soon springs began to squeal. I raced to get out of earshot.

THESE WERE STRANGE times that the safest place in my world was the public third-floor hallway, whose fluorescent fixtures lit me like a rock star. I had the food for my colony, yet I couldn't be sure that it and I wouldn't be barbecued together when I offered it. If they did accept it, what good would it do? A few more days of feasting, then a return to lethargy and futility? I wouldn't have another chance. I had to make more of American Woman's earlier self than that.

I propped her between two bricks in a joint missing its mortar. When James and the mop came by the next day, I had to squeeze in behind her. Even dead, she filled me with rage and fear, and also, I'm afraid, lust. But it was useful torture: I realized how American Woman could help me in the long run as well as the short. Now I had to wait and be patient.

Each day I checked the mail laid on Ira's welcome mat. The letter didn't arrive until two weeks later. I dragged American Woman to the threshold. I got under her like an Indian under a bison skin, and carried her into the apartment.

"Invader, invader!" Krazy Glue screamed. I was flattered. The few citizens on the floor fled for the baseboard. I walked up the hall.

Several of the Vibrams were tugging on a piece of dust stuck in the door hinge. The sole survivors of a hearty family, they were a lucky find for me. I trapped them against the door. In my deepest voice I said, "Do as I say or you're antipasto."

Goosh Vibram looked at me carefully and said, "OK." I was disappointed.

"Up there, to the mantel." I had them go first. For me it was arduous to climb carrying the shell, and also to preserve my disguise. On top I said, breathlessly, "That white pawn. Push it up one square."

Legs slipped and scraped against the marble until the pawn crossed the line. My citizens shouldn't have been so industrious in the service of the enemy.

I set them free. Goosh said, "Why don't we move them all, Numbers? That would really mess up the board."

We all laughed. I pushed American Woman off the mantel and picked her up when I reached the floor. After stashing her in the bedroom I returned to the living room.

THE MOMENT Ruth walked into the apartment, Ira said, "I got a letter from Lev Dubalev. I was just about to open it."

"That was quick," said Ruth. "It can't be more than four months this time."

"That's what worries me." He lowered the chessboard to the coffee table. "I'm afraid I missed something."

"Don't be so pessimistic. It might just be a thaw along the Trans-Siberian burro trail."

He opened the letter. Ruth stood behind him, hand on his shoulder. He stared at the board and started mumbling to himself. I was lucky—Lev had played in the center of the board, as we had. "I can't believe it. See this? Queen to bishop six. That's his move. I can take it and he's beaten. Five moves, tops. It doesn't make any sense."

"Then what's the problem?"

"He doesn't make mistakes. It's a ploy."

"Russians make mistakes too, Ira. That's why they have Club Gulag."

"Not this Russian."

Ruth examined the envelope. "Maybe the KGB steamed this open and changed his move, so you'd lose respect for Lev and stop harassing your congressman." She kissed his bald spot. "Why not see how it looks after dinner."

"I'll be right with you." As soon as she left, he pulled a stack of similar letters from the drawer of the lamp table. They documented every play of this game, from the first move. Ira reset the pieces to starting position, opened the first envelope—he had written little numbers on the corners—and made the designated move.

Ruth left him alone until it was time to eat. By then he had gotten through about half of the moves.

"How was your day?" she said at the table.

"OK."

"Findley found some obscure clause in the original leasing agreement that might destroy the entire acquisition I've been working on. Everyone was running around like chickens without heads, including me." She was very animated.

Staring into his dish Ira said, "I can't believe it."

"All right, Ira." Ruth put down her knife and fork. "But eat a little more first."

It took him another half-hour to reach the current move. "The pawn!"

The Vibrams had made Lev's move into a pointless, graceless sacrifice: his actual position was sharp, dominating the area in front of Ira's king. Ira smiled, for the moment more relieved by Lev's competence than threatened by his own predicament. That would soon change.

This was the crucial moment. Fault had to be assigned. Had he misread the letter? Had Rufus, or maybe Oliver, moved the piece?

Ira rose from the table and walked to the kitchen. Ruth was drying dishes. "Well, is his goose cooked?" she said.

"You never did take the game very seriously, did you?"

"Of course I take it seriously. I know what it means to you. I just let you walk out on my best dinner of the week."

"Then why did you move the piece?"

"I don't even play the game. Why would I do that?"

"That's what I'd like to know. It's the only thing in the whole apartment I ask you to leave alone."

"Ira, you're being ridiculous. I never touch that board."

Ira looked at her suspiciously. "Then how do you dust it?"

"I don't. I just told you, I never touch that board."

Ira strode back to the living room and drew a finger across the marble. He looked at his fingertip, then rubbed off the grime.

A few minutes later he returned to the kitchen. "I didn't mean to accuse you. I guess I'm a little too caught up in the game."

Ruth dismissed it lightly. Once again she refused to play her part by issuing a just reprimand. I would make her see reason tonight.

Ira turned off the lights after a vapid evening. I moved a piece of cellophane, peeled from Rufus's cigar pack, from behind the sofa, where I had stored it, and put it into the middle of the hallway.

Ruth was sitting in bed in one of her nicer nighties, a white lacy number that made the most of the line of her breasts. It was as if she thought he would be unsettled by his accusation, and require extra incentive.

But Ira's routine was on my side. He always stood on the same spot beside the night table as he undid his watch, and this is where I pushed American Woman.

Preceded by a wave of mouthwash, Ira entered the bedroom. Ruth said, "Forget about Lev. Come on in here and make a few moves."

A moment later his large toe split American Woman down the center with a violent crack; if only it were her in the flesh. He grabbed his glasses. "There's a fucking waterbug in here!" He jumped onto the bed. I loved the term "waterbug." So demeaning. I wished I had remembered it down the hall. "Ruth, I have lived in this apartment for twelve years, and I have never seen a waterbug here before."

"What is that supposed to mean?"

He was trembling. "I am only stating a fact. This is not the first incident. Since you moved in, vermin have taken over the bedroom."

Ruth returned to her side of the bed. I pulled American Woman back into the shadow of the bed leg.

"And since life does not generate spontaneously. . ."

"Yes?" Finally, after all these months, anger was rising in her voice.

"You want me to spell it out? OK. Then we must assume that it has something to do with your hygiene."

"My hygiene? How dare you! How about that slob who lived here before me? I'm still cleaning up after her. My hygiene!"

"Don't you talk to me about her," yelled Ira. "There were no waterbugs while she was here."

"No, she was so petite she probably brought crabs."

Ira said, "Let's not change the subject. Why don't you see your guest out of the bedroom."

Ruth snorted. I had her now. "If that will spare me any more of your juvenile hysterics. Get out of the way." She slid across the bed and looked over the edge. "Where is it?"

"Right under your nose."

That covered a lot of area. "Well, it's gone."

"I stepped right on it. It's got to be there." American Woman was safe; Ruth didn't care, and Ira wouldn't go down on all fours to look for a live waterbug. "I'm not going to sleep while some disease-carrying vermin walks all over me. I'm getting the spray."

Teeth gritted, he made an impressive leap from the bed toward the door, then strode down the hall as if playing Giant Steps. His feet were angled perfectly so that on his fourth step my cellophane shot up between his toes. Ira's scream brought Ruth running heavily down the hall.

He jumped onto the living room sofa. "That does it!" He snapped on the lamp and held up his sole for examination. Then he lowered it, perplexed, even disappointed that it wasn't tattooed in red and brown.

Ruth said, "What happened?"

"I landed on that disgusting thing again."

"Let me see."

"Take my word for it."

Ruth had already reverted. Soothingly she said, "Whatever you stepped on is a long way from here now. Let's go to bed. If you want, I'll call the exterminator tomorrow."

"I'm sleeping here. I'm not up for any more adventure tonight." Ira thrust his head into the pillows and rolled on his side.

She stroked his back. "Come to bed, baby. You'll catch your death of cold out here."

After several minutes she left.

I ran to the bathroom and took position under the toilet seat; I had to gauge my effect on her. As soon as the buttocks landed, her sphincter whistled a happy tune, and the bowl smelled like the bayou. She had learned her lesson.

I heard a click, like the clasp of her pocketbook, then the crinkle of cellophane. She had found it in the hallway. I didn't care; its job was done.

A quick rasp, and I smelled a match, a cigarette. Once I thought I had seen a pack of Virginia Slims in Ruth's pocketbook, but she had never smoked in the apartment. Why now? Why do anxious women smoke?

This was the unpardonable offense. If Ira drove Ruth away, Elizabeth, or someone else—it didn't matter—would have been present for the shiva. Even if he didn't, Ruth would be forever tainted in his eyes, and every other woman would look better, especially those who already did look better.

I wished I could see that cigarette glow, a little pyre for their romance. But her beefy thighs sealed the bowl.

Then I had a disquieting thought. These thighs were trapping methane. Her cigarette was burning down and there was only one place to dispose of the butt—in here. The second that ember hit the gas we would blast straight through the ceiling. Ruth's head would lodge in the toilet trap and she'd get a chance to watch the Howards in 4B the way I watched her. And I. . .

How could I hide, where could I run? The last exhalation. The cigarette was spent. Her thighs were parting. I bolted. Her hand lowered between her legs and she bowed her head. Daven, please! Give me time! But she released it.

I was dead. I listened for harps but I heard only this: *hisss*. And it was over. I shamefacedly ran back under the seat.

Ruth stood up and turned to look at the floating butt, turning slowly in the bowl. She seemed to be debating whether to leave it as a gesture of defiance. But she flushed, opened the window, and sat on the edge of the tub, sniffing.

It was up to me. I raced out of the bathroom and up the hallway wall. I was breathless by the time I climbed into the housing of the smoke detector.

This was a photoelectric-type detector. Ira refused to let the landlord install the cheaper ionization type—which I could not have manipulated—because its element would have subjected Ira to about as much radiation as he got from a hot knish.

I knew this would be a tremendous shock. I tensed myself and walked across the little mirror, blocking the light beam and setting off the alarm. The shriek hit me like a leather sole. My intersegmental membranes felt like fault lines that would reduce me to a family of little grubs.

I fell from the violently vibrating mirror into the bottom of the housing; I knew from Ira's weekly tests that the torture would last only a minute.

By the time my hearing returned the assault was already in full force.

"You do this often?"

"This is the first time."

"It's vile, disgusting. How could you do it in my house. Don't you know my father died of lung cancer?"

"Stop already, Ira. I'm sorry."

"You're sorry. Great. First the waterbugs, now this, and you're sorry."

"Stop it! You're so unfair!" And then she began to cry.

That's it, honey. You don't have to endure this abuse. Leave him. Just let him try to replace you.

But as she hunched forward to hide her face, her fat gathered at her sides and pushed out beside her thighs. She was a victim of the look of the times and a prisoner of the tardiness of her generation. It was too late to go. Poor Ruth.

MY PLAN WAS to open the cabinet, and I was pleased with my progress. I didn't care why, or for whom, Ira spent the money, as long as he did. Ruth had her own problems. Now that I had made my point I expected her cooperation, and I would involve her no more than I had to. I was taking no pleasure in causing her pain.

Elizabeth Gets Cold

IT WAS ONCE again time to squeeze the bellows of discontent into the Wainscotts' hearth. I could pick out their apartment with my eyes plucked out. Their mark was blandness—the absence of spice, the soft odors of boiling and buttering, of frozen meals and canned goods. Undisturbed clothing, furniture, and carpets grew colonies of pallid WASP microorganisms. The small resident *Blattella* colony, chronic sufferers of spiraclitis, never welcomed visitors or word of the outside, where they were certain life was better.

If undertaken in Ira's apartment, this expedition would have led me deep into the closet, through piles of neatly stacked boxes. It could have taken days. But here in the Wainscotts' apartment my objective sat clearly visible and easily accessible, atop a mesa of debris on the desk.

I climbed a leg to the desktop. Dust lay thick and bitter. I scaled a pile of yellowing, unopened newspapers to the "Bernsteins'" box, which Ruth and Ira had given Elizabeth on her birthday weeks earlier.

I slid into the box. The scarf was taupe, with the folksy-artsy kind of design Ruth loved. The pattern ran down the center, leaving plain borders on both sides. These were mine.

I descended to the desk drawer. Behind the pointless pencils and topless pens was the rubber cement jar, with its cap glued on permanently askew. Lumpy lines of dried glue ran down the outside. I pulled loose the top end of one of these lines, where it was thinnest, and walked down the side of the jar, peeling the cement as I went. Finally it pulled free and fell to the drawer bottom, coiling like a watchspring.

Though the outside was very tough, the underside of the glue was still somewhat moist and malleable. I tore off six small chunks and packed one around each of my feet.

I did three sets of jumping jacks—which I'd learned from Elizabeth—twenty repetitions each. During the first I clapped my forelegs together over my head, while the back four jumped in and out. In the second set the midlegs clapped, and in the final set the rear legs clapped, while the other legs did the jumping. At the end I was an exhausted aerobic roach wearing rubber cement flippers. I felt ridiculous; I could barely walk. In the spell of the vapors from the glue I thought about leaving terra firma to return to my roots in the sea, as the whale had. But the idea passed quickly—I could never risk becoming a developmental blunder so pathetic that humans would beg for it on bumper stickers.

I tripped over to a red pen and fell on my side in front of it. I padded my flippers over the tip as if I were walking a treadmill. The pen did not write first time or any time. I shimmied up and injected my potent piss into the tip beside the ball. Now the pen yielded like an oasis spring. I saturated all six flippers and walked off dripping red, as if onto the set of a horror movie.

I quickly returned to the box and stomped around one of the borders of the scarf, leaving clashing red cuneiform that even charitable Elizabeth would be pressed to think of as folk art. When my steps faded I pulled off the flippers and left them in the box. I wished Oliver and Elizabeth were keen-sighted enough to find them; I would have loved to hear them argue about what they were.

I WALKED ACROSS the wall to the thermostat. I could slip under the clear plastic face and pull over the setting needle, but Oliver would have seen it and easily corrected it. Instead I worked my way into the back of the thermostat, to the bimetallic strip that moved the room-temperature needle. The small metal pieces that connected the two were so fragile that I kicked them apart. The room temperature needle would read just what it did now, no matter what the actual room temperature was; the radiators would not come on. Wind blew through the myriad cracks in the aging window frames, and the apartment cooled fast.

Elizabeth came home and immediately started cooking, which buffered her from the cold; Oliver's martini protected him. I was freezing.

It wasn't until after dinner, when the stove cooled, that Elizabeth looked at the thermostat. "What's wrong with this thing?" she said, tapping the plastic. Glowing from his third drink, and swaddled in blubber, Oliver would not move. Elizabeth put on a heavy sweater and hugged herself.

Finally she said, "Ollie, I don't think it's working."

With a groan he rose from his chair, tipping a wave of his fourth martini onto his pants. He looked at the thermostat. "It's seventy-two degrees in here. What do you want, a sauna?" He rapped it so hard that the cover flew off.

Oliver returned to his reading. Elizabeth sat beside him, feet curled under her tight little buttocks, rather than his capacious ones. Hands in armpits, she looked vacantly around the room. Finally she saw it.

She walked to the desk, opened the box, and gently lifted out the scarf, smiling as she rubbed it against her cheek.

Oliver looked up. "How much did you blow on that?"

"Ruth and Ira gave it to me for my birthday. Don't you remember?"

"Well, don't you forget their birthdays, or you'll be hearing about it."

"Oh, please." Elizabeth folded the scarf lengthwise; I was afraid she had turned my art to the underside. But then she held the scarf up to the reading lamp and gently rubbed it with a finger. "Ollie, I can't get this off."

"What, the price tag? Let me see." He scratched at the flipper marks with the nail of his chubby thumb, then tossed it back to her. "That, my dear, is filth. Filth is what Ruth and Ira have given you for your birthday."

"Do you think it will come out?"

"It's hard to know with that Korean polyester."

"Stop it. It's wool challis. Do you think it would be terrible if I told them?"

"Why not? At Bernstein's all they have to do is give their Christkiller number and they can make any exchange they want."

Elizabeth wrapped the scarf around her neck. "Ollie, I really don't like you talking like that about people who went out of their way to buy me a birthday present—which is more than you did."

"Mine will get here. Didn't I take you out to dinner? That was romantic."

"At Burger Brigade? The Custer Trough for Two?"

He dropped his paper. "What do you want from me? Is my love for you measured in dollars? Should I have blown for something ostentatious and empty? Or maybe you wish I'd grown up in a faith where the bottom line is God."

Bless him, he pushed her much farther than I thought the scarf was good for. "They're the best friends we have.

They're kind and generous. But everything you say about them is ugly. You seem to want me to feel dirty about our friendship. Well, it won't work, OK? It's your problem."

Later that night Oliver climbed into bed aflame with alcohol. When he tugged on Elizabeth's shoulder, she slapped his hand and said, "Not tonight."

THE COUPLES were in the perfect mood for Friday dinner. I had only to make final preparations.

The Table Is Set

I GOT HOME several hours before dawn, the safest time to forage. I had hoped that the Julia episode would prompt more searches of our floors; instead it seemed to have discouraged the colony altogether. I heard only one deviant, from around the corner: "Workers of the world unite! You have nothing to lose but your chains." For once I wished someone had listened.

But I was filled with purpose, and today's was to locate my vacuum cleaner nymphs. I spotted the first one late in the morning, after Ruth and Ira had left for work, loitering with his peers beside the baseboard. As I approached, his front legs shot out and struck the wood. "Got you, sucker!" he said. The others laughed.

They were stomping bacteria. There was no sport in it; the slow, defenseless microorganisms had no chance. It was pure viciousness: the adolescents had learned from watching, or hearing about, humans doing it to us.

I lifted the nymph by his forelegs. "What are you trying to prove?"

"Fuck yourself," he snarled. What had happened to his self-preservatory instinct to make him risk his life with his foul little mouth? His chitin cracked in my grasp. He made little whining noises, but he would not beg, not with his friends watching. I wanted to squeeze until he broke. But I needed him.

He was far too light for his age. When we fixed the Wainscotts' lock he was a second instar. He should have been an adult by now, but he was still a fourth instar, and even those two molts hadn't been completely successful; he was long and slender, with thin, weak limbs.

I dropped him. He rubbed himself. When I asked for his help he mocked me.

"There's a big meal in it for you," I said.

He soon found all seven survivors; the eighth had been rolled up in a table cloth and perished in the spin cycle. They were all as sallow, anemic, and foul-tempered as he was, which upset me. A spoiled child of the Gypsy generation, I refused to accept that every new generation could be anything less than we were, princes of the ecosphere, master survivors.

I told them their reward was American Woman; I knew the Vibrams would have blabbed by now. On the open floor the nymphs were determined, indifferent to sights and sounds that had terrified them a few months earlier. They climbed into the back of the vacuum cleaner without hesitation.

"Six pieces of wire this time," I said, "each twice as long as the one we used in the lock. I need them by this afternoon."

I RETURNED to the baseboard to a barrage of accusations. It seemed that I was now a hoarder as well as a murderer. If the citizens knew American Woman was in the apartment, why hadn't they gone out and found her? I would have. Hunger was paralyzing them, making them cowards.

"Hold on," I said. "I was the one who went out to defeat the waterbugs. I will share her with you, but only if you do as I ask."

They wanted the meat without making the motions.

A voice in the back piped up: "Every present state of a simple substance is a natural consequence of its preceding state, in such a way that its present is big with its future." It was Hegel, orating with impunity.

I took him on: "Which is just what I was saying. How better to make your present big with your future than to make your gut big with waterbug meat?"

"In the world everything is as it is, and everything happens as it does happen: *in* it no value exists, and if it did exist, it would have no value."

My spirits began to fade. Who was I to direct these loud, demanding citizens, when *Blattella* has resisted direction for 350 million years? Each of us was designed to do it our way, and our individualism has everything over the alternative, communalism. Its lowly avatar, the bee, like the human, thrives only in its assigned caste, unable to sustain itself alone. The good little fascist worker performs its "dance" (would entomologists say galley slaves "dance"?) to endlessly collect food of which it barely partakes, to tend a hive it rarely inhabits, to indulge a female so obese, so grotesque, that she is never let out for fear the species would be laughed out of the animal kingdom. And at what cost the honor of worker beehood? Half of all chromosomes, all gonads, and all independence. Everything.

It had to be *Blattella* ways, first and always. The problem lay not with my fellow citizens, but with my own defective individualism. I wanted to open the cabinets, to reclaim the kitchen for the entire colony. It was too grand, too collective. Why wasn't I looking for grape nuts or hot *Blattella* babes for myself? I wasn't being selfish enough.

I left the baseboard. Under a kitchen toe-kick I saw a backside of distinctive stiffness. Bismarck. "What have you got?" I said.

His leg flew apart to defend his food. He had it right—every roach for himself. But when he saw me he said, "A bran flake. I stayed here all through breakfast, and I got lucky. Ira's plugged up again."

We shared the flake, and a moment later shat uncontrollably on Ruth's clean floor. "Good stuff," he said. "I don't know how he holds it in."

Bismarck's generosity turned me around again. This time I felt sure. I could not give up my plan after months of work. I was as selfish as the rest, only mine was an enlightened selfishness; if I received no immediate reward, the future prosperity of my colony was certainly my selfish interest.

I said to Bismarck, "I'm going to play it out tonight during dinner, and there's an awful lot to do. The others won't help."

"We don't need them." Within minutes he assembled Barbarossa, Sufur, T. E. Lawrence, Clausewitz, and last of all Snot, who could not meet my look after his cowardly retreat from Julia. If these citizens didn't quite share my vision, they did share my disgust with the torpor of baseboard life.

THE THEORY of boric acid holds that a human lays the fine white powder where we, the quarry, are likely to pass. Too primitive to notice, we stroll through it, if necessary plunging into drifts shoulder high. Then, ignoring the chemical's astringent taste and all our knowledge of its effects, we preen—a primitive instinct of primitive animals—to transfer the powder, now stuck all over our bodies, into our mouths. This is how it kills us. Humans don't think much of the intelligence of insects; but if I filled Ira's living room with barrels of toxic waste, I would not expect him to jump in.

We picked our way through the line of boric acid just inside the pantry. The floor was clear from there to the back wall, where Ira had put more poison. I never understood why.

But it had worked. Half-buried in the white powder were three *Blattella* cadavers. It was a terrible sight. Bottomless white sockets stared at us from where heavens of eyes had sparkled. Powerful wings and thoraces had weakened to a translucent brown; extremities had turned a rotting guppy green. Most unsettling was their posture, contorted like prospectors caught in an avalanche. These were careless deaths, which had to date from the bounteous generations before Ruth. It angered me to see lives casually squandered, and it hurt to be reminded of the prosperity that had passed us by.

I handed out fragments of a toothpick that Rufus had spat onto the living room carpet. I kept one for myself.

Bismarck and I walked into the pile. Planting myself securely in the deadly powder, I swung the sharp edge of my wooden pick at the body. It bounced off; the chitin was tougher than it looked. I planted the pick on the membrane in between two of the body's segments. With a cellophane pop it was pierced. Bismarck speared the body the same way near the head.

We hoisted the cadaver up out of the pile. Boric acid poured out of the eyeholes and limb joints, and the spiracles trickled like a salt shaker. Snot and Sufur moved into the drifts and extricated the second carcass. But Barbarossa adamantly refused to work with T. E. Lawrence on grounds of homosexuality, even though Lawrence was most adept in the boric sands. Clausewitz took his place, and the third body was removed.

Laid out on the oak floor, the dusted bodies looked like wraiths. With my toothpick I started to carve out a hold so I could pick up my cadaver without touching acid. Chips of chitin flew; dust to dust. We all cut holds, then carried our charges slowly, like pallbearers, through the perimeter of acid and out of the pantry.

In the kitchen the pots and pans hung from a pegboard beside the stove. When I first saw the board, as a newborn, I figured that with its body-sized holes it would make a good advanced position. But Ira caught a patrol there and decimated them even as they clung to the back, like ladies in a knife-throwing act. Raid shot through the holes and killed them on the ricochet.

Ira wasn't home, and we quickly got the bodies up the board. Now I had to make a crucial tactical decision.

There was a seven-pound chicken defrosting in the sink, which was certain to be roasted. This did us no good, because the roasting pan had no holes, and therefore did not hang.

Ruth was a firm believer in the four mythological food groups purported by scientists to be essential for good health (although quintillions of us have thrived on fewer for 350 million years). For starch, I guessed potatoes or rice. Baked potatoes were also out of our control, but she might boil or mash them; rice, too was workable.

The vegetables would arrive fresh with Ruth. But what would she do with them? They could be boiled in a small pot, steamed, sautéed in the small frying pan, or even turned into a casserole. There were too many variables.

I had to guess. A roasted chicken the size of a booby is bland. So are potatoes. I intuited that there would be at least one spicy dish tonight, which probably meant frying or sautéeing; or else rice would be the medium.

This was it, then; the rice pot and the two frying pans would each get a cadaver.

With the toothpick fragment Barbarossa scored his stiff lengthwise and snapped it in half; the sound made me shiver. The shell slid through the hole in the pegboard and dropped into the smaller frying pan. Since Barbarossa relished the exercise, we let him break and deposit the other two cadavers as well. The mines were in place.

I needed large-scale help now, but I was still reluctant to use up American Woman. I asked Barbarossa if he could scout up about forty more bodies for a little while.

"As you wish," he said, clicking his back legs together smartly. He headed back toward the baseboard. I wished I too had the power to bully instead of bribe.

In a niche between the refrigerator and the neighboring base cabinet was a small pile of debris left over from the Terror. Though it was only plaster dust, the similarity to boric acid made us very tentative. It took twenty minutes to pull out two pieces of an old plastic spoon, which could be fitted together like the arm and fulcrum of a primitive catapult. We also extracted a dry, crusted watermelon pit.

Once, as a nymph, I tried the raisin bran escape, the maneuver that later doomed Rosa Luxemburg. Caught on top of the refrigerator by oncoming shoes, I raced across the top of the bran box and made a dive at the tab. I was thwarted; the box was unopened. Not yet familiar with real pain, I decided to jump to the floor. I was lucky that the young quickly heal and lost parts grow back. But I didn't learn that until after my excruciating crash, whose exact spot was where we now set up our plastic launcher. I believe in physics.

We hoisted the watermelon pit into the hollow of the spoon. By this time Barbarossa was returning with hordes of citizens. "Where do you want your volunteers?" he asked.

"The top of the refrigerator," I said.

No one moved. I was about to explain the plan, then realized, from watching Barbarossa, that reason was pointless; this mass had to be led. "White is right!" I cried, and started up the alabaster rise. The others swarmed up after me, picking up the call.

"Why you go use some asshole line like that for?" said Sufur.

On top of the refrigerator, guarding the raisin bran, sat a big black box with *Periplaneta*-sized letters: ROACH MOTEL. One viewing of *Psycho* on TV had kept us away from it. And in case anyone missed the show, the box described its adhesive, even the recipe of its cloying bait, right on the side. Only an illiterate with a taste for Kandy Korn would ever walk into a Roach Motel.

But Ira believed in them. I once heard him cluck, "Poor bastards!" as he put down a fresh one. Before the Terror we regularly booked the motels with debris from around the apartment, to multiply in Ira's mind the magnitude of his conquest. Delighted by their success, he continued to buy us new motels. We enjoyed watching the evolution of their graphic design.

"Yo, check this out," said Sufur, pointing to the writing on the façade.

Barbarossa walked over. "If you check in you can't check out. It says so right here."

The crowd was getting uneasy on the revealing surface.

"Citizens!" I cried. "Let's relocate this eyesore to the floor, where it's darker."

Again those of us who were convinced quickly swayed those who were not. Within a minute we were packed side by side, like a burnished xylophone, heads butting against the box, united for a noble purpose. I tingled, thinking that if apartment 3B lasted for a thousand years roaches will still say: "This was their finest hour."

Ira's ammonia had left the top of the refrigerator spotless and almost friction-free. "Now!" I commanded, and with surprising ease we got the motel moving. "Faster!" Feet screeched on the enamel and citizens groaned, their depleted bodies no longer fit for exertion.

Still is was an inspiring sight, hundreds of hairy *Blattella* legs thrusting, a hundred antennae bent back by the weight of the motel. The front slid over the edge of the refrigerator door, and suddenly our side tipped up, the outer paper tearing in our grasp. In an instant our sworn enemy crashed to the floor, hitting the spoon. The plastic cracked sharply, and the pit flew. I miscalculated; it didn't make the counter. It just barely reached the edge of Ruth's seat.

I noticed a white hole in our line across the top of the refrigerator door. Someone was missing. A scream echoed through the kitchen: "Mutha!" Sufur. He had forgotten to let go.

We rushed down to him. He was lucky that the motel had fallen sunny-side up. He pulled me close by one of my mandibles and said in a hushed, concussed tone, "Free at last!"

"Yes you are," I said, helping him up. He staggered off. The volunteers slid the motel across the flooring into the gap between the refrigerator and the cabinet; I didn't want to risk gaining Ira's attentions.

Snot had climbed onto Ruth's chair and was sniffing the pit. "Smells like haddock."

"Get closer," I called.

Bismarck appeared, dragging another hair from Elizabeth's pillow; the one I had brought had long been lost to the vacuum cleaner. Bismarck and I climbed to the seat and knotted the hair securely around the watermelon pit. We all took hold of the hair and climbed up the chair back onto the counter. The pit bounced and spun, the twisting hair burning in our grasp.

We crossed the counter and continued up the wall, above the line of canisters, a family of instars growing from dainty "Nutmeg" to burly "Flour." I figured Ruth would rest her shopping bag near the edge of the counter, then take out the box, and next to it put the platter, which would end up beneath the sugar canister. Splendid! Ruth rarely cooked with that evil food.

We walked the hair up one side of the sugar canister and down the other, maneuvering the pit on the handle. Barbarossa chewed off the hair with his huge mandibles and I dropped it behind the stove.

"Where'd you get the pumpkin seed?" said Junior.

"Just you watch," I said. I whispered to Houdini, and he climbed onto the handle beside the pit. After all these months he still stank of horseradish.

He said, "Ladies and gentlemen, for this trick I need a volunteer from the audience who can spit. You, sir, step up and show us what you can do. Right on that seed. Good. Now, that wasn't too bad but isn't there anyone out there with a little more juice. . . ?" Soon the white pit was running with spittle, Houdini turned his back and mumbled portentously, "Liver of blaspheming Jew, gall of goat, and slips of yew. . . cool it with a baboon's blood, then the charm is firm and good." He stepped aside. The pit was black and shiny as the day it dribbled off Ira's lip.

"Dinner will be served in the main dining room at nine o'clock this evening," I said.

BISMARCK, BARBAROSSA, and I entered the utility drawer in the base cabinet, the one truly chaotic site in the apartment—when Ira had transferred the contents from the old cabinets he had resignedly dumped it all in. The nails, tacks, tape measures, can openers, corkscrews, plastic bags, wrapping paper, twine, screw drivers, oil can, plastic straws, scissors, glue, and so on had over the years formed an organic whole. Our interest, the flashlight, lay on one side of the drawer.

"Do you think we could get something between the bulb and the batteries, or in between the batteries?" I said.

Barbarossa shook his head. "Forget it. How are you going to get in there?"

"Break it open, you animal," said Bismarck. "Shatter it with your very might."

Barbarossa's face lit with joy and fury, as if all his life he had been waiting for such an invitation. He burrowed to the bottom of the drawer and returned with a small finishing nail. He rocked rhythmically, then hurled it against the plastic lens. While he was still following through with his motion, the nail ricocheted and struck him between the eyes, knocking him into the eye of a ball of twine.

Bismarck laughed. Suddenly the flashlight lurched to the side, nearly crushing him and me. It wasn't the force of the nail. Barbarossa had set off some Rube Goldbergian reaction while he was rummaging.

Bismarck climbed to the top of the lens. "See this? If somebody pulls open the drawer, it's going to drive the screwdriver right through the bulb."

I climbed up beside him. "Looks a little low to me." We could no more lift the flashlight than the refrigerator. So Bismarck and I pulled on twine, string, and ribbons, and Barbarossa, now recovered, pulled on the big stuff. But a half hour of strenuous labor didn't move the flashlight another micron. We were ready to quit.

Almost as an afterthought, Barbarossa lifted the end of swizzle stick topped with the NAACP shield. Things started to rumble. Bismarck and I ran for the corners, tacks sliding and batteries roiling past us. When all was calm I raised my head. The flashlight had moved again.

"I can see the lights of Paris!" said Bismarck from the tip of the screwdriver.

IN THE HALLWAY we ran into Goosh and Mayhem Vibram, who were carrying two huge chunks of rubber cement. We all walked to the hall closet.

The fourth instar was lying on the floor between a pair of galoshes. One wire lay beside him.

I said, “We agreed on six.”

“Get the rest yourself,” he said. “Where’s my food?”

We walked up the cord into the vacuum cleaner. Sleeping nymphs lay beside three more lengths of wire. I hadn’t expected even this many.

We paired the wires and girdled them with the rubber cement. Barbarossa carried one pair to Ira’s kitchen, and the Vibrams took the other back to the Wainscotts’ kitchen.

One last touch remained. I had brought a strand of Elizabeth’s scarf back with me to Ira’s living room. Now I laid it in the black matte ashtray, which he kept spotless to discourage people from smoking. It set off the wool perfectly.

Now hurry home, Ira. We’re waiting.

Last Licks

THE DOOR OPENED, and in came my hero. He took the hall in a jaunty step, whistling spiritedly off-key. Seated in his favorite chair in the living room, he spread out the newspaper on the coffee table and skimmed the headlines. This was usually an intense search, scissors ready, for the urban horror stories that were grist for his moral mill. But today Ira didn't seem to really read anything.

When Ruth arrived, he sprang up and met her with a kiss just inside the threshold. "Princess!" he said, bowing like an eighteenth-century courtier. Somehow chivalry couldn't wear brown double-vents.

"Ira?" She squeezed her three shopping bags past him and put them on the kitchen counter, then turned warily to face him. "Good day?"

"Why yes!" he sang. "And you?" A formality. He wanted to talk.

"Not particularly," she said, on her way to the closet with her coat. Ira followed like a well-trained pup.

"Then let's start with the good day." He took her hand and led her to the living room sofa. I trailed them in the long shadows of the late-afternoon light. Ira bounced as if he had bladder trouble. "James Jackson has been granted a retrial."

"James Jackson, James Jackson. Oh, wasn't he the one who put his common-law wife through a meat grinder and tried to sell her to McDonald's?"

"Burger King. 'Special orders don't upset us.' No, that was James Johnson, now Abdullah-Aziz Johnson. He's still at County being evaluated."

"James Jackson. Let's see. He sprinkled angel dust on his malted and went for the land speed record in his, let's see, Plymouth, right? Down the sidewalk at rush hour?"

Ira beamed. "That's the one. You'll never believe it. I didn't find out until today that he wasn't read his rights."

Ruth got up. "That's great, honey. I've got to start dinner. I told them seven o'clock."

Ira and I followed her to the kitchen. He said, "The arresting officer said it would have been a waste of time because the perpetrator was so high."

"Well, maybe he had something there." She pulled packages from her shopping bags. Ira scored a pastry before Ruth shut the box on his fingers.

"Come on, Ruth. How can you say that? In an adversarial system the police are hardly the ones to decide when a suspect should be read his rights." He reached for another pastry. He was impishly buoyant tonight. The timing was all wrong.

Ruth snatched the box and put it back in the shopping bag. "So are you going to have him released?"

"He did kill four people, so the judge will insist on some psychological rehabilitation, probably group therapy. Vehicular homicide groups have sessions in a parking lot so they can understand what they've done wrong. But the guy has been sitting in an overcrowded jail for three months. That is cruel and unusual punishment."

"Well, let's hope James Johnson gets what is rightly his," she said pleasantly.

"James Jackson."

"Him too."

Ira went to change out of his good shoes, then returned to wash the vegetables. To my surprise Ruth started disjointing the bird. It would not be roasted after all.

Ira quickly finished. "And now?"

"The salad. And after you have to wash the mushrooms one at a time. They were all gritty last time."

He did as he was told. "Done. How are you doing the chicken?"

"A stew. I thought it would be nice for a change. First I have to sauté the parts."

Ira stretched on tip toes for the frying pan. "Isn't it handy to have a Titan around the. . ." As soon as he pulled it from the pegboard he saw the body. "Jesus Christ!" he screamed. The pan bounced off the iron stove supports with a terrible clang, and came to rest between the burners.

Ruth and I flinched; I cracked the last joint in my back left leg, and she gashed her thumb with the cooking knife. "What?" she cried. "What happened? Are you all right?"

Ira pointed at the pan and hissed. "Look!"

"Oh dear." Wrapping her bleeding thumb with the other palm, Ruth stepped over to the stove. Awkwardly grasping the pan handle, she dumped the body into the sink and washed it down the drain. She swirled water around the pan and replaced it on the stove. Blood from her thumb dripped quietly to the floor. "There, all gone."

"No, it's not all gone. You don't just rinse away bubonic plague, typhus, dysentery, and all the other disgusting things they carry." Indeed? "I renovated this kitchen for you, Ruth, and you have to put some effort into keeping it clean."

"Don't start that again. You did the renovation because the old one was a monkey cage. I keep this room spotless. I don't know what a harmless little roach was doing in a clean pot, but it is not my fault. I am not the ringmaster of the animal kingdom." Her blood continued to drip.

"You know what? Give the roaches my portion. I just lost my appetite." Ira tried to stomp out of the room, but the carbonified outsoles, and double-density medially stabilized insoles of his running shoes muffled him.

That's it, Ira? You're in danger of dying a terrible, disfiguring death. Don't be taken by these false denials. Ruth is turning your kitchen into a shelter for pernicious vermin. Don't walk out and let her think it's all right.

He wasn't interested in combat today. That damned Miranda ruling must have really juiced him up with endorphins.

But now my long work on Ruth paid off. A week or two earlier she would have gone after him, perhaps even applied the sexual emollient, and after a short break the evening would have continued as if nothing had been said. But tonight she took off her apron, opened her newspaper on the kitchen counter, and tried to read. When Ira finally returned and reminded her of the imminent arrival of the guests, she shrugged. Only when he began to produce strange odors from the pots did she return to the kitchen helm.

WHEN THE DOORBELL rang, dinner was not nearly ready. "Can I help?" said Elizabeth.

Ruth said, "Oh, no, everything's under control. Make yourselves comfortable in the other room. I'll bring something to munch on." Her voice betrayed nothing.

As Oliver walked by the mantel, he reached for the chessboard. "Don't," said Elizabeth. He shrugged and fell into a chair. It was all right; he'd get his chance to do worse.

"Ira, you in there?" he called to the kitchen.

"Yeth." Ira was eating.

"You're helping? Be still my heart. What, did your goldbricker union get you some bogus holiday today?"

Ruth appeared at the doorway, thumb bandaged and wooden spoon in hand. She motioned Ira out of the kitchen. "Why don't you tell Elizabeth and Oliver about your big day."

Oliver said, "Another killer nigger walking free, eh?"

Elizabeth pulled on his arm. "Please don't use that word."

"I'm sorry, dear," he said to her, then loudly, "I mean another killer nigger strutting free, eh?"

Ira said, "He's getting a retrial."

"I have faith in you," said Oliver.

Ira said, "As you might put it, it will be a black day for America when innocent men don't walk."

Ruth arrived with a tray of cheese and crackers. Chévre—an excellent choice; it was impossible to smear this cheese and pick up and chew the cracker without hailing crumbs onto the carpet. Oliver began to gouge the cheese before she set it down. "Manners," said his wife. I would harvest later; there was about twelve hours until the Saturday morning vacuuming. My ambitions tonight were much greater.

Oliver licked the side of the knife. His wife slapped his arm. "Nice," said Ira.

Oliver said, "Ira, I want to bet you that within two months of the walking date—and I know you'll get him one—he'll be back. Whatever he did, and whoever he is." His wife subtly dug her fingernails into the pendulous underside of his arm. "That is, of course, regardless of his color, creed, sex, or previous condition of servitude. But he'll be back."

Ira usually took these provocations with a smile. Not tonight. "It makes me uncomfortable when all we talk about is my work. Tell us what's new in the world of contracting and organized crime."

Oliver looked surprised. "What's wrong with the construction business? You must be confused by the idea of men going to work before they pick up their paychecks."

"No. It's the idea of people ending up at the bottom of the river in concrete Reeboks."

Oliver paused. "That may happen, Ira. I don't deal at that level so I don't really know. If there's a rubout every now and then, to make a big job go smooth, well, what can you do? At least my money's doing something. But when my tax dollars go to you to spring a spook who has been living on the dole so he can blow somebody else away for another hit of drugs, and then go back to court and back to jail on my money, that bothers me."

Ruth turned to him. "That's one of the most awful things I've ever heard."

Oliver shrugged. "Don't be naive. That's what it's like in the real world, where people earn a living."

"Please, Oliver. I am senior financial officer. . ."

Elizabeth interrupted in a startlingly bright voice. "Ruth, this wool looks like the scarf you gave me. Did you get one for yourself?" She had found the strand I left in the ashtray.

Ruth took it from her. "It does, doesn't it. No, I just got the one."

"Come on, Elizabeth. We all know a scarf like that wouldn't do for Ruth," said Oliver.

Elizabeth's face issued a powerful warning.

"Oh, I don't know," said Ruth. "If gifts started coming my way I wouldn't mind at all."

Come on, Oliver. Tell her you're on to her, that you know she's a cheap kike who buys Korean polyester for her friends and expects Thai silk in return. Tell her, thank you very much, but your fashionably thin wife does not wear filth on the nape of her delicate neck or beneath her single chin.

Oliver looked at his wife and sighed. "I wonder if there is any more Tanqueray." She declined to move, so he waddled back to the kitchen. His thirst for free premium gin was my first miscalculation of the evening.

They moved to the dining room, and Ruth shuttled in the serving dishes. I waited for someone to grow pale and shake as the planted *Blattella* body rose ethereally to the surface of the stew—the Ascension in 3B.

It didn't happen. The table was simply a portrait of earthly injustice. These fugitives from natural selection crammed while we, the apple of nature's eye, starved. I went back to the bedroom for American Woman and dragged her up the hall to the dining room threshold.

Smack, slurp. "It's wonderful, Ruth."

Hum. "Yeah, really."

Clink. "Oh, damn."

"Quick, pick up the glass. Pour salt over the spill. Get the whole thing. Keep pouring."

"Not the bottle, you sot. The salt."

This was my break. I dragged American Woman across the dining room floor and under the table. The lace table cloth draped to the ground, lending bordello floridity to the setting. The leaves lengthening the table spread the shoes elegantly, and safely, apart.

I called to the baseboard, and Bismarck's head emerged. "Are you inviting me to be the sacrificee?" he asked.

The dialogue above continued:

"Heirlooms get dirty. That's what they're for."

"That's not what they're for."

I said to Bismarck, "You'll never get safer pap than this."

He raced across the floor and skidded right into the waterbug shell. He leaped away, a *Blattella* reflex.

"Bismarck, please meet American Woman." He shuddered.

Sufur appeared at the opening, and was soon launched by Barbarossa, who climbed out after him. Citizens now came steadily. Everyone I had invited showed up, even the instars from the vacuum cleaner and the extras on the Roach Motel. American Woman could not accommodate all of us at once, so Barbarossa, snarling and straining, snapped her in half along the line of Ira's toe fault. Now we had two dinner tables, two dinners: my friends and I ate one, the Raid orphans, Listerine, Toe Nail, Spic 'n' Span, K-Mart, Ponds, and the rest of the volunteers at the other. The book cripples were there too.

We ate ravenously, Oliver-style. I felt as if our enemy had foolishly granted us a cease-fire, a chance to replenish and rearm, in the heat of the final battle.

"A wonderful meal," said Bismarck. "To you, Numbers."

"A wonderful meal, Ruth," said Elizabeth.

"So let me get this straight," Oliver said. "These two clients of yours have already generated five cadavers."

I was congratulating myself for nurturing his animus with vaginal deprivation when I saw something terrible—T. E. Lawrence, pale, almost yellow, was weaving slowly across the open floor, clearly visible to everyone at the table and beneath it, staggering back every few steps and leaving a bud of green vomit.

I screamed to him to come under the tablecloth. He stopped, and said grandiloquently, "I loved you, so I drew these tides of men into my hands and wrote my will across the sky in stars." He threw up again.

Barbarossa confessed. "The fairy was trying to mount a nymph. It was disgusting. I threw him into the boric acid. I'm not sorry."

"Don't do it," Bismarck said to me. "They'll get you both."

But I went, straight across the floor, timeless *Blattella* precepts howling their violation through my head. I grabbed Lawrence's antennae and dragged him under the table.

"I'm sorry," I said, to no one in particular. "I couldn't just leave him out there."

Bismarck said, "You could have and you should have. Here he can only bring us attention. Be sure he doesn't."

Bismarck was right; if Lawrence waltzed out from under the tablecloth, Ira would take a look and we were dead. Why had I done this? Cold fear blew me whispers of Saint Matthew: "Is not the life more than the meat?" Matthew and Lawrence both had to go.

Oliver was saying, "When you spring them is it like in the movies? The warden says: 'Boys, we went easy on you this time. But if we see your candy asses around here again, it's going to get rough.' He hands them a bus ticket and a pack of Camels. Felons hanging on the window bars are yelling, 'See you next month, James. Don't forget your KY.'" He was tapping his eleven EEEs on the floor.

"Ollie, we're at the dinner table," said his wife.

I said to Lawrence, "Come, the Turks are asking for the White God." He primped, then it was easy: I led him under the shoe and Oliver crushed him without knowing. A good soldier to the end, Lawrence rode out the conversation stuck to Oliver's leather.

My compunction had already passed. No one reviled me for this execution; no one bothered to look up from his dinner.

"Where do you read these things? I mean, what channels you watch these things on?" said Ira with a cough, which worsened, then stopped his words. Someone smacked him on the back.

He wheezed. He was still breathing. He would never die so easily. "Are you all right?" said Ruth. Foolish design; if you breathe through your back, food can block your airway only if you roll in it.

I went back to work on American Woman. Snot, who was working toward me, had already eaten his way across the centerline. "Don't eat so fast," I said. "Damn it, it's my shell."

"Don't eat so fast," said Ruth. "It makes you sick, and you won't want dessert. If there's any left."

Dessert!

Without waiting for distraction or cover, I raced from the table to the kitchen. I should have been in position already. Now I was in trouble. Ruth brought in the first load of dishes and stayed while Elizabeth retrieved the rest. I climbed to the underside of the counter, to within several feet of the canister shelf, but I could get no farther. Ruth was only placing dishes in water; she would wash them later. Her back wouldn't be turned long enough for me to make my move.

She raised the shopping bag to the counter, put the pastry box beside it, and placed the serving platter beside that, all as I had anticipated. I smelled the lardy sweetness of the pastries as she arranged them, and heard her lips smack after she licked her fingers. Oh, to have her place me into the arrangement! I cursed myself. If the platter left the counter without the prepared garnish, all my work could easily come to nothing.

The crackle of wax paper. The pastries were all on display. Maybe I could salvage a little icing before I took the bad news home.

The doorbell rang. Could it be Rufus already? I didn't care. As soon as Ruth went to the door, I raced over the counter, up the wall, and to the top of the sugar canister.

"Yo, what's goin' on?"

I pushed the pit off the handle. It slid down the shoulder of the canister, glanced off the shelf, and landed in the platter.

"You're so early," Ruth said.

"No, right on time," said Rufus. "I'm a businessman."

The pit stuck in the thick glaze on the edge of the top pastry. This was no good; during her final inspection Ruth would pluck it off.

"You're right," she said. "I forgot, we got held up. . . we were delayed. Come in. We're about to have some dessert."

As soon as I heard the awkward syncopation of her heavy steps and his taps, I leaped. I landed on the pastry beside the pit, and my legs sank to the first joint. The glaze was like flypaper. This was too cruel.

Ruth's pumps were quickly scuffing back. I flattened against the pastry. I was lucky—this time she chose to take the coffee pot. I had about thirty seconds before she would come back for me. With the superhormonal strength generated only by pure fear—the strength that lets old ladies lift cars off trapped sons—I managed to get one leg free, pry the pit up on the edge, and kick it between the pastries. With a soft *ping* it found the platter. Pulling myself onto a walnut, I eased out my legs, almost losing the back left to the glaze. Then, despite my exhaustion, I sprang farther than any *Blattella germanica* has in 350 million years, from the middle of the platter to the countertop—a feat I never announced in the baseboard, knowing I would not be believed. Not even the glaze caked to my legs could slow me now. I raced across the counter and made it behind the toaster just as Ruth returned.

This time she took the coffee cups. My heart was pounding; I wished I had known. By the time she brought the platter into the living room, I was sitting with the others, who had moved to the coffee table.

"So, Rufus, old man, how've you been?" asked Oliver.

"I been good, Oliver boy."

Elizabeth said, "We haven't seen you in ages."

"Not in a coon's age," said Oliver.

"I've been busy, mindin' the store."

Oliver was tapping his foot again. "Rufus, you'll be glad to hear that Ira rectified a serious breach of constitutional justice today."

"A refund from the tax man? He musta owe you what, five, ten green easy."

"No, no, it was a Negro. Someone neglected to read him his rights after he ran twenty people down with his car."

Ira's head swung back and forth as he made a futile effort to intervene.

Rufus's voice fell to a whisper. "Sound like the Miranda Gang. Buncha bad-ass nigger love to be read to, like little kids. Forget, *Pow!* you nothin' but dust."

"Wow!" said Elizabeth. "They must be a well-educated gang." Oliver dropped his head.

"You dumb enough to get caught, not hearin' your right don't buy you nothin'," said Rufus. "Only on TV."

Oliver looked at Ira. "That's it! The TV defense. It's every bit as good as the San Francisco Twinkie defense. Rufus, do you eat Twinkies?"

Rufus stuck out a tongue like a lizard's. "I like to lick out the white part."

Ira quickly passed him the tray. "Why don't you try a pastry?"

"That's the longest tongue I've ever seen," said Ruth. "Can you touch your nose?"

Rufus said, "I can touch your nose."

"What are you doing?" Oliver said to his wife, whose little tongue was straining over her own upper lip.

"See what you started?" Ira snapped at Oliver.

"I can do it," Ruth said to Ira, as she painted the bottom of her promontory. "Can you?"

With an expression of contempt, Ira picked up the winning pastry and opened his mouth. The watermelon pit, stuck lightly to the bottom, fell to the platter with a *thwack*. The conversation halted.

No one spoke for several seconds. Finally the host said, "Where did that come from?"

Elizabeth was watching her husband. "The pastry was fruity tonight."

I signaled to Crest, in the doorway, who passed word to Bismarck in the kitchen. It was time to dispatch the contingent up the wall.

I had gone through all the effort of placing the pit to spur Oliver's racism, which would humiliate his host and infuriate his wife, thereby consolidating their alliance. Oliver took his cue. "Ira, you devil, you've been filching from the Legal Aid coffers."

"Shut up," said Ira, then to Elizabeth, "Did he put that there?"

"I'm not saying you're not entitled to your pits. But are you declaring them to the IRS?" Oliver chortled. "Rufus, you're a businessman. Would you accept this as legal tender?"

Ira looked defeated, Oliver mirthful. Elizabeth's apprehensive eyes darted from face to face; Ruth was not quite as concerned. Rufus tapped his outstretched fingertips against one another. The pit sat in the middle of the white platter, a black hole with profound cultural gravity over the orbiting humans. I had done it—pushed them together and left them with nothing dignified to say. I was stripping their civilization, abandoning them to their naked humanity.

Finally Rufus broke the silence. "Let's do business. I ain't got all night."

Ira leaped up. "In the kitchen."

I sent a second signal to Crest, and Bismarck relayed it up to the fusebox. Holding the rubber cement girdle, a squad of citizens pushed the copper wires from the vacuum cleaner into bare points on a connection in the main line. *Pop!* The apartment went black.

"What the hell was that?" said Ira.

Oliver laughed. "The Miranda gang. They want their story."

"The lights are on across the street," said Ruth. "It's just our old wiring. Don't worry."

Rufus's shins cracked against the edge of the table, and he fell back into his chair, cursing and massaging. Ira felt his way along the wall to the light switch and yanked it up and down.

"That's not it," said Ruth. "The hall and kitchen went out too."

"It must be the fusebox," said Ira.

"And they say Jews aren't handy," said Oliver.

Oliver's wife said, "Why don't you help him?"

"I'm not the kind of guest who gets in people's way."

Ira worked toward the kitchen like a mole; he had walked the route thousands of times, but without sight, *Homo*'s only adequate sense, he was lost. I easily kept up with him. "Nice work," I called to Bismarck.

Ira fumbled for the utility drawer. Feeling the resistance we created, he gave the handle a brutal yank. The shattering glass rang out; the flashlight was eviscerated.

He picked it up and tried the switch. "Damn it, Ruth. Shut the flashlight off when you put it away." He threw it back in the drawer.

"What?" She smacked the table with her legs and sat.

Ira felt his way back down the hallway wall. "Turn the thing off. The flashlight. Never mind. Oliver, you must have taken one from work."

Oliver patted his pockets. "I seem to have left it at home."

"Shit, I ain't got time for this." Rufus rose and stumbled over Elizabeth's foot but still kept going.

Ira said, "Wait, Rufus, I'll get the lights back on."

"But it's so cozy like this," said Oliver.

"Next week." Rufus left.

This was the critical moment, and Elizabeth rose to it perfectly. "Come on, Ira. We have a flashlight."

WHEN WE GOT to her apartment, she turned on the kitchen light. Two squads from our colony were in place; we had negotiated with the natives for operating time.

"There's one in here, I'm pretty sure," she said.

Ira said, "I'm really sorry about this. What a mess. Sometimes I don't know what she's thinking."

"You're lucky. I always know what he's thinking." She dug into her utility drawer, a mess like Ira's. Her perfume filled the tight, poorly ventilated space, and soon his pate began to turn pink.

He watched for a moment, then plunged his hands in beside hers. When their shoulders brushed he flinched. Lusty, impulsive Ira. She said, "Oh, yuch!" and pulled out a khaki L-shaped flashlight, which looked like war surplus. The batteries had eaten through the base, and the switch was corroded. She dropped it back in and closed the drawer.

Clausewitz gestured impatiently from a socket box at the end of the counter. I signaled him to wait. This was the culmination of months of work. We could not risk it by striking a measure too soon. The animals in my humans, like gas in bread, needed time to rise.

But what was I thinking? Animals in these players? My male lead's big Jewish brain was most adept at holding down his little Jewish penis.

I gave the signal.

Clausewitz and the others pushed the second pair of copper wires into the socket, and the kitchen lights blew.

"This time it must be a blackout," Ira said.

"I don't know, Ira. The clock radio is still on in the living room, see?"

Side by side in the doorway they stood, watching the illuminated squared-off digits mark the passing minutes. Alone in the dark beside the pretty blonde, oblivious to everything, I imagined, except for her hand on his shoulder, and the perfume tantalizing his nostrils, what else did Ira need? And Elizabeth, alone in the dark with a man built more like a human than a huge slime mold, who had shown her consistent sensitivity and generosity over the years. What were they thinking? Was plain, stout Ruth, the appointed cause of more and more of Ira's woes, suffering beside the sleek, redolent blonde? Was fat, crass, offensive Oliver suffering beside the gallant, scrawny defender of the downtrodden? After I had pushed them together and polluted their domestic lives, were they finally ready to relinquish themselves to the natural course?

"Where's the light?" The question struck me like a mallet.

But beautiful Elizabeth said, "Wait, Ira, I want to let my eyes adjust for a minute."

She's offering herself, you shmuck. Look at her, Ira, a blonde! You've never had one. Kiss her! Then you can make up for your deficiencies with expensive gifts.

"Take my arm," he said. "Now, where's the switch?"

Go ahead, turn it on. May the sweat from your cowardly hands get you electrocuted.

Ira and Elizabeth stumbled into the hall, kicking each other like karate warriors, then apologizing like librarians. If Oliver and Ruth weren't so contemptuous of each other, they would have long coupled by now next door.

"Turn right," Elizabeth said.

But by propensity Ira turned left, and her spike heel drilled into his instep. He yelped and tore his foot back. She screamed as she fell, and clutched the back of his jacket, which split up the middle with a quiet *zip.* Tangled and off-balance, he toppled over on her.

Never had I flattered myself that I could fell and stack these two so quickly; I was giving up hope that it would happen at all. My mind danced with visions of Elizabeth's tight skirt pushed up, quickly, desperately, her panties peeled down, no, torn off, zippers racing, and mad rutting to words of eternal fealty. Even if Ira and Elizabeth later tried to dismiss the event as blackout madness, their groins would be sure that things were never again as they were. As the primitive Arab knows, magical rays flow from the hair of women; Elizabeth's gleaming mane would levitate Ira's stash from the cabinet. And then, for us, a quick midnight relocation into the back of the cabinet, followed by endless generations of peace and prosperity, served up by Ira and the next woman of his choice. I wished the whole colony, even my detractors, were here to see the birth of a new age.

The lingering silence began to unsettle me; a few whimpers would have been reassuring.

"I can't believe it!" Ira said passionately. A premature ejaculation? Impotence? These things happen. Keep the tip in the soup, man. Try to relax. Breathe deeply; inhale the perfume. Still furled? Stick your face into her pooze. That'll buy you some time.

Elizabeth surprised me even more by asking, "What is it?"

"I think I tore my pants. Oh, God, I can feel it. A brand new suit."

She reached up and switched on the light. Ira was sitting, legs bent, fingering an arrow-shaped tear over his knee. Both of them were still fully clothed, buttoned, and zipped.

"Brand new, Pierre Cardin. Cost me three hundred bucks wholesale. Damn!"

The woman, Ira, the woman!

"It doesn't look bad," said Elizabeth. "A tailor could mend it."

"No," he whined. "It's never the same."

I did all the work—all I asked was a token of cooperation. Sure, I'm just a little bug, and I couldn't really understand the reproductive principles of higher life forms—cowardice, impotence, and marriage. But didn't they hate themselves for being like this? No, they didn't. And that was the most mysterious thing about the perpetuation of this species.

Elizabeth listened compassionately as Ira went on about the venality of tailors. I had turned to leave when he caught himself, took her hand, and said, "Thanks for listening. I know I carry on sometimes."

But that's as far as I would get with them. Elizabeth was about to reply when Oliver opened the door. "Just as I suspected. Pulling my wife in here so you could show off your kneecap."

I DRAGGED to the outside hallway and sat on the ceiling. How could I face my colony now? What excuse could I offer, what plan, what future?

The fluorescent fixture, with its mocking buzz and blinding light, was like Ira: dumb, unnatural, unrelenting. Maybe it was time to admit that I was obsolete and that he represented the new order. I was tired of fighting. I decided to join him.

I squeezed into his liquor cabinet and found in the very back the inevitable bottle of Manischewitz. Two long purple scabs ran from the cap down to the stained label. Belly up to the bar, boys, this one's on me.

My saliva turned a segment of one of the clots into a frothy cocktail. At first I felt dizzy and a little nauseated. But then I settled into a gentle, expansive state that was not all unpleasant. I should have been more suspicious of anything humans pursue with the ardor that they do alcohol.

Suddenly a vision of Oliver appeared beside me. He looked contrite. Have I been too harsh on you, big fellow? Maybe I've made too much of our differences. After all, we are neighbors, and we live for the same things—good food, good pussy, and deep sleep. No reason to fight over that.

Wait. You can't bamboozle me. You're a fat slob, a selfish, foul-mannered boor, and the others tolerate you because they're too decent to tell you what they think of you. But what the hell, Ollie, your wife is dim and has no tits, so maybe it's not your fault. Underneath it all you're probably just a frightened 250-pound puppy, albeit with the heart of a jackal. Never mind, Ollie, you're OK with me.

And Liz, you oversanitized little fox, you golden-haired twit. If you had half a brain in your adorable head you'd dump the oaf. He drains you like an enormous, flat-footed leech. I gave you a shot at Ira. He respects you—or pretends to. But what the hell, I can't listen to him, so why should you? I forgive you, Liz. You're sweet and harmless and I like smelling your perfume and hiding under your high heels. You're all right with me.

Ruth, you're tougher to excuse, you porker, because you're smart and you have class. What are you doing with this sanctimonious whiner? It can't just be your jello-thighs or aspic-ass, can it? Follow the dictates of your superior mind. Don't shrink from cellulite; it's inescapable, all around you, like spores. Am I wrong? Is this the presumption of an animal blessed with pheromones? Maybe you're right, Ira is the best humanity will offer you. that case it is a nice apartment you've chosen. Damned cozy before you let that alien into the kitchen. I still don't know why you want him, but you must have a good reason. You're OK with me, Ruthie baby.

As for you, Ira, you skin-headed, limp-dicked little pansy. Can I ever forgive you for destroying my home? Or for your nasal voice, which injects putrid humanisms into every crack you've left me? But I'll give it to you, Ira, you're a scrapper. You were willing to sacrifice to stop me. I could hear those glands screech to a halt. I toppled the blonde onto you, didn't I, those pointy little tits and that bony mound jutting into your soft, undeserving body. And what do you do? Lower your head and take a whiff, cop a feel, or just cram her one, like any normal male? Hell, a slug would have scored enough slime to brag about. No, you let her lie there, dreaming to be had by even a circumcised dick, but feeling unsure, then unwanted, then humiliated. Her blonde pubic hair glistened with dew while you whined about your hideous suit. It's not as if I didn't know you'd suppress your hard-on by concentrating on the Republican convention or calamari. Being a gentleman, you'd spare her that embarrassment. Still, Ira, giving up shikse snatch just to get at me? But never mind. You've got a good woman, so why don't you go buy her something nice? Women love gifts; money is the pheromone of *Homo sapiens*. Complacency could lose her, Ira, and you're a cheap, cowardly jerk, but, I don't know, you're still all right with me. . .

I awoke later that night on my back on the bottom of the cabinet. The bottles towered over me like bad futuristic skyscrapers. I was very cold. When I moved, I could feel the beginning of a hangover in every ganglion, a carillon of pain. But at least my mind had cleared.

Scarves, watermelon pits, fuseboxes? What was all this bullshit? Too complicated. Too human. Scars of my youth in the bookcase. The problem was simple: I wanted the money out, which meant I wanted Ira and Elizabeth together, which, I realized, couldn't happen in this pathetic monogamous household until Ruth was gone. Who was the better woman? Who would prevail? I decided to find out right now.

LIKE THE PRINCIPALS of a wake, Oliver and Elizabeth lay on their backs, parallel, the blanket over their chests as smooth as if the bed had been made with them in it. I watched for some time, but neither of them budged. Elizabeth might have been trying to win on congeniality, but there was only one criterion in this contest. I had already marked her down for playing dead with Ira in the preliminaries.

I slipped under the blanket beside her shoulder and walked down the sheet next to her arm. I had never tasted her perfume so thick and moist. It was lovely. But tonight perfume would not be important. I continued a long way over the slick satin, repeatedly slipping and spraining my joints, as I looked for some biological landmark. The first flesh I found was her wrist. But her nightgown seemed to continue into black eternity. I didn't want to go that far. Did Oliver ever feel that way? Though I was tempted to declare Ruth winner by default, I had to go on; I couldn't live with the doubt.

Knowing the hand of a supine woman is at vulva level, I was doubly irritated walking down the outside of the gown, as I would have to walk just as far again up the inside. And as far as I had already come, I still hadn't picked up the faintest whiff of pheromone. Maybe this wasn't the most inspired idea after all.

It must have been an hour later when I got to the hem, suspended primly between her ankles. The first mark in her favor; the tension offered me a clear path up her leg. The foliage there had been felled to the skin, and this part of the trip was very quick. I passed her knees, and continued easily over her upper thighs.

But if I was where I thought I was, I should have been awash in vapors. Under the blanket I could not see anything. I wondered if I had taken a wrong turn.

Just then I ploughed into something slick and springy. It was the same fabric as the nightgown. The bounce seemed to be the work of a cushion of hair. Which meant that I had just walked into a matching pair of panties.

How could Elizabeth do this to herself, incubate her vaginal parasites with dense satin? She must have had iron control to keep herself from scratching; or maybe she was a magician, expert at misdirecting people's attention while she dug in.

I wished she would go at it now. I circled her thighs and crossed her waist, but elastic bound the panties tightly to her. And still I hadn't gotten a pheromonal hit.

I had gone a long way today, and I had a very long way to go. Couldn't I be, just for the moment, the Cyrano of insects, the mosquito, and shove my proboscis through the weave to sample the goods from here? I started raking my rugged mouthparts angrily against the fibers of her panties. To my surprise, they broke and unraveled quite easily.

I carefully pulled back the flap I had cut, expecting a blast of hot funk. But all was calm. I poked my head inside. The blonde hair was sparse and straight and fell neatly, with a part, as if it had been combed. A stinky sweet powder precipitated onto my back; the more I tried to wipe it off, the more I collected.

A summary of my depressing examination will suffice: her labia majora were cool and dry. The footing around her clitoris was firm, and the clitoris itself was tiny, no larger than my head. I pulled and twisted it, and provoked not the slightest reaction. Disappointed by her odor, her texture, her talc, and her response to a skilled lover, I gave her more than a fair chance to prove herself a sexual animal: I stuck my head into her vagina. The arid walls chafed me. My antennae finally detected some vague sexual presence, roughly the strength of a *Blattella* female dead a week three blocks downwind. Oh, there were powerful tastes in there. One was vinegar. The other was a poor chemical imitation of strawberry. Elizabeth had poured herself a TV pussy, which is probably exactly what her tin-can husband liked.

Back out on her mound, I saw a straight airspace extending all the way to her feet. If only I were one of those lucky insects who flew. But *Blattella* wings are cosmetic and ritual, used only during foreplay and copulation.

Hours later I finally left that antiseptic bed. What a waste! I was angry and depleted. I went for another belt of Concord Grape to soothe me, and later realized that I also needed it as a scientific control, to be sure Contestant Number Two got a fair shake.

I SURVEYED the Fishblatt bed from the tip of Ira's big toe, which stuck out from under the covers. It was unusually dark in the room. It took me a minute to realize it was because the clock-radio was out; Oliver had refused to fix our short circuit. Unlike their tidy neighbors, Ira and Ruth slept like victims of a bomb blast. Blankets and sheets which this afternoon had been impeccably anchored with hospital corners were now loose, strewn over their contorted bodies.

The toe twitched and I jumped. "Not in this house!" said Ira, twisting violently. A moment later Ruth groaned softly and rolled away, her flannel nightgown rising slowly around her chubby thighs; somehow I was sure it had no matching panties. However, because she seemed to respond to him even asleep, the interval between Ira's indignations was all the time I would have for my expedition.

I mounted Ruth's shin, figuring the bone would offer the fastest route up. I was wrong. Ruth was not a shaver, and her foliage grew thick. Advantage: Elizabeth. Hundreds of sturdy shanks tapered to sharp points. There would be no shortcut here, just tough careful slogging. Where were my elephants, my litter-bearers to carry me through the forest?

Soon the hairs were so long that my legs wouldn't even reach flesh. I had an inspiration: I would Tarzan-swing up to her knee. Halfway up the first hair I reached for the next one, but before I could grab it the first one gave way. I landed on my back, and her spears gouged my tender spiracles.

I learned the rhythm of the curly hair. I moved quickly and smoothly, minimizing the risk that a sleepy hand would lay me forever to rest in the brush. Even so, the distance I traveled from Ruth's ankle to her knee was many times the distance as the fly flies.

From a clearing in the knee I looked back with pride at the wilderness I had crossed, but with trepidation that soon I would have to cross it again.

I looked north. I was right. Unlike Elizabeth, enlightened Ruth wore no panties (*Candida* said panties were *agents provocateurs* of itch), and so it sat there before me, the Hairy Grail, alluring as the jungle's hidden treasures, frightening as the jungle's vipers and cannibals. The first hormonal warning shot struck. The organ had looked so furry and friendly from the toe, like a cuddly toy; now I wasn't so sure I wanted to play. I remembered Junior in the bookshelf, when we were nymphs, deriding the sages who had derived "pudendum " from the Latin *pudere*, meaning "to be ashamed." "It's not totally ridiculous," he said. "But get close to me, if you can bear it, and you'll know why it derives from the English 'P.U.'"

I pushed myself forward. The forest thinned as I passed the knee, but a new peril appeared. Trenches, pits, sinking deeper as I traveled on. Surely this had been the site of a terrible artillery duel. The footing was treacherous, and the vestiges of gas made me afraid the shelling would resume at any moment.

I jumped into a crater. I could see some rare good news—the foliage up above had been shot completely away. If I could avoid the ditches it would be a clean run, almost all the way home. I caught my breath. Then I went over the top.

I jumped into the next crater. Why go at all? Why didn't I just stay here until the end of the battle?

But I couldn't. If my Jewish Valkyrie rolled over she'd crush me between her thighs: the *Liebestod*, the love death.

It was no-man's-land, and I was running as no man had. Her muff dominated my view, and the beacon scent grew sharper almost by the step. It was not a pleasant odor, complex, musty, tinged with urine. At ten paces its character changed; the same elements were all there, but the balance of the blend had tipped. My discomfort gave way to pleasure, the way a tight genital chamber that chafes against your member can suddenly become heavenly. Was I being lured by an illusion into the wire? I wondered if the Manischewitz had been fermented to the specifications of the Jewish genitals.

I pushed on. The tops of her thighs had rubbed each other smooth. But then came the bush itself, a military masterpiece that looked completely out of place on the soft, chubby flesh. It was an impenetrably dense breastwork of tough coiled hairs, spikes bristling in every direction. If I got caught in it, I could be mashed during morning fornication—a repellent thought—or Ivoried to the shower floor and flushed with steaming water down the drain to the great unknown. And even if I made it past her outer defense, what awaited me? The inner surfaces of this organ had a glimmering, treacherous look, like flypaper, or maybe quicksand.

But damn it! I'd tried everything else. I wasn't going to stand here, a few inches away, as my last chances for glory and a decent life vanished I charged straight into the bush. It was a terrible mistake. Within two steps I put out twelve of my eyes, and my legs were all snared. I dangled like a POW on the wire. Ruth's pelvis started to shift. But she settled back. It was a warning, perhaps my last one.

I backed out carefully, leaving painful chunks of chitin on the wire, signing her guest register with blood. I retreated to the top of the thigh.

I didn't know what to do now. I saw no way in. As I preened, a nervous habit, I tasted Ruth's musk, which must have stuck to me in the bush.

Immediately I felt a stirring in my wing muscles, the very ones that never moved except in response to a female's chemical magic. This was all wrong. It's not that Ruth wasn't from the right side of the tracks; she wasn't even from the right side of the animal kingdom. For God's sake, she had a spinal column! But a moment later my wings opened.

It was impossible. It was embarrassing. But I figured: if my wings could spread—and since I had no option—why not try to use them? What did I have to lose, a few more eyes? I retreated down Ruth's thigh and picked out the runway with the fewest potholes. I came running back. The faster I went the stupider I felt, these two huge plates bouncing wildly on my back, catching the air randomly, awkwardly, twisting me side to side.

Two steps from her bush I made my leap. It wasn't a thing of grace, no eagle's soar. No, I'd call it a desperate lurch that got me about one leg's length above her spikes before I came plunging down. The back of my abdomen scraped and burned against the wire. But my front legs landed in labial soil. I pulled myself onto it. I made it. I hit vulva.

Now I was certain she had felt me. Quickly to work. I started up the mountainous outer lip. It was bouncy and moist. I jumped. The flesh gave under me softly, but not obsequiously. Advantage: Ruth.

I hiked north along Labium, which had the dark pigmentation of her Mediterranean ancestors. Her aroma: a complex woman, I would describe her as honest but not self-righteous; earthy but not vulgar; spicy but not ostentatious. Balanced. Impressive. Elizabeth was not in her class.

I walked to the apex. A shimmering layer of ooze surrounded a black hole whose depth challenged my imagination. I reached out, but recoiled from the heat.

Again, from habit, I preened. Again her taste surprised me. This fluid was fresher and even more potent than the stuff in the bush. But I was a zealot for absolute truth. These fluids had been oxidizing for hours and I insisted on sampling Ruth's hottest jazz.

With two legs planted on the outer lip, I moved my middle legs to the peat bog between so I could grab her nib, a dicier maneuver than it had been on the dry flesh next door. "Nib" didn't do the organ justice—it was a huge irregular pyramid, hooked at the end, shaped something like a nose, like Ruth's nose, in fact, only with more wrinkles and without nostrils. It was impossible for me to get my legs around it. For scale, imagine Ruth rappelling down Mount Rushmore and onto Thomas Jefferson's schnoz.

I hooked on the spikes of my forelegs. When I pulled they slipped off, and if I hadn't made a lunge for a curl lying inside her labium, I would have tumbled into the abyss. That would have meant a horrible end for me. But then I might have risen! Catholics all over the world would have to wear little golden vulvas on neck chains, and carry big ones during ceremonies. But I wasn't cut from martyr cloth.

I tried the spikes closer to the apex of the clit, where the slime was thinner, and carefully shifted my balance. I pulled and my grip held. I started to rock back and forth, tugging what I could of the organ. I was careful not to over-excite her—I didn't want her moaning to wake Ira, who might then wake her.

After several minutes of skilled manipulation, I dipped my antennae into her fluid. The same oxidized dross.

Just like Elizabeth after all. What did I have to do to get her to secrete? Foreplay? No wonder some Africans used to cut vulvas completely off.

I tried not to dwell on the fact that I had worked on Ruth long enough to satisfy twenty of my own kind. I tried hard to remember that this was research, not biological slumming.

But putting my mouth to a human genital, how could I keep perversion from my mind? Come on Manischewitz! Make me want it!

I worked my tongue against her mountainous clit, walking over it and down the other side, and then back and forth to where I started. And back and forth and back and forth and on and on until I became dizzy and nauseated and my legs ached and my tongue felt like a cactus. Yet when I checked her chemicals there was still no change.

By God, I've filled a lot of smiling females in my time, a sight sexier than her, with gleaming carapaces and great succulent glands. The impudence! I should have been the one on my back receiving ministrations.

I stretched forward and chomped down on the tip of her clit with my mandibles. The dormant nib suddenly came to life. And then, like an earthquake, the whole area started to shift. The labia stretched and undulated. Planted on different levels, my legs threatened to pull apart. But Ruth soon settled back. "Oh, baby." She meant me.

I dipped my antennae once again, and sure enough, here was fresh lava. It was impressive stuff. Ruth's worry about the texture and shape of her thighs blinded her to the vast power between them.

Emboldened, I stepped onto the steaming inner lips. The great hole, big enough to accommodate half my family side by side, yawned just below me. There had been coitus here tonight, which meant that my plan to antagonize her and Ira had failed; he didn't perform when he was upset, and not that often when he wasn't. Ruth was proving more formidable than I had ever suspected.

What exactly was her magic? Legs braced on her flaps—as if I had any chance of holding them open during a sexual quake—I invoked for the one time in my life the *Blattella* god and stuck my head in.

I was transported. Was she really human? She seemed more like the universal, primordial animal. Chemicals I never knew existed exploded through my body. I was helpless, out of control, spinning and speeding, though I was not sure I was moving at all.

Her soft flesh closed gently around my head. Blood pounded through the walls of her vagina, just as it had through my own mother's vestibulum before my birth. I hadn't thought of mom in eons.

I pulled my head out into the cold night air, bowing a thousand pardons to humanity, which I had so often maligned—not because of the *sapiens* part; oysters are better thinkers—but because of the greatness in that vagina.

As the secretions dried and crusted on me, my walking became labored. The view from the labium was sobering; the defensive works were just as formidable from the inside as they had been from the thighs, with no room for a runway. Stealing and bushwhacking, I had to get out before she rolled over; there was no reason for her to protect me now.

I was out of tricks; the retreat would be a struggle. I shat to drop some weight. Then I licked from my body the white crusting, which would slow me going through the wire.

It shouldn't have come as such a surprise that the white powder, which was just dried hormones, again ignited my body. My back rippled with power.

With the next flex, I dipped my antennae back into Ruth's slop. My muscles tensed. They were going to move; I was sure now. I sucked in one last dose of pheromones. That was it. My wings popped apart and started beating like a dragonfly's.

I lifted straight up, pulling my legs from the ooze with ease. I was airborne, a fucking flying cockroach. I was really soaring this time. My mind reeled with the possibilities—I could catch falling crumbs in midair, or strafe waterbugs, or shatter Ira's glasses as I broke the sound barrier. I flew above the depths of the bush, then quickly passed over the no-man's-land of the thighs, the knee plateau, and the jungle of the shin. This was exhilarating! I swore I would never crawl again.

I passed Ira's toe, where it all started, and soon I was over the end of the bed. I zoomed through the bedroom doorway, strictly by luck, and down the hall. I flew a great circle through the living room, watering the plants, and patting the white queen's bottom with a wing.

A moment later, narrowly missing a reburial in the pages of the Bible, I met the wall. I slid down the plaster to the floor. Slumped against the baseboard like a bum against a lamppost, I could think of only one thing: Ruth Grubstein. Ruth, Ruth, Ruth. The sound dominated my mind as if I were a pimply adolescent human in the grip of first love. But I didn't care. In fact I was proud. Ruth. If I'd had the energy I would have carved hearts all over the apartment. N + RG FOREVER.

DAWN FORCED ME to think of safety. When I got up, my head still spun from the collision. My wing muscles ached from their singular exertion. But this did not explain the odd list to my gait.

Then it came to me. The missing weight was my spermatophore. My excitation had been so wild that I had ejaculated into my beautiful Ruth without realizing it.

I was thrilled. A perfect consummation to our new love.

But I soon started to worry how our little one would come out. A boy four feet three inches tall with a chitinous head covered by black curly hair, fairy wings drooping uselessly down his back, fronted by a *Blattella* phallus? A girl, soft-fleshed like Ruth except for her chitin-plated breasts, a six-legged Brunnhilde? The possibilities were too grim. Poor Ruth. She would be ecstatic as she swelled. Then everything would go wrong. Ira would throw her out of the apartment. She would become the darling of the *National Enquirer* and perhaps the science section of the *New York Times.*

How could she account for the birth? If she were smart, she would use Mary's line and say she had been inseminated by a divinity during the night. How far would it be from the truth?

THE CLEAR VICTOR in the vaginal joust was Ruth. Though by the standards of the magazines Elizabeth was more visually attractive, Ruth had crushed her in every other way. I've always been convinced that everywhere in *Kingdom Animalia*, even on this rotten branch, the fittest pheromones get their man. So my plan to have Elizabeth topple Ruth had been doomed from the start.

What could I do now? Find a woman with more sexual swat than Ruth? Not likely. It would take a hormonal barbarian, a woman not hindered by the limits of good taste or any accepted social standard.

It took a whole day before the proper questions pushed through the fog of my hangover. Who defiantly refused to bathe regularly because it was germ genocide? Who thought grooming was a conspiracy of the plastics conglomerates? Who refused to use tampons because they interfered with the self-expression of her vagina? This barbarian had been a crucial part of our lives—she was, in fact, the Savior in our original, short-lived plan—yet somehow in all my plotting I had overlooked her in favor of Elizabeth.

It was now April. I climbed onto Ira's desk and rubbed a leg across the tip of his pen and added a digit "1" to the front of his taxable income on his 1040 form. Anything that got Ira thinking about needing extra money could only help us.

I spent the week in the upper molding. The following Friday, Rufus the businessman returned. In the foyer, still humiliated by the previous week's events, Ira subjected him to a double dip of self-effacement. As Rufus shifted from custom-made shoe to custom-made shoe, I lined him up and dropped from the ceiling onto the soft cured skin of his hat, cushioned by his thick bush—a perfect landing pad. As Rufus started down the stairs, I scurried over the rim of the hat and into the dense matting of his hair. It felt impregnable.

"To the Gypsy's, boy," I said. "And step on it."

On Tenterhooks

RUFUS AND I stopped on the second floor, waited for Ira's three locks to snap shut, then crept back to the third floor. Rufus glided down the hall. Where were we going, to eavesdrop on Ira? No, we passed his door. Certainly not to see Oliver. Perhaps a play for his wife? But we passed her too.

He slowed. I said, "No, not here, Rufus, buddy. Any apartment but this one. Please."

But he buzzed. Hector Tambellini opened the door. "Hey, Rufus baby, come in out of the rain." He bellowed, "Hey, Violetta, look who's here." Rufus quickly closed the door behind us.

Clutching his hair, I scanned the floor for the *Periplaneta* perverts who had defiled me. The door slam must have scared off the cowards. But they were out there.

Wait. What was I worrying about? Barring a suicidal charge up Rufus's body they could not get me up here. And even if Rufus OD'd and fell to the floor, I could dive into the tight woof of his bush, which would give me a natural advantage over the monsters. Rufus was my fortress.

"American Woman!" I sang. "I'm back, lover. Please come out. I can't see you." The floor was covered with reddish-brown smears, the waterbug palette, painted by the soles of Hector's orthopedics. She would make a lovely silhouette.

Violetta walked in, at work on a sandwich. As she bit, slices of American cheese and cold cuts greased with mayonnaise slid out into her palm. She pushed her face into her hand and ate them. I liked the way she luxuriated in food, so unlike the modern women down the hall.

"Rufus," she said between bites, "you're so skinny. Look at him, Hec. He don't eat. Get him something. Get him the other half of this sandwich. It's on the counter. I'm on a diet."

"No, it's cool," said Rufus. "I ate."

"Don't nobody feed you? You got a girlfriend?" A triangle of bologna stuck to the corner of her mouth.

"Don't embarrass him, Vi," said Hector.

"There's nothing to be embarrassed about. You got a girlfriend?"

"Why, Bi, you got a niece for me?"

"Well, I mean. . ."

"Don't mind her." Hector gave Rufus a roll of bills. Rufus counted. "It's all there," said Hector.

"People make mistakes," said Rufus. I counted twenty dollars less than Ira paid; the wages of liberalism, and probably the reason for the secrecy of the visit.

Rufus pulled off his hat and took a small, clear bag of white powder from inside the sweatband. I burrowed a little deeper. He handed the bag to Hector.

"Happy trails to you," Rufus said at the door.

"Yeah, you take it easy."

"Get yourself a girl who can cook," said Violetta.

On the street, Rufus reached into his pocket for a silver case, from which he pulled a thin cigar. The night was calm and the smoke rose straight up, driving me further under the hat. The hair made a good filter.

We stood there for a minute, and suddenly the hat lifted off. I panicked and dove. I was about halfway to the scalp line when a line of sharpened black spikes ripped through the bush, barely missing me. Hairs *pinged* as they snapped. The spikes retracted, and an instant later came cutting through again, even closer to me than before. I knew this had to be the dreaded Afro-pick.

Pulling myself through the thick tangle of hairs in the deeper levels was nearly impossible. The thought of being skewered like a shish-kebab was awful. Would I end up suffocating in the grimy clogged drain of a ghetto tub? Or would I gradually starve here in Rufus's hair, so weakened by the wound that I couldn't escape the confined stench of my own putrefaction?

By the eighth pick plunge, I managed to reach the scalp. Serendipity landed me on a patch of psoriasis, a pip of a disease which causes human skin to come loose in micaceous scales. I slipped between one and the skin beneath, and lay as snug as if it were a freshly made bed.

After a woman's length of preening, the hat went back on. I slipped out of my little bed. My back leg caught and tore the end of the scale. I froze; this blunder could bring him down on me with perfect accuracy. But nothing happened. The skin had to be completely dead. I took a nibble, but it was so bitter that I spat it out. Too bad. Rufus and I could have had genuine symbiosis: I would have eaten, and his leatherwear would be dandruff-free.

Laboring for air, I was about to climb back up when I noticed a clump on the neighboring scale. It was a group of nits, baby head lice, using Rufus for warmth and food. No wonder he was coming down so hard with that pick; nits are notorious for their deadly sharp claws. I kept my distance.

"How's the digs, fellas? I'm aboard now. Anything I should know?"

The voracious little suckers wouldn't stop to answer. There was so much I wanted to know. How often did Rufus shampoo? How long had it taken them to get used to his taste? How could they live in the air down here? I couldn't.

I surfaced and peeked out from under the hat. The cool evening breeze felt terrific. Rufus and I were in full stride. Soon we turned into Reggie's Bar and Grill.

"Yo, Rufus, how you be?" came a deep voice.

A huge black man placed a hand the size of a pizza on Rufus's shoulder. His gigantic head sloped sharply from his receding forehead to an enormous, powerful jaw. The top of his head was shaved except for a thick mohawk stripe down the center. In his right lobe he wore a golden earring shaped like a pistol; a matching amulet hung from a golden chain around his neck. A cigar sporting the El Producto label nestled in the gap where one of his yellowing front teeth was missing.

The three of us took a couple of torn vinyl stools at the bar. The bartender, with lazy, addict-red eyes, approached. "What it be, gentlemen?"

Everyone in Reggie's was black, except for a fat bleached blond across the bar from us, whose thin white T-shirt was intended, I supposed, to show her descending breasts to their last advantage. She wore steel-framed glasses so thick that they gave her huge frog eyes—myopia probably explained why her flaming red lipstick had pretty much missed her mouth altogether. She sighed impatiently as a graying man on steel crutches tried to light her cigarette without falling over backward.

"The usual," said Rufus.

"So what you been up to?" said his friend.

"Not much. Runnin' the store."

The bartender returned and mixed Rufus a glass of Courvoisier and 7-Up. Rufus took a sip and smacked his lips. "Ah, good shit." A few vile sprinkles landed on me. I wiped them onto his hair; I was permanently on the wagon. "Junior, I seen you with some mean trim the other day. In Blimpie's."

Junior smiled broadly and laughed. The cigar rose with his upper jaw. "Yeah, ain't she fine?"

"Built for speed, Jim." Rufus laughed and offered a palm, which Junior slapped so hard I was afraid he'd break it.

Another voice said, "Built for speed is right—that cow needs a diet pill." I was astounded by this challenge, and even more so when Junior ignored it.

Rufus said, "So you shacked?"

"No way," said Junior. "The bitch look fine and she got a pussy that drip honey. But all she want to do is get high."

"Can't blame her. Look at this ugly buffalo. He's so dirty you can't tell the grease from the nigger," said the voice. Yet Junior again let the death wish go ungranted. I couldn't understand it.

Suddenly Rufus dropped his head. A quick grab at the wire saved me from falling onto the bar. He clapped his hands and gave a falsetto yelp.

"What you laughin' at?" said Junior.

"You got the biggest nigger nose I ever seen. You mama shoulda named you Hoover."

"I like a line or two. Sure. But the bitch, that all she want, line after line, all day long."

"Yeah, just like you. Only you gotta put up the dead president. Cause she got a pussy and you don't, right."

Junior was getting upset, and he was easily powerful enough to drop Rufus to the bar with one blow. I looked down to see where we would land. The *Blattella germanica* population was quite large, protected by the dim light and brown laminated surface, living on beer-nut and popcorn spills. There was no fear of frenzy in their motion, as had always been the case at Ira's apartment. It was a nice easy life.

Junior said, "You know what I mean. The bitch ain't got no conversation."

Rufus laughed again. "All you gotta hear is the sound of thigh upside your ear. 'Ain't no disgrace to bring your face below her waist for a little taste.'" He slapped Junior on the shoulder and I almost fell again. But now I noticed the citizens on the bar had a weak, unnatural color, left incomplete by the neon light. Like the humans around them, they were products of generations of alcoholic overconsumption.

"Shut up, Rufus," I said. "Don't antagonize this large man anymore. I don't want to live here."

Junior said, "The bitch take my paycheck right up the nose. I don't know, my man."

"That's *welfare* check, not *paycheck*. Three hours on line yesterday, remember?" I had to stop this voice. How much razzing could Junior take?

"I mean, what you do? How you stop the bitch from spendin' all the green and still keep her doin' her thing?" said Junior.

Rufus said, "Don't ask me. I don't go for them skanky bitch you like." I grabbed his hair.

"You see the jive?" said the voice. "Five minutes ago she was mean, built for speed. Now the skinny guy hears money's low, and suddenly she's a skank. But watch this—because of the drugs Junior won't even remember."

"I can't shove the beefaroni into the bitch unless I feel somethin'," Rufus continued.

Now it was Junior's turn to laugh. The El Producto waved in his teeth. "Like what, you swipe get stiff?"

"I don't go for the coke-nose bitch. That strictly business. Speakin' of business, you seen my man Lester around?"

Junior drained his beer and ordered another. The reflection of the Miller High Life clock on his sweaty head said it was getting late. "You hear about Lester? Made one of them sign, say: 'I am blind, God bless you.' Every day he sit on the sidewalk outside them big office buildin' downtown with one of them blind-man cane. By fall he gonna have enough scratch for a Continental. What you want him for? Make a contribution?"

"Man borrow money from me about six month ago and develop a bad case of amnesia."

"No shit. I thought you be friend."

Rufus finished his drink and wiped his mouth with the back of his hand. "Only friend I got is the green dollar."

"The first true words out of your nigger's mouth," said the voice.

He had seen me. I dove. But halfway to the scalp, I thought: *My* nigger? What did this guy think, that I was taking Rufus for a walk?

But who would notice me here? Who would talk to me this way? And why had Rufus and Junior been ignoring this inflammatory voice? Of course—it was a roach's voice. The constant company of humans was eroding my basic sensitivities.

I resurfaced to look for the presumptuous, ill-mannered citizen. The *Blattellae* on the bar were absorbed in gluttony, as were the ones on the floor and in the popcorn dispenser.

"Getting warmer," said the voice.

Finally I found him, perched on the front of Junior's mohawk. "This pack animal is not my nigger," I said. "Don't project your problem onto me, fella."

"So? You think this is mine? No way. I live downtown with a professional relaxation expert. Her name is Nirvana."

"What are you doing way up here?"

"I was sleeping with my baby one night and the next thing I knew I was riding the subway in this skunk patch. Grease must have sucked me in."

Rufus stuck out his palm for punishment. "I got to hit the trail. Be frozen, Junior."

"Enjoy your new mobile home," I said.

"I'm out of here. You'll see. If only he weren't such a drugged, destitute halfwit."

"Why don't you walk?"

"With guard rats on every corner? Pigeons? No chance."

"Well then, start a tab at the bar. *Bon Appetit!*" Rufus was rising from his stool.

"No I won't. I won't stay here. I'm going back to Nirvana. He promised her, and this time. . ." He carried on, stamping on Junior's head like Rumpelstiltskin, until he hit a slick. With a terrible scream he slid down the mohawk, bounced off Junior's forehead, and disappeared with a small *plunk* into his beer.

Junior didn't see him. "Yeah, be cool, Rufus my man. Don't take no wooden trim." He held up his glass in toast and drained it in one swallow.

"Thanks," said a new voice. This time I paid attention; it was another *Blattella.* I soon found him, perched in the front of the bartender's pompadour. "I was getting sick of that Nirvana rap, night after night, week after week. I thought we'd never get rid of that guy."

"My pleasure," I said.

A MOMENT LATER Rufus and I were walking up the street. I heard a primitive percussion. As it got louder I could hear a voice rapping. It wasn't music; there was no melody, no harmony, not even a change of pitch. He spoke only of infatuation, seduction, and sex, with an occasional reference to money. This was a refreshing distillation of human ambition; if Ira were so clear-headed, I'd be safe and warm at home right now. The advent of rapping probably marked a circle in human development; when *Homo* first chattered and banged on a log, could it have sounded much different?

I soon started to see gutted buildings, windows and doors sealed with cinder blocks or sheet metal. Bums slept in doorways on newspaper bedding. I was glad to see scores of *Periplanetae* having to snuggle with them for heat on this brisk evening.

"Damn!" said Rufus, shivering, stepping into the street. He flagged a gypsy cab.

Soot puffed from the decomposing upholstery when Rufus sat down. The plastic barrier, which looked glazed with spittle, slid open and the driver said, "Where to?" Tires screeching, we took off.

"Whoa!" cried Rufus. "This America, Jack. Red light mean stop."

"Sorry, man. I'm beat. Last night them Ricans was havin' a party next door." He turned toward us, and through a mouthpiece formed by his thumb and first finger, gave a creditable impression of a salsa trumpet. "Kept me up till five A.M. in the mornin'."

"Watch where you drivin'. One time them Latino did that to me. I call 911. They say they send a car over. Nobody show. I call back, use my whitey voice, and say I hear a shot. Four car come flyin' in, siren goin', G-men in bulletproof vest. No more noise that night."

The driver laughed. "I try that next time."

The car pulled over. We had been driving the wrong way, away from the Gypsy's apartment. I could stay in the cab and hope it turned around. But it was so stuffy and grimy that I decided to stick with Rufus.

He paid the tab plus a five percent tip. As we got out of the car, he reached for his armpit. From the peak of his hat I saw the mother-of-pearl handle. *Click.* A safety? A bullet in the chamber? Where was I going, the OK Corral?

If I jumped from Rufus's head now, what were my chances of getting out of the ghetto alive? Guard rats on every corner. I couldn't risk it.

Only one thing could protect me—Rufus's skull. Unlike Ira's ovoid head, Rufus's rose on an incline from his forehead to a peak, then fell sharply to his neck. I moved behind this peak, and periodically ran out to see what was happening.

Rufus kicked open the cracked glass door of the tenement. A middle-aged man slept on the floor beneath the mailboxes. A younger man leapt off the windowsill and came at us with a malevolent smile.

"Easy," said Rufus.

The man looked at Rufus's hand, still under his jacket. Still smiling, he said, "What you got there, my man?"

"Start walkin', or this roscoe blow you back to Africa."

The man retreated, still smiling, and went out the door. We backed into the elevator.

Rufus opened the door to an apartment. The air was filled with a choking carbon haze. A big black woman sat on a sofa that was mostly springs and stuffing, in front of a small TV set perched on a pile of newspapers. The antennae, with small balls of aluminum foil wrapped around the ends, reminded me of me.

Setting down her Coke and potato chips, the woman jumped up, wrapped her arms around Rufus's neck, and kissed him wetly on the lips. "Where you been at, lover man. You a cruel nigger not callin' me for days. I didn't know what to think."

Rufus gave her capacious ass a loud slap. "What you worryin' about. Who pay the rent?"

"I need you around, Daddy. I get lonely for you."

He sat down on the sofa, but sprang up, hand gripping his crotch. "Why don't you throw this shit out. Almost took my ball off."

"Oh, no, Daddy. I guess you need Ambrosia special massage."

"Yeah, I don't want no infection."

She began to rub him, pressing her tits against his body. With a sweet smile she looked up and said, "Got a couple line for your little Ambrosia?"

"Sorry, baby. Sold out today."

I went back under the hat. There were still several bulges in the sweat band. Tightwad.

"Come on, sugar," she purred. "Just one?"

"I can't give you what I don't got." He turned away from her.

She fell back into the couch; its spears did not bother her. Rufus said, "Look, bitch, I don't got it. You keep on, and I'm goin'."

"No." She pulled him down onto the sofa. His hands went to his testicles before he landed. She said, "I need somethin' cause I get bored, Daddy. I be talkin' to Emma today, and I say, 'You know, I love my man Rufus, but I get bored sometime,' and she say, 'Yeah, I know what you mean, cause before Ramses go to the joint he away a lot, course not as much as now, cause he in the joint,' and I say, 'Sometime I like to go out of my mind,' and she say, 'I know what you mean, cause I feel just like that before Ramses go to the joint'. . ." More and more of Ambrosia's animated face came into my view as Rufus nodded off.

"Rufus, you listenin' to me?"

His head jerked back up. "Course, sugar. Let's go to bed."

"OK, lover. I got to use the bathroom for a minute." She pranced down the hall, buttocks rippling. Rufus turned the TV to professional wrestling. She finally returned in a nightgown, hair braided, glowing like a Buddha.

"What the fuck you do to your face?"

"Vaseline, Daddy. Keep me young and pretty for you."

"Girl, stay young and pretty some other night."

"Every night, sugar," she said, leaning over to kiss him.

He pulled back and wiped his face. "Don't get that shit on me."

Soon we were in the bedroom. She made him sit on the bed while she stood before him and slowly peeled off her nightgown. She was a mammal among mammals. Her breasts descended to her navel, but were firm and full and extended to the sides almost as far. Her dark, flat nipples were about a water bug's length in diameter. Her shoulders and arms were fleshy and strong, and her belly plump. Her bush was as full as any Afro I'd seen on the street.

She turned so Rufus could see her from every angle. From profile she showed the hairpin line to her pelvis, advertising her ass while tucking her belly under for better protection, a superior configuration I've seen only on black women. She held herself as if she loved being a big, full-bodied, sex object; I doubted that even someone as exceptional as Ruth could match her as a reproducer.

Rufus stripped except for his hat, which he pushed back on his head. He took his face below her waist for a little taste. I had heard this never happened among this tribe. His hair and her muff locked, indistinguishable. I didn't move; ending up with Ambrosia would maroon me forever. Not that her vapors were unpleasant. Not at all. In fact, the musk pouring from her vagina was a world apart from anything I had ever sensed, even from Ruth.

Ruth had intoxicating hormones. But Ambrosia was history. Hers was not simply a sexual essence, it was more like a chemical missing link. Like our pheromones, hers told the whole story, from the beginning. I could smell beyond humanity to the little primates, first venturing out of the trees. I could smell the first four-legged creatures, and the amphibians rising desperately, determinedly, from the water. I could certainly smell fish, and the primitive marine creatures, back to the first multicellular organisms, and then the first unicellular ones, darting around in the primordial ooze, the soup where it all began. Rufus wasn't just eating pussy, he was finding his Roots.

Ambrosia was frighteningly impassioned, growling and thrashing and inciting Rufus with breathless talk of his prowess. She screamed and her body convulsed, her thighs locking around his head while her fists pummeled the bed. I ran under the hat for safety. "Oh, Daddy, you killin' me!" A few minutes later she was sufficiently revived to say, "Fill me up, lover. Fill me to the top."

I walked back out to watch Rufus rear up on his knees, his pencil-thin penis poking out from his withered thighs. He made Ira look like a prize bull. When he mounted Ambrosia, her reaction was so extreme that I had to wonder if she was responding to Daddy's dick or Daddy's rent payments.

"Bless my soul!" Rufus said a few minutes later, and rolled away. Ambrosia fell asleep immediately. I expected we'd be on our way, but Rufus dropped his head to the sheet beside her fecund crotch.

I slept well, though I had vivid dreams of the Serengeti. Sunlight was filtering through the soot-covered windows by the time Rufus woke up. He started to dress. Ambrosia awoke. She propped herself up on her elbows and cupped her breasts provocatively. "Mama got a present for you cause you so good last night."

"Gotta go, sugar. I got business."

Suddenly she was furious. "Stop callin' me sugar. Probably call every whore you fuck sugar. Don't you know my name?"

Rufus was moving around in front of the cracked bathroom mirror, searching for an image of his entire face. "Sure, sugar."

"When am I gonna see you?" she said petulantly.

"When I come back." And we were out the front door.

It was a beautiful day, cool and crisp, with Rufus's head providing just the right amount of heat. The gutters in this part of town were lush with chicken bones and skins, cigarette butts, dog shit, condoms, sputum, and much more. I could hear the happy hum of thousands of my larger cousins at harvest.

Rufus was popular. "What's happenin'?" he said to scores of people he passed. "How you been?" to many others, and they invariably answered him with the same words.

Ragged men wearing clothing stiff with dirt staked their claims to empty doorways with stuffed shopping bags. In front of one building sat a teenager on an upturned wooden box, annotating a copy of *War and Peace.* I was astonished. When we passed him I walked out to the end of the hat. The pages were covered with little circles; he was picking out every letter *j*.

The character of the neighborhood soon began to change. There were no more abandoned buildings. Bag ladies joined the men. The streets were cleaner; this was a whiter, voting district. Courting behaviors became more subtle. Men did not accost women or whistle or hiss at them; they just looked slyly. Women of the ghetto occasionally smiled at the obscene compliment, but these wealthier, whiter women showed nothing but contempt for the men who admired them.

We were in the university neighborhood. I knew this not because of classroom buildings, libraries, or youths with books. It was the three Iranians who had chained themselves to a fence, surrounded by signs insisting America free them from the tyranny of the mullahs.

They called out to us. Rufus turned. "You get what you deserve, swami. Don't go takin' American hostages. Don't go bringin' that shit into the USA or we bomb your ass." I wondered what Ira would have said.

Street activists came thick now. On the next block two overweight women in flannel shirts sat at a bridge table covered with pamphlets. Their sign read, PORNOGRAPHY IS VIOLENCE AGAINST WOMEN. They chanted lifelessly, "Stop porn, respect women! Stop porn, respect women!" One of them rose and approached us with a yellow petition.

Rufus said, "You kiddin'? Bitch like you be violence against pornography. What size head you got? I'm gonna buy you a bag."

There were two scrawny men with closely cropped beards at the next table. They did not bother to ask Rufus for his signature. The woman with the sign-up sheet for the local tenants' union also let us go by.

Then a man about Junior's size, black, with a shaved head, came right at us. He had a tatoo *carved* into his right bicep that said ATTICA 1970. Even Rufus tried to sidestep this one. But he took Rufus's arm and said, "Yo, brother, put your name to the list here. The brothers upstate need vocational trainin'."

I told Rufus to give him what he wanted so we could get out of there. But Rufus looked at the list and said, "Who you tryin' to shit?"

"Say what?"

"I look like some lily white fool? Put my address down so the con know which door to use their vocational skill on when they get out? Shit."

In a moment I knew I would be in the bloodied gutter. But the Attica man broke into a smile. Two of his front teeth were black. "Yeah," he said, and released Rufus's arm. His face again became stern as he turned to intimidate approaching pedestrians.

Then came a block of ridiculous causes, epitomized by Jews for Jesus—the human version of Roaches for Raid. It made me think. Entomologists draw a distinction between two routes of insect development. In incomplete metamorphosis the larva grows into a nymph and the nymph into an adult. The nymph is essentially a small adult, lacking only certain details. Isn't this true of black humans? Adolescents loiter, jive, strut, and take drugs like adults.

Complete metamorphosis has an additional state, the pupa, which is completely alien to the adult it becomes. Compare hirsute, unkempt Jewish teenagers espousing Thanatotic causes with the carefully coiffed careerists they become. My guess is that the trauma of seeing their own pupae is why Jews and butterflies can't touch the reproductive success of blacks and roaches.

I KNEW THE Gypsy's address from the envelope of the one hate letter she'd sent Ira, and Rufus had brought me within four blocks of it when he made his first wrong turn. I jumped from the back of his hat, slid down his smooth leather pants, and bounced on the sidewalk. I was sad to see the old felon strut off.

Without a hat to hide under, I was blinded by the intense sunlight, and certain that every foot in the city was coming after me. The sign at the curb said that the streetsweeper, a bristly monster which made the vacuum cleaner look like a cotton-candy machine, would soon arrive. I couldn't stay in the gutter.

I sprinted along a groove in the hot sidewalk, and jumped behind a garbage can in front of the nearest apartment building. The building of the block were all contiguous, so this part of the trip was easy.

When I reached the end of the corner building, I realized that I would have to wait there until late at night, when the traffic cleared. I burrowed into a crack in the concrete, where I was warmed from the evening chill.

Pedestrians passed:

". . .but he wouldn't listen, and he's the fucking boss, and now equities are off fifteen percent. On my record! I need a drink. . ."

". . .she's such a jerk-off. Two days late. Big deal. And she drops me a whole grade. What a retard. . ."

". . .I don't care what you think. Do as your mother says. . ."

". . .but if I blow him he'll give me the part. At this point in my life, what's one more blowjob. . ."

". . .coke, weed, speed, acid, dust, crack, yellows, reds, you want it, we got it. Hello there, missy. . ."

". . .the bitch want a hundred dollars to show me the color of her drawers. Shit. I tell her she could leave by the window. . ."

". . .Mama's sorry she was so late, but that big mean boss of hers made her stay late and do some typing. My little Fifi must be stuffed like a kielbasa. Heres's your spot, sweetheart. That's a good girl."

This monologue didn't recede like the others. I was slow to understand. Suddenly a deluge of hot, acrid piss engulfed me. I felt myself lighten as the crack started to fill, and then, as hard as I gripped the crags of concrete, I began to float. Soon I'd be up to street level, taking Fifi's stream directly in my face, helpless when she turned around to admire her work.

But Fifi ran dry just before I surfaced. That's a good girl. As the concrete slowly absorbed, I settled back down into the crack. The piss turned cold on my body and left a stench I would wear for days. I climbed up to watch Fifi depart, the shitty brown of the white miniature poodle's ass twitching to the click of her manicured claws. The thought of her, and the fat-assed bleached blonde in sweat pants holding her spangled tether, running through the woods just ahead of a pack of laughing wolves, did my vengeful heart good.

Traffic didn't die until after midnight, and then I made it easily to the Gypsy's apartment building. I had expected a rent-controlled dump; this was a fancy place, with a large, ornate lobby and a doorman in livery who sat inside the double doors, head against the marble wall, asleep. I passed him and walked across the mailboxes, where I found that she lived in apartment 8B.

That was too far to climb, so I went into the elevator. I knew I was in for a wait, but I needed the time to figure out exactly what I was going to do when I got to her place.

The Gypsy. Esmeralda Kosar. The story of her introduction into Ira's life was considered an essential piece of local lore when, as a nymph, I first entered the cabinets.

Ira had been on the phone. "Lenny? Ira. Listen, you're not going to believe what happened tonight. I went to the Lefkowitz Mahoney party. I'm talking to Mrs. Lefkowitz—a real cow—and some clod hits her arm. Dumps red wine on my beige suit. The one I got at the Bernstein's clearance sale last year. Right in the crotch, if you'll excuse my French.

"I tried blotting it, using soda. No way. And listen, this is when it happens. This woman walks over, stares at my crotch, and says, 'So, you're a feminist. I like that.'

"Huh? Kinda short, nice looking. Everybody else is pretty formal, but she's in this floral hippie dress. But she got away with it.

"Wait. Then she says, 'Get me a drink, would you. These heels wear me out.' She's holding them right in her hand! 'They're supposed to make our asses look nice. What do you think, are they worth the trouble?' I couldn't believe it. What? I didn't say anything. Oh sure you would. That's easy to say now.

"She tells me her name and says it's the only one in the book, and she leaves. Just like that.

"What do you think, should I call her? Or is she nuts?"

Lenny probably figured this promised grand entertainment, so he insisted Ira call her. The following Saturday she made an entrance the likes of which our colony had never seen.

She walked into the middle of the living room, dropped her brightly colored cloth bag, pirouetted, and said, "My, how very clean." There was subversion in her tone, in her eyes.

Ira stood off to the side. "Thank you," he said uneasily. It was clear right away that she was out of his league. No one in the colony had any idea why she was here.

She reached down and took off her shoes. "Let me see. It needs to look more lived-in." She threw one onto the sofa, the other onto a chair.

"Please don't do that. You were just walking outside."

"No, not nearly enough. Let's try this." She pulled her dress up over her thighs so she could unhook the garters and roll off her stockings; one she draped over the couch, the other over a chair.

Ira opened his mouth in protest, but nothing came out. He retreated a step.

"No, still not enough." She reached behind her neck and unfastened her dress, then slid it off. She was naked to the waist, as proud of her adolescent buds as Ambrosia was of her full udders. The Gypsy spread her dress out on the sofa so that it looked half-upholstered in flowers. She sat down, in garter belt and panties, and drew her feet up. "Now, that's much better, don't you think?"

Ira didn't venture an opinion, because he was already hiding in the kitchen. She laughed. It took her an hour to subdue him on the living room floor, undermining the order of his apartment and his control over his life.

Under her spell, he soon begged her to move in. She thrilled him. She could anticipate with her dark intuition just how far she could bend him without breaking him. He relished the bending.

Why did she stay? The guess was that it was a lark that went on too long. Then it became an exercise in sexual power. Staying saved her a lot of money, and she was poor. And who knows, maybe she even developed a fondness for the wretch.

After riding up and down for several hours, the elevator finally stopped at the eighth floor. It was very late, so I walked right down the hallway and under the door into 8B.

I knew immediately that I had made a mistake. The place was immaculate, reeking of cleansers and disinfectants. There was no sign of insect life: even the bacterial population was low. There was no clothing on the furniture, no food on the counters. I had misread the damned mailbox, and now I had to go all the way back to the lobby.

I sat at the elevator door for hours before it opened. During the morning rush I buried myself in an overstuffed chair in the lobby. The mailman made his deliveries. Then I again crossed the polished chrome boxes, feeling exposed and vulnerable in the light of day. An elderly lady, opening the box beside me, yelled "*Shoo!*" and banged the metal. I slipped through the slot into someone's L. L. Bean catalog. When I was certain she was gone I came out and finished my run.

8B did say Kosar. But there was another plastic tag in the same slot, almost totally obscured by the Gypsy's. I felt the letters under my feet; they spelled McGuire.

So the Gypsy had again wangled her way into someone's apartment. Defiance was so integral to Esmeralda's relationships with men that McGuire could only have made her submit to the impeccable household order if McGuire was immune to the puissance of pussy. It had to be Ms. McGuire.

As I waited for the elevator, I thought about strategy. Because there was no *Blattella* community, McGuire would be my sole ally. But the more I thought about the burden she had chosen to assume the harder it was for me to picture her. Nor had I ever fully understood the Gypsy's arrival to or departure from Ira's life. Could I revive her feelings, whatever they were, and get her back to him? I was beginning to fear I had set myself up for another defeat.

I finally got back to the apartment. This was a strange couple. McGuire came from a Danish modern, steel and glass world. In the bookcase were the Gypsy's dog-eared volumes of Ouspensky and Gibran, but McGuire had relegated them to a corner of the bottom shelf; the books at human eye-level were thick and had flat blue covers with gold sans serif titles.

I climbed up the case and soon found myself on a spine reading *Uprighting Inclined Mandibular Molar in Preparation for Restorative Treatment.* To my left towered *The Apically Positioned Flap.* I looked out into the living room. There was crocheting on the arm of McGuire's sofa ("like making our own chains" was the Gypsy's feeling about needlework). A peerless housekeeper, a scientist or doctor, a handicrafter—how could this McGuire live with the Gypsy?

Maybe she wasn't immune to the Gypsy, just not as servile as Ira. I remembered when, one night a month before she left, the Gypsy belittled Ira's scant sexual experience by comparing it to her own. She yelled through the pillow Ira wrapped around his head. "I can't even count the cocks, Ira. I've had more pussy than you'll ever have, too." Was McGuire's one of them?

I sat on *Guide to Occlusal Waxing* the rest of the afternoon. The sun was setting when the door opened and McGuire came in. She was short, with neat, closely cropped brown hair and a pleasant face. She wore an attractive blue pin-striped suit. She put a bunch of flowers into a vase, and placed it on the coffee table in the living room. She tuned the radio to an easy-listening station, and crocheted, humming the tunes she knew. I watched her closely. I couldn't see her with the Gypsy as friend or roommate, and certainly not as lover. They were too different.

Some time later the door opened again and a man entered. Now I was baffled. He was pasty and unfit, with narrow shoulders and wide hips, maybe a few inches taller than her. I was quite sure he wasn't the type for a ménage à trois. Maybe he was a gay roomer. I wished I had checked the number of bedrooms.

When McGuire kissed him that theory died.

"Have a good day?"

"Fine. And yours?"

"Fine."

"Nice flowers," he said.

"Thanks."

They made the Wainscotts seem hot-blooded. How could the Gypsy stand it? I wished she'd get here already.

McGuire disappeared into the kitchen. The man sat in the living room. From his briefcase he pulled a copy of *American Plaque*. So he was the dentist! The group portrait was not developing for me.

Boiled smells reached the living room. McGuire called him, and we retired to the kitchen.

They ate pretty much without talking, mouths carefully sealed while they chewed. Knives and forks crossed hands for cutting. Napkins dabbed lips. Wine was sipped from crystal goblets. The gypsy used to stick a knife into a large chunk of meat and gnaw on it, and drink wine straight from the bottle. Were they eating early to avoid her? Was she coming home late to avoid them?

When dinner was over, the man helped McGuire carry the dishes to the sink. As she began to wash them, he kissed her lightly on the cheek and said, "Very good, Esmé. Please brush your teeth before you do this."

Esmé. Esmé? Esmeralda? The Gypsy? Impossible. She hated the name Esmé. She had hair to her waist. She would never wear a suit. The deportment, the manners, the smell, the crocheting. No. However unlikely it was that there would be two Esmeraldas in one household, this was not the Gypsy.

They spent the rest of the evening watching sitcoms. Esmé continued to crochet. The Gypsy did not show up. Still wild.

"I'm going to get ready for bed," said Esmé a few hours later. I followed her to the bedroom. I wanted to be sure.

Esmé wore a frilly little bra; the Gypsy called bras "tit-cuffs" and never wore one. Esmé hung up her clothes; the Gypsy used to leave hers where they fell. When Esmé removed her bra, I had to admit that she had the same little teen-tits. But beneath her skirt she wore panty hose, which the Gypsy reviled as a "muff muzzle." The clinching evidence snaked through Esmé's thin, mousy bush; the string of a tampon. The Gypsy was a sworn enemy of the "vaginal gag."

As Esmé showered, she shaved her legs and underarms. How could this be my Esmeralda?

Doubt still gnawed. I went under the toilet seat. First the tampon—out with the old and in with the new. She fumbled a bit with the applicator, unusual for a woman of over twenty years' experience. Lemon-lime vapors rose from the tampon in the bowl. The Gypsy would rather die than pollute herself like this. But the hormonal smell was too maddeningly faint to make a positive identification.

Esmé urinated, which did not help. I couldn't stand it anymore. As she crumpled her toilet paper, I raced across her buttocks for a quick lick of her pussy. I had to know.

Everything happened very fast. She must have had a most sensitive bottom, because she immediately reached back and brushed me off. I fell into the bowl, right onto the disintegrating tampon, and my questions were finally answered. The tampon kept me afloat long enough to watch her wipe; for the first time I noticed a gold band around her fourth finger. This woman was married to the dentist. This was Mrs. McGuire. And the chemicals in the spreading fibers told me the rest. Beneath the lemon-lime, it was her. Mrs. McGuire was the Gypsy. The wild one, the free-loving anarchist—now shaved, douched, disinfected, tamponed, and married to a dentist.

Another plan shattered. Even if I could get her back to Ira's, after this metamorphosis she was useless. Ruth's secretions would waste her. As if in retribution, the instant I concluded this the Gypsy reached back and flushed. At least she still had a touch of the old venom.

She stood up. Her receding silhouette spun slowly as it pulled up its briefs. Pushed up against the side by torrents of cold water, I started to circumnavigate the bowl, faster and faster until my guts pressed against my back. Eddies rippled over me, dimming my dizzied senses; but the weak taste of Esmé's hormones stayed with me. Poor me. Poor Esmeralda. Can civilization ever compensate you for your loss?

With that lament, I whooshed through the bottom of the bowl, and careened through the trap.

Bless the Rat and the Roach

BLOODY TAMPON fibers and clods of toilet paper wrapped around my legs as the torrent of cold water washed me downward. Falling from the refrigerator had been scary, but at least I could see the end of it; this pipe was a black eternity.

How long could I continue at this tremendous speed? I prepared for impact. Suddenly my free fall was stopped—but I hadn't reached the bottom. I was pinned by a sideways blast from another waste line. If not for the cushion of shit it provided, I might have been cracked open on the galvanized pipe.

After a few seconds of intense pressure, the flush was spent. But it had stripped me of the cellulose fibers and the resistance they provided, and I fell at an even greater velocity.

A moment later I skidded against a pipe, then shot through a short flume. The fall was over. I was unharmed, floating in a pool of calm colloid. I was in the sewer. I never would have believed I'd be so happy to be here.

To me the sewer had always been an unimaginable

Hades at the bottom of the sink drain. Now I saw that my imagination had failed me. How awfully decent of humans to have constructed a vast network of impregnable tunnels so we could get safely around the city. This was the perfect way to check out new apartments, to visit friends and relatives, or, for the singular individual, to limp home after the stillbirth of a lame-brained plan.

My mind was swarming with new tactics that I wanted to discuss with Bismarck and the others. All I had to do was swim home. I extended my legs and pulled them back. My body didn't move but the sewage did, washing over me, little clods of feces settling into my spiracles, like jimmies on an ice cream cone. I tried to wipe myself clean, moving gingerly so I wouldn't tip over. I'd always supposed everyone just knew how to swim; I never imagined it was something you had to learn.

The current of the sewer carried me slowly; I was sure I was headed straight for the ocean. I thought I could already hear the surf beating on the shore. The ocean. The thought of it made me cold. Animals that looked like sea weed, or glowed in the dark, or generated electricity. All that weird protolife stuff, neither animal nor vegetable. Slime everywhere. My ancestors rose from the oceans hundreds of millions of years ago, and I was certain they'd had damned good reasons.

My legs were quivering, poised to churn. But why bother? I was doomed. There was nothing I could do.

In my despair it occurred to me that Ira's apartment could be on the way to the ocean. Where was I now? There was some light in these larger conduits, and I could see letters and numbers on the ceiling; but they had nothing to do with any coordinates I know of the city. I prayed I would be able to crack the code before I hit the breakers.

All my hours under the toilet seat served me well; I could read the neighborhood by the excrement. Just now I detected the lardy taste of refried beans shot through with flatulence, yellow rice and oil, and the inert seeds of tomatoes. The urine was sharp, acidic, also from tomatoes. A small slick of coconut shavings trailed the meat. I was passing under a neighborhood from south of the border.

This sample had been unusually pure. Readings soon became far more difficult because many areas of the sewer were outlets for small neighborhoods with fuzzy boundaries. To prevent myself from becoming saturated, insensitive to nuances in taste, I was careful to sample only occasionally, always from the mouths of the smaller pipes, before their flow blended with the main line.

I continued to watch for clues to my location. Large chunks had fallen from the ceiling of the ceramic pipe, which looked over a hundred years old. There was no glamour here; humans wouldn't bother with it until there was a major collapse. I could see it: a sweltering summer day. Heat would penetrate the asphalt, and one small shift in a teetering section of pipe would bring the whole thing down. Within hours shit would be backed up and running down the avenues, trapping old and infirm humans, small dogs like Fifi, and best of all, a good number of water bugs. Fancy footwear sucked off well-heeled pedestrians would bob in the sewage. Virulent disease would gestate in the moist heat, then erupt through the human population, defying attempts by health authorities to treat or contain it. Local news trucks and helicopters would race to the head of the flow to transmit important video footage. Some people would swear it was all caused by political corruption; others would detect a message from God.

From the looks of things down here, I wouldn't be surprised if the whole city substructure were about to go, water supply, power supply, and phone exchanges too. The foundations of the buildings would crumble. The great vertical city would turn horizontal. Then nothing could stop *Blattella germanica* from the conquest and domination of every apartment, every office, every kitchen and bathroom. It was glorious thought.

I passed through a small ripple and into the next section of pipe. Suddenly it was very dark. The air was hot and filled with a carrion stench. I didn't think I was anywhere near the business district, yet the smell brought cannibals to mind.

It didn't last long. I soon passed under a neat row of yellowish stalactites, down another small fall, and back into the prison light and bracing aroma of fresh sewage.

I looked back. A dull orb floated in the sludge, but didn't drift with the current. There was another one much like it on the other side of the pipe. Then I understood. The ripples I thought were being caused by soiled paper and tampons were in fact the work of leathery hide. The stationary turd in the center of the pipe was the tip of a snout. I had just floated through the mouth of an immense alligator.

A gift from Florida, the alligator was probably flushed when it was about nine inches long. Now it must have been thirty-five feet long, its jaw five feet across. Its camouflage was superb. It was almost as if the animal had evolved right there.

But it didn't. The alligators had survived out in the world. How did they do it? Or maybe the real question is why did the rest of the dinosaurs die out and leave them here? The Jurassic roaches thought the dinosaurs would reign forever. *Homo sapiens* thinks of himself as lord and master, but he has had an unsteady hand on small swaths of the planet for a mere blink of the eye. The dinosaurs *ruled.* They were huge, fantastic animals. The swift ones would have made a slug of a cheetah, the powerful ones a flea of an elephant.

Above the rest stood the *Tyrannosaurus rex*. Roach nymphs did not play Bats then, they played Tyrannosaurus. And not only did they emulate the beast, many of them lived off it. The spindly forelegs of the Tyrannosaurus could barely hold kills up to its mouth, so plenty dropped; more slipped between its huge teeth. Because of this, every Tyrannosaurus had an entourage of thousands of roaches.

What happened to the noble dinosaurs? Ira, who took his nephew to the natural history museum once or twice a year, adduced several theories (which changed with the vogue in the current glossies). One year it was the Ice Age that wiped them out (but not us). Then it was the competition with smaller, supposedly smarter animals. (The shrew pitted against the Tyrannosaurus.) According to the following year's theory, a change in the earth's magnetic field had done something to release the ozone layer, letting in excessive ultraviolet radiation. (The Tyrannosaurus succumbed to freckles.) And last year he decided that an asteroid smacked into the earth 65 million years ago, causing a violent explosion whose cloud darkened the planet for years, killing off the plants, then the herbivores, and finally the carnivores. (But not the roaches.)

Every roach knows the truth: one day in South Dakota a Tyrannosaurus was finishing up a baby stegosaurus. Thousands of *Blattella*, *Periplaneta*, and *Corporata* roaches were harvesting the falling blood and scraps. When the carcass was tossed away, everyone ran to it. Usually the dinosaur burped and went off to nap under a giant fern. However, this time it stopped to watch the roaches and, for no obvious reason, stomped to death every one.

There had never been a single conflict between a large reptile and an insect. But the next day there were fifty more similar incidents. The peace was over.

Battle plans were drawn up by the *Corporata* roaches and transmitted coast to coast. The following day *Coroporata* battalions shadowed and mounted every Tyrannosaurus on the continent. On top of each one's head they divided into two groups, about five hundred in each. Right at sunset they struck, running into the dinosaur's nostrils and locking their bodies tightly together. The last ones used the Tyrannosaurus' own mucus to seal the passages.

Two anatomical defects in the species proved its undoing: the short forelegs could not dig into the nostrils; and because of the depth of its skull, the Tyrannosaurus could not breath through its mouth. Within half an hour of sunset on the west coast, *Tyrannosaurus rex* was extinct in America and soon after around the world. Other carnivores vied for their spots, and the *Corporatae* did them in too.

The herbivore population quickly grew. They were slovenly animals which stood in swamps all day, chewing and drooling. The roaches killed them off without a twinge. Most got the Tyrannosaurus method. The dinosaurs with thick nasal armor got the stopper treatment: several score of *Corporatae* ran up their urethrae with dirt and twigs, which either burst their bladders or killed them by infection. Only the small lizards were too quick, which is why they still exist to this day. The alligators survived by staying offshore.

We could have killed them too. Now I could see why we didn't. Dumb, docile, and slow, but large and fierce-looking—the welfare class of the era—the alligators were the best, safest possible souvenirs of the Jurassic period. Ironically, the *Corporata* roach colonies soon collapsed under the weight of their organization, and the species died out.

I RODE ANOTHER small cataract into a huge pipe. Spikes of light pierced through manhole covers. Ladders led up to a walkway beside the conduit. But the current moved slowly, and a sewage sample revealed such diversity that it told me nothing.

Thousands of turds floated down the sewer. Now, for the first time since I was flushed, I saw something moving against the current. It looked like a tiny boat, a racing shell with almost no wake, powered by long, beautifully coordinated strokes. I was amazed to see that it was a *Blattella germanica*.

I tried to swim across the pipe to her, getting nowhere and earning myself an extra helping of jimmies. She stopped and said, "New down here?"

"Yes, and not by choice."

"A lucky break for you. The sewer is a wonderful home—endless food, complete safety, climate control year-round. Perfect for retirement." She was good advertising—sleek, exotic, graceful. Very exciting.

"I have some business at home before I can consider retirement." I explained my excrement navigation system.

She said, "Tell me what you're looking for."

"It's a mix. The staple is chicken, in all forms. There are traces of hip ethnic foods. The "100% natural" component means high concentrations of sugar, mold, fungus, and bacteria. And there will be a good amount of antacids, laxatives, aspirin, and Valium.

"Easy. Everybody knows that neighborhood. We're going to have to turn you around. You're heading for the sewage treatment plant."

Visions of vats the size of apartment buildings came to mind, of huge drums stenciled with the skull and crossbones, acids dumped in by droning mechanical arms.

"Yeah, let's turn me around."

But she had disappeared.

What did I say? Why did she leave me? Oh my god, a sewage treatment plant. I'd disappear like a fudgesicle on a hot sidewalk.

Like her, now. Smooth. Pull. Pull. The turds flowed over me as I drifted closer to the plant. Come on. Pull. Pull. But I just couldn't get it. The debris on my back was making me gag. What an awful way to die. I so desperately wanted one last shot at Ira.

Suddenly I was lifted out of the water. I was standing on hard chitin; she had swum underneath me. Why did I think she had abandoned me? There must have been human toxins in the shit.

We started upstream. Her sweeping strokes were a pleasure to watch. I lowered my hindquarters onto her cuticle to feel the vibrations—a sexual thrill without pheromones. Very provocative; very unusual.

We passed through three long segments of pipe, each narrower and darker than the one before. She said, "We'll wait here."

Swarms of large pointy gray forms cut through the sewage. When one came close I could see fur tufted with turd, strands of shit hanging like brown tinsel from whiskers, little beady eyes with crusted yellow frames. Nervous, driven. The legendary sewer rats.

I said, "You don't know them, do you?" They were aquatic nightmares, with their insatiable appetites and their merciless ways. One of our oldest enemies.

"Don't worry. The ones down here are practically blind. One of them is going to take you home."

I looked down at her. "Take me to the treatment plant."

"They're extremely primitive creatures. They run daily routes that hardly change during their lives, and they have little interest in anything else. That's why they're the stars of human labs. The one who goes to your neighborhood every day just came in."

She started swimming me toward the rat. Its twitching whiskers flicked shit in the air. The eyes were blanker, more red and murderous, up close. I didn't want to go near the thing. When I got a whiff of rodent stench, I almost jumped off her back.

"It will put its snout on that ledge for a short rest," she said. And it did. She pulled up beside it. "Now grab hold of the fur and climb on."

"I want to stay here with you. It is great down here."

"It's perfectly safe. You'll see."

"I'm charming and well-read. I'd make a perfect companion."

"Up you go." She bucked, and I rolled onto the rat's back. It was disgusting, covered with cold clammy shit, quite unlike the cold clammy shit I had been floating in all along.

When it twitched, its entire body spasmed, primitive and brainless, like a jellyfish. I had thought better of rats. I settled into the long, secure fur of the nape. I faced the back, doing my best to forget whose paws my fate was in.

My savior moved away, blowing water through her spiracles like a fire boat. "Thank you," I said.

"Drop in any time." I hoped to.

After a few minutes of rest, the rodent turned and headed back up the pipe, as she had said it would. It swam determinedly, drawing its paws through the sewage, saying to itself, "Left, right, left, right. . ." At first I thought this was a joke, but it didn't stop. Did it fear it might get the stroke wrong, or let its mind stray? Or was this just another discharge of the regimented brain?

I climbed across the side of the neck and said into its ear, "Right, left, right, left. . ." The rat flicked its ear. When I persisted it shook its head, almost tossing me into the drink.

It was a foolish thing to do, because I wanted to get home as soon as possible. But this was too enticing a challenge. I climbed back to its ear and said, "Rat pussy. Nice warm rat pussy. Hot juicy rat pussy. Just behind you. If you let her catch up. . ." There was no reaction, so I tried, "Rat tits. Nice big full rat tits." I assumed this was a male rat, though I was not going below to check. Still, there was no harm either way in "Rat cock. Nice big hard rat cock."

And the rat said, "Left, right, left, right. . ."

The innocent-looking can be the most deviant, so I said, "Rat feet. Rat feet in black high heels." Though this human perversion is the only one to have caught the imagination of other species, my rat was indifferent. Next I tried, "Rat babies. Illegal rat babies, smuggled from a sewer out of state." And finally, "Rat whips. Rat whips held by rat dominatrixes in black leather rat corsets, flaying your little rat behind."

"Left, right, left, right. . ." Nothing would stay this rodent from swift completion of its appointed round.

I returned to the nape. The route was so complex that even if I knew how to swim I never would have made it. Bless the rat and the roach.

An occasional wave of shit washed over us; it was still too complex for me. The codes on the ceiling remained impenetrable. Since we were going upstream, it was safe to go too far; I could always float back to Ira's.

The rat paddled tirelessly for hours. Other rats passed now and then, but were too absorbed in their little quests to take notice of us. When several rats were close together, the pipe would echo with a chorus of, "Left, right, left, right."

Blattellae were riding quite a few of them. "Where are you headed?" I called. Visiting. Shopping. One was going surfing. The rats were mere mass transit.

Mine took a sharp turn. "Whoa, Nelly!" I cried. The sewage that broke over us indicated a change in neighborhood. Small bits of carbon were suspended in large slicks of oil, remnants of things overfried, along with potato chips and other junk food, lots of sugar, and a great deal of alcohol end-products. We had passed Ira's area and reached the ghetto.

"So long, Mickey," I said, and leaped into the scum. The rat paddled away upstream with unflagging concentration. "Left, right, left, right. . ."

Legs spread in a float position, I watched for hints of my location; I didn't want to get out too soon and have to face keen-eyed ghetto rats on the surface. I still couldn't decode the ceiling. Pipe after pipe expelled refuse in my path.

I felt a nudge from behind. "Take it easy," I said. It bumped me again. "Look, pal, there's plenty of room to pass."

It wasn't until the third hit that I turned to look at it. I had never before seen this species, a mutant of the sewer. It was my length, but our proportions couldn't have been more different. It had a huge swollen·head, bent down and tucked over its belly. Its eyes, pointing out to the sides, were closed; I wondered if that's why it hit me. The short forelimbs look like pieces of cauliflower, the rear ones like stubby paddles. It was the only creature I'd ever seen with two tails: a segmented reptilian tail extended beyond the body; the other was wispier and far longer. The creature's skin was a naked pulpy purple brown, which looked like something's innards. It made me queasy to think that it had touched me.

I was streamlined and balanced compared to this thing. I said, "Look, Romeo, if you want to go faster, do it over there. I'm looking for something."

It closed in and butted me yet again. This was it. I leaned to the side and blasted it with my back leg. It reared as if I had shot it, its repulsive head rising completely out of the water. Then the head dunked back in, and the miscreant rolled over.

It lay there for some time. I prodded it with my leg. "Turn over, you ugly scuzz." It didn't try. This was no more an aquatic animal than I was. I must have killed it. I didn't mean to. I felt bad.

What was wrong with me? I was attacked and I responded. That's what animals do. So the stupid thing was dead.

The Bible was kicking up in me, the meek shall inherit the earth and all that. But I wasn't buying. I retaliated with a salvo from Psalms: His enemies shall lick the dust.

The critter hit something and turned over. The long tail had wrapped around its neck. That's what killed it. Not that it mattered.

Why have a tail that can undo you? Was it prehensile, while the other one was for balance? Did they meet the body at a common trunk, or were they completely separate? It was hard to tell in the shit, so I rolled the beast over again.

I should have seen it from the beginning. The longer tail didn't begin anywhere near the segmented tail. It came out of the middle of the gut. This was no tail. It was an umbilical cord.

This was not a disgusting new creature. It was a disgusting old one. It was a human fetus. I didn't kill it. It had never lived.

A primordial rage gripped me—this was the only time in my life I would face a human my own size. "Had you lived, you would have been the same as the rest. Boric acid. Motels. Sprays. Stepping on us, mashing, squealing. And we've never done one spot of harm to your species since the day it fell to earth." I couldn't contain myself. I cracked it across the swollen head. It bobbed back. I kicked it in the gut and then in the sliver of exposed thorax. I loved the impact. I kicked it in the eye, which was still closed. The lid caved in, and my leg punched into the hollow. It was revolting. I planted the other legs on the face and yanked myself free.

Covered with bruises and gouges, the fetus drifted downstream, its head bobbing, as if to apologize for all of its kind.

I climbed up the next conduit. A crack of light led me to the street.

It was great to be on terra firma. A bus blanketed me with exhaust. I didn't mind. It helped dry me off. I walked down the curb. At the intersection the signs told me I was only five blocks from home. I was so excited that I didn't wait for nightfall.

Checking In

3B—GRAVEYARD of friends and family and many to follow. Why had I come back? Hadn't I suffered enough here? Yet as soon as I crossed the threshold, I realized that this was my true home, and I would do anything to keep it.

Since I had avoided the colony the week after the Defeat, I didn't know how they had taken it. The hallway was empty, and I feared the worst.

When I turned into the dining room I saw the unimaginable: a herd of hundreds of citizens, slowly crossing the center of the floor in the bright light of day, with the deliberate, exaggerated motions of creatures in a trance. On their backs some hauled useless mementoes—hairs, dust, slivers of wood—while others leaned on makeshift walking sticks, an unaccountable affectation for six-leggers. They were trying to look even more hungry and long-suffering than they were. I hadn't imagined deterioration would take hold this fast.

I trotted to the front of the pack. The leader held the longest stick, almost half a toothpick. His mannerisms were the most pronounced. It was Exodus. I was not surprised.

I said, "What are you doing? Where are you taking them?"

"Who are you to ask me this, you, who smelleth as if the goat and the cow and the chicken hath taken you to wipe their dirty bottoms upon!"

"I'm your brother. Don't you recognize me?"

His eyes focused way beyond me. "If you are one of us, join us. If not, be gone."

"Ruth and Ira are going to be home in a few hours. You're leading everyone to slaughter."

He said, "I am bringing them out of that land unto a good land and a large one, unto a land flowing with milk and honey."

"In the living room?"

"The place of the Canaanites, and the Hittites, and the Amorites, and the Perizzites, and the Hivites, and the Jebusites."

I said, "But Exodus, we're in the land of the Fishblatts, and the Grubsteins, and the Wainscotts, and the Tambellinis. There's death all around."

"Sojourner, the only death I sense, it radiates from you; a fabulous stench, like the corpse of the boar in the summer sun. If you have suffered and it was not just, I pity you. But do not lead astray my flock." He motioned with his back leg. "A mighty six hundred thousand."

I grabbed his stick, but he ripped it back. Faith made him strong. "It's that book, remember? This is not Sinai, Exodus, it's apartment 3B. Lead them back, I beg you."

But he kept on. I saw many of my once perceptive and quick-witted friends in the pack behind him. How had they been divested of their reason? I approached Snot. "Why the living room? There's nothing there. You know that. You'll be killed."

"The route might be a long one, and difficult," he said. "But the land is promised to us."

"We used to laugh at lines like that."

"We blasphemed. We should have made the exodus long ago, as it was intended to be."

Exodus intoned, "At evening ye shall eat flesh, and in the morning ye shall be filled with bread."

"Amen!" roared his flock.

They continued across the hall into the living room.

When they reached the far wall, beneath the windows, they stopped. Unable to divine whether to turn left or right—there was no verse concerning this choice—Exodus just stood there.

Prophet's block had come at the perfect time—they were in the safest part of the room, hidden from human view by the couch back and by shadows from the standing lamp. If he agonized for six more hours, I might have a chance to get everyone back to the baseboard during the night.

Ira and Ruth came home. After dinner they repaired to the living room, but a TV documentary on Seminole pottery protected the flock from their attention. If they would just stay still. . .

Exodus was more demented than I suspected. This was no pose; he was living in ancient Sinai. He turned and walked through the flock to his sacred mount, the coffee table. He climbed to the glass top, reared, and held his mighty staff over his head, proclaiming, "If a man shall steal an ox, or a sheep, and kill it, or sell it; he shall restore five oxen for an ox, and four sheep for a sheep."

"Huzzah!" cried the colony.

"Jesus Christ!" cried Ira, looking over the top of the newspaper. He brought the business section down on Exodus, who made a crunching sound that made me feel very mortal. When Ira lifted the paper, Exodus was gone; but IBM, which a moment ago was up one point for the day, had surged to close up eleven.

The others were sure he had gone to confer with God. They would be very patient. I could come back for them later. I returned to the dining room. Fresh boric acid was scattered along the baseboard. The Exodus phenomenon began to make some sense.

I carefully entered. No one was inside, dead or alive. If there hadn't been a slaughter, what had happened? Perhaps Ira had seen a poor starving patrol in the area, and then laid down poison. The colony had crowded at the cracks to watch. The vigil must have been hell: would he see the opening and pour in the boric acid, massacring them all? The first bitter molecules wafting inside terrified the colony, making them desperate to flee. Who could resist the promise of a land flowing with milk and honey?

I jumped from the opening over the acid.

It was late night now, and the kitchen was dark. Before I returned to the living room, I had to quell my hunger—no easy task, because my sewage marinade made it hard for me to smell anything but myself. I looked in the usual places without success. But when the fan beneath the refrigerator went on, it issued an aroma of pure sweetness that defeated even the sewer. Why hadn't Exodus led his flock toward this honey?

I tried to locate the source of the scent. At the edge of the refrigerator I heard the muffled sound of full-mouthed revelry. The aroma became very strong in the gap beside the refrigerator. The voices rose, shrieking and growling. It was a bacchanal. I was more than willing to pay for my meal with sperm.

I followed the voices through the black. Three days wasted. Instead of drifting in shit I could have been here, overeating and overfucking. Now it was my duty to catch up.

When the voices were close, I bounded in beside them, yelling, "Let us eat and drink; for tomorrow we die!"

Two steps. That was it. Then I was stuck, my legs sunk in something absolutely unyielding. Maple syrup, I figured. I would just have to eat my way out.

But I figured wrong.

Now I could hear the voices with perfect clarity.

"Help me!"

"Pull me loose, I beg you."

"Numbers, don't let me die here."

A stupid illiterate with a taste for Kandy Korn—I had walked into the Roach Motel.

It was my idea to push it here, out of the way, in the dark, where no one could read the warnings. How could I forget so soon? How could I fail to recognize its disgusting odor?

"Well-chosen adage, Numbers. Here's another one for you to think about—and you'll have plenty of time. 'As a dog returneth to his vomit, so a fool returneth to his folly.'" It was Bismarck. I had doomed him too. "You taught me that."

I pulled up my left foreleg so hard that the adhesive rose into a small cone around it. But when my joints started to crack I had to stop; if I broke off a leg my body would settle into the mire, and I would have no freedom of motion and absolutely no chance of escape. As if I had one now.

Once my eyes had adjusted to the dark, I saw that my legs were caught on a pad of adhesive which looked like chewed, flattened gum. Bismarck was far worse off than I was. Not only his legs, but one antenna and the front of his head were stuck in it too, as if he had used them for leverage to try to pull up the legs. There were eight other guests, some grunting and cursing, the rest silent and still.

Bismarck said, "We checked it out, and we checked in after all."

I said, "In that case, get the manager. The decor stinks. Room service doesn't answer. The rug is an abomination. And there are cockroaches in here. I say we check out."

"I'm with you." His laugh sent an eerie, muffled echo through the motel. "You said that putz Ira would never miss this thing. We really put one over on him."

"*No!*" A scream from the back. The motel jerked as someone thrashed.

I was caught in a Roach Motel. I was going to live here for a long time, get thin here, then die here. Years from now, when the refrigerator breaks, or the alien's work is redone by a new tenant, someone will find the motel, throw it away, and it will end up in a dump. Other garbage will bury and compress it. Millions of years from now, long after humans are extinct, my fossils might be uncovered by a scientist of a wiser species.

Eternity in the motel was the single most unbearable thought of my life. I started to jump up and down. Then I calmed myself. It was time to accept my fate: no more grape nuts. No more pastry crumbs. No more pheromones (that one smarted). But then again, no more disinfectants, and vacuuming, and overstuffed baseboards. No more boric acid and poison sprays. No more waterbugs. And thank God, no more trying to get Ira Fishblatt's penis into a woman he was too terrified to touch.

Howls from the back of the motel threatened my equanimity. I needed chatter, distraction. "I've got to tell you, Bismarck, you don't want to go out with your head stuck to the floor like that. Not at all elegant."

"That really hurts, Mr. Muff Diver. What did you think this was, one of those kinky motels?"

"Very kinky, watching you suck tar."

We heard exploratory scratching outside the motel. Bismarck yelled, "Get away! This is a trap." Anxiously we watched the opening. The steps receded. He had saved a life.

The event sobered me. I said, "A couple of months ago we were smart. The colony had purpose. And look at us tonight, divided between hopeless places: the living room and a motel. What happened?"

Bismarck paused, then said, "I've had a chance to think about that, and for what it's worth, this is my opinion: when we were nymphs, anyone who came out of the bookcase with a scheme to improve the species was laughed at. We had our instincts; we knew exactly how to manage.

"Then you began your operations. The vacuum cleaner, the lock, the wires for the circuits, and let's not forget the Roach Motel. I supported you because you were practical, not ideological. I still think that with a little luck we would have won our new life. And you made the colony believe in a future even as food was running out.

"But at the same time, the operations bred a subtle organization in the colony. Citizens began to think of the plans, the future, the colony, first, before their own immediate welfare. They got used to being told what to do. Their faith in the future was based not on their own competence but on yours.

"The night of the dinner party—when you didn't return, you coward—they were lost. After months of dependence, they didn't know what to do. They had forgotten how to take care of themselves.

"Now they're prey for anyone who will promise them anything. Going to the land of milk and honey doesn't sound any more bizarre than a lot of your schemes. And look at you and me. How can we explain this?"

I was astounded. Except for my close friends, I had never felt the slightest support from the colony. I never got help without offering a bribe. If citizens had been corrupted by my vision, I didn't see it; I couldn't believe that doing a little labor for a Cheerio or a waterbug shell once or twice could have such a profound effect. For the most part the citizens had watched and waited in the baseboard, selfish and lazy, while I worked.

I never represented myself as a savior. When I offered a strategy, citizens followed me out of pure self-interest when they thought I was right, and reviled and rejected me when they thought I wasn't. How did that instill self-abnegation or organization?

Bismarck said, "If you're blaming yourself, you're an unbearable egotist. I'll have to ask you to step aside so I can die in humbler air."

"I don't feel the slightest guilt or responsibility. I was the only one who tried to change our fortunes. No offense."

Bismarck used his only free part, the one antenna, to strike the top of his head in applause. "Well done, lad. You have edited the truth so you can have a peaceful death."

"Bastard, I *remember* the truth."

His laugh was labored. The posture made all expression strenuous. He fell silent and soon he was asleep.

I lost track of time. Suddenly I was startled by the clomping and shuffling of shoes. Ira and Ruth. The shoes passed within a yard of us. So close yet so safe—like being in the middle of an artillery barrage, knowing you couldn't possibly be hit.

Aromas soon permeated the motel. Bismarck was wakened by the clamor. He sniffed. "I have to cut down on my cholesterol. Thank God I'm here so I don't have to eat any of those eggs."

As the dishes and pots were washed, I could smell the moist detergent and hear the abrasion. "Pinky!" I said. "I just remembered. That's you're real name. You were one of the Brillo boys!"

"Who told you that?"

"You did. A long time ago."

"You'd take the word of someone named Pinky?"

"I think it's adorable. Why did you change it?"

"Ask Soapy Barbarossa. . . And grant a roach his dying request: never call me that."

The shoes left, and the motel was quiet. The others were still. Were they dead? Asleep? I couldn't sleep; there would soon be ample opportunity for that. The compressor of the refrigerator, just beside us, kept switching on and off, our relentless timekeeper.

Ira and Ruth didn't return to the kitchen until the following morning. Bismarck looked much worse. The specks of gray that had appeared overnight in his carapace were a terminal sign. He was going to die long before I did. The thought of dying had become bearable to me because I had pictured it in his company, joking and jousting. Without him I would be prey to my howling fear.

"Bismarck!" I cried.

He woke. "What?" His weak, crackly morning voice was Caruso to me.

"Good morning."

"Good morning? You woke me up to say good morning? Leave me alone until check-out time. Can't a roach get some sleep around here?"

He dozed for several more hours and awoke in a serious mood. "You know you can get out of here."

"Great. Let's go."

"Not us. You. Look at your legs. Only the tips are caught. If you're very careful you can leave them behind."

I laughed. "Then what would I walk on?"

"Your new ones. When you molt. Are you a total ninny?"

"Molt at my age? Who's the ninny?" I struck my back with an antenna. I sounded hollow, like a gourd.

"Let the dead bury their dead. I'm going to save you. You'll always owe me for this one, and all I regret is that I won't be around to remind you. . .

"In a day, maybe two, I'm going to die. Eat me. Don't grimace; compared to most of your diet, I'm champagne and caviar. I will fill you out for a quick molt. And that, my friend, will set you free."

My mind would not accept the idea. But he was waiting for a response, so I said, "I'd rather you didn't die before I do."

"Numbers, you're hopeless."

The motel was quiet all day. Our starvation was marked by the compressor.

Ira and Ruth, our other faithful markers, returned and ate dinner. That night several more citizens died. As far as I could tell the motel now had eight dead guests and two living. And the register was going to change again.

In the morning Bismarck looked still worse. He was grayer, his back shedding flakes of chitin.

"Bismarck," I said.

There was no answer.

"Bismarck!"

Still no answer. No movement.

"Damn you, Bismarck, answer me!" I screamed.

"More pressing business this morning?" His voice was low and weak.

"Don't ever do that to me again!"

I let him doze. The switching of the refrigerator was unbearably loud today. By midday I couldn't stand any more. "Hey, Bismarck, remember when I walked up the wall when Ira was fornicating. He got so mad I thought he was going to die in the saddle. Bismarck?"

"Sure."

"And remember when I set off that smoke detector when Ruth was in the bathroom? That was a good one, wasn't it? Bismarck?"

"Why are you asking me this?"

"I'm reminiscing."

"I'm tired."

I let him be. I was glad when Ira and Ruth reappeared and filled the motel with aromas of corned beef and cabbage. Their shoes and voices broke the maddening rhythm of the compressor. I said, "Good thing we don't have to clean up after that meal."

Bismarck did not answer. I was too scared to repeat myself. In the morning I didn't bother trying to wake him. It was no longer possible.

I rubbed his back with my antennae. "Pinky," I whispered, "you scoundrel. First you let me walk in here so you won't be alone, and now you leave me. Where are your manners? What am I going to do now, just watch you decay?" The compressor went on.

Later in the day I heard *Blattella* footsteps somewhere in the kitchen. My mind raced: what if the citizen approached? Would I warn him off, assuring myself a harrowing death in this rotting wax museum? Or would I let him distract me, as I had distracted Bismarck, during my last days? I debated with myself passionately.

He approached. My heart pounded. I knew I was about to speak—but to this day I don't know if it was going to be a warning or an invitation—when I heard a voice.

It was a silverfish. "Check this out. A Roach Motel."

Her friend said, "You know, not even a roach would fall for that thing. You'd think they'd give it up already."

It was a terrible night. Every time I started to nod off, I was certain I saw someone move. I would strain in the dark to see a sign of life. The effort of examining all nine bodies tired me, but each time I grew sleepy I would imagine something stirred and go through it all again.

When sleep came it was punishment. In my dream all of the bodies came alive. A set of stairs appeared in front of each of them, leading out the top of the motel. I did not get one. They easily stepped out of the adhesive and started to climb. I begged them to let me come. "Someone has to watch the motel," said Bismarck. Fuck the motel; I was going after them. But I was still stuck fast. I yelled, "Tell me how you got free." "Faith," said another voice. It was Exodus, who was standing at the main opening. "I'm going to lead you to the land of milk and honey. Do you believe me?"

"Yes, yes, lead me," I said. He raised his forelegs and incanted. The adhesive pad started to ripple and flow toward the sides of the box, parting down the center. My legs were freed. I was amazed. Exodus beckoned me from outside. But just before I reached him he cried, "Liar! Infidel!" He raised his forelegs and the adhesive was released, crashing down on me, coating me, securing me like a hundred manacles.

I woke trembling. I vowed never to sleep again.

Now I noticed the first specks of gray on my own back. So soon? I didn't feel as if I were dying. I wasn't even tired. But then, I had just seen that death is not announced with cannonades and crashing cymbals.

Bismarck's eyes were already beginning to decompose, to flatten, making him look gaunt, determined, as if death were not the last rest, but rather the next shift. I knew this was decay, not emotion, but it was hard to discount the expression on the face I had trusted for so long.

"Why do I want to live so badly, Pinky, when I really don't want to live at all? We used to say that we were the only animals freed from genetic prejudice, that we lived the true life. You may have, but I can't. You knew when to give up. I'm a prisoner of the survivor instinct."

I looked on my little world with new eyes. In front of me sat a hunk of flesh in early decay. That's all. Fillet of human, rat steak? I didn't know and it didn't matter. I looked it over, my salivary glands colluding in the deception, trying to choose the site for the first bite. I let my eyes wander to the face. Suddenly it was Bismarck again—the meal was gone.

I steeled myself and concentrated on his rear legs, far from the knowing eyes. Quickly I tipped forward and opened my mouth. My heart was pounding so violently that my antennae wrote figure eights in front of me. I lunged and bit into the thigh.

The chitin crackled between my mandibles. I spit it out. I couldn't do it.

Come on, Numbers. Listen to the refrigerator; time moves on. We are all flesh, but his is carrion and yours lives.

I concentrated on that as I closed in again. I took another bite. I suppressed the gag reflex and swallowed. Before I could think I took another bite, then another. I finished the thigh, then worked down the leg, stopping safely above the adhesive. With the last bite, the leg cracked in two, and the body lurched toward me. I couldn't stop, couldn't allow my mouth to begin to empty. I leaned over him and ate the other thigh. The cercus was one bite. It was flesh now, good flesh, cool and fragrant, tender from its brief aging.

I was eating on instinct. My motions became automatic, efficient. It was not a matter of hunger; I ate because there was food. I consumed the thorax and abdomen back to front, top to bottom, ever faster, loving the motions, being a cockroach again after so long. Soon I could feel my gut swell against my carapace.

When I reached the tegmen, I stopped. I didn't want to look into those eyes. I was sure I had had more than enough meat.

Leaning back, I looked at what I had done. The head was intact, but the rest was a husk ravaged by locusts, a bombed-out plane. I was a glutton, a cannibal! It made me sick. But at the same time the first nutrients from his body were clearing my mind. Though I was nauseated, I refused to vomit, which I knew would cost me my only chance to survive. Soon the horror passed.

For the first time since I'd checked in I slept well. The next day I felt sick, as my withered digestive system was unequal to the richness and volume of what I had eaten. My guts churned, but the food crept along. And oh, for a crosswind to clear the motel of my foul, foul flatus.

On the second day I could feel new tissue reconstructing my body. Unlike the other nine guests, I was getting fatter. I was a survivor.

The call to molt is a general pressure which feels as if you want to shit in every direction at once. When I was young, molting was as easy as shitting: one contraction and the cuticle would split between my wing muscles. Flexing would work the slit open, and in a few minutes I would step out of the old carapace, a newer, bigger model.

I could already tell it wasn't going to be like that this time. I was beyond normal molting age, and my thick, tough shell was not meant to split. Though I was filling it nicely, I wasn't sure I had the strength or the endurance to get out of it.

During the third day I felt I was at peak plumpness. It was time. I opened my spiracles all the way to increase the volume of air inside my shell. Then I shut them and flexed my wing muscles, slightly engorged ever since the flight from Ruth's mound. Soon I was trembling. I contracted my abdominal and thoracic muscles. The pressure was so great that the damned carapace should have cracked in six places and flown apart. But it didn't. My eyes bulged, magnifying the cadaver set-piece that surrounded me. I would not end up like them.

But I ached with effort. I couldn't push any harder. What more could I do?

Then I heard scratching just outside. I was sure these were *Blattella* legs.

"Don't come in! This is a trap!" I yelled.

But in walked G-string. "Did you say something?"

In a moment she discovered she had checked in. "Hey, I'm stuck! Help me, will you? Don't just stand there." When her eyes adjusted she said, "So it's you. I should have known. You want to get us all."

G-string was a pill. She had none of the charm suggested by the stripper's garb of her name, which she had in fact taken from a piece of gut on Howie's guitar. Now I was sure I'd escape; I couldn't imagine living out my life in her company.

"Get me out!" she shrieked, contorting as the others had, locking herself in a position of perpetual discomfort. She began to curse me.

Her execrations were music to me. Strength redoubled, I flexed. Come on, split, you bastard!

G-string's struggles only succeeded in coiling her body even tighter. This may have been tragic for her, but it was grand comedy for me; now each threat or insult squeezed excrement from her body. "I'll get you!" she screamed, and two pebbles dribbled from her anus. "Are you laughing?" A puff of piss atomized from her rear.

When the cloud drifted over to me I stopped laughing. The urine was mixed with pheromones.

Imprisoned in a Roach Motel, a cannibal, bombarded by G-string's verbal venom, about to die, and all I knew, all I cared about, were the pheromones.

Immediately my phallus sprang to life. But my abdominal muscles were locked so tight that it could not pass through its normal channel. Penis pressure built. Chemistry could not be denied. Chitin cracked, and then my masculinity tore through the carapace.

I flexed again, and the seam in my shell raced around me, top and bottom, like tearing cellophane. *Whizz! Zip!* The sounds were wonderful. My guts felt the invigorating air. Soon I pushed the old shell in half. G-string had done it! I was free!

You emerge from a molt larger and stronger, but at first as soft as a clam's guts, and as pasty as Ira. Half an hour later melanin browns the hardening new shell. I wanted to let the new armor set before facing the world again, but I couldn't risk being trapped inside the shell of my old legs.

As I pulled out my front legs I felt them expand like dough. I carefully climbed onto the back of the corpse at my side.

The view was disquieting. I was up here, but I could see myself still down there. Up here I was mushy, off-white, unsteady. Down there I was brown and hard, posed, as I would be for all time, beside Bismarck, my irreplaceable friend. But down there I was dead among the dead. Up here I was just steps from a new life.

Only G-string stood between me and the exit from the motel. Still wrestling with the adhesive, she had lost interest in me. As soon as she stopped to rest, I hopped with my mushy legs onto a clear spot on her back. One short leap and I was free!

Then the rising pheromones struck again. My phallus slid easily from my pulpy flesh, crooning: G-string, beauty, lover! The mat below screamed: Agony, starvation, death! I had never had to weigh the pros and cons of sex before, and the debate was over in a second. The only issue was mechanics: how could I stuff it into her from up here, when the normal position would place me back in the adhesive?

"What the hell?" shrieked G-string. She grabbed one of my legs with a free antenna—I had thought her parts were all pinned—and planted it in the glue.

Lust shut off; self-preservation switched on. I leaped for the opening, twisting awkwardly in the air because of the trapped leg. But the other five hit vinyl.

I was exhilarated and enraged, but most of all curious. In all my time in the colony I had never witnessed, or even heard of, a single instance of sadism. "Why did you do that, G-string? Can you tell me?"

"A life for a life, Numbers. You're the one who said it."

Not this life. The hostage leg was pasty and slick, like a maggot I was taking for a walk. I pulled on it, but the maggot would not heel. I had no choice but to cut it loose. I did not worry about cannibalism because the flesh was mine. I bit into the joint. The sharp pain quickly faded. I was free!

"I hope you die," she said. "I hope you get stepped on and crushed and sprayed. Don't leave me here."

"My leg is a memento. Look at it and think of me."

I went out into the kitchen and sat quietly under the toe-kick, allowing my body to firm. I had a feeling the walk back to the living room would require thicker skin.

The Breach

"ALBANY. . .Pierre. . .I know this one, Baton Rouge. . . Portland. . . What? Salem? Are you kidding me? Salem?"

It might have been just an absurd dream, until an explosion woke me. The sight of a pair of vicious alligators made me leap. I was clubbed on the head and fell to the floor. The scene slowly cleared. The toekick of the cabinet was above me; I had struck my head on it. These alligators were Ira's wing-tips. The master had slammed the cereal box with the offending quiz on the counter above me. The molt and escape had so exhausted me that I had slept here the whole night—not the wisest choice.

As I massaged my bruise, I realized that the new shell had hardened and browned. My life could begin again. The refrigerator fan blew straight across the floor at me. I no longer minded it; it had helped my chitin set.

Ruth came in for breakfast. "I wonder who paid off who to make Salem the capital," Ira said as they left together for work.

I walked out onto the floor, heavier now, and stronger. My joints cracked, as new chitin will. I moved surprisingly well on my five legs. What bothered me was the sound. Accompanied by a six-beat every step of my life, I hesitated after each five-beat, waiting for the last one. I supposed I'd get used to it.

Before I returned to the living room, I had to decide where I could lead the colony. Five legs were a greater liability climbing than walking, but I struggled up the cabinet face. The sharp edges of the door trimmed my new carapace.

Nothing in the cabinet had changed. The bills were still camped over our hole. "Snug as a bug in a rug, there, Ben?"

Ben's epitaph said that his body was food for worms. Since there were no worms around I decided to take a taste. I snapped my mandibles on him. I could not tear the paper. He was a tough guy. The fermented stench of a hundred human hands rose from him. Ben wanted to see to it that I ate not to dullness, that I ate not at all.

I felt behind the roll of bills. The hole that led to the sanctuary was still there.

But the old man stood between me and the future, and he would not move. I became enraged at the idea that he would make me play the victim again. I leaped to throttle him, forgetting for the moment that I was short a leg. I landed askew on his shoulder. One of my foreleg spikes stuck so I could neither climb up nor back down, and when the other legs tired and slipped, all my weight hung on it. I could not tear loose. Ben smiled a little wider, as if he were thinking: if we don't all hang together, assuredly I shall hang you separately.

Ben began to shake and let out a shriek, as if my spike had struck a nerve. He sprang, knocking me over, and fell hard on top of me. I was sure he really had returned to life.

On my back, under his formidable bulk and fetor, I was able to slowly work the spike loose and crawl out. I climbed up the borders of the piled Bens and assorted patriots, to the door of Independence Hall on the top layer. The hole in the wall above me was clear! The future was mine!

These slips of paper, the center of my life for months, the focus of my efforts and suffering, were suddenly moved—not by elaborate psychological manipulations, but by one botched jump. Until this moment I was certain I was right to have involved other citizens, fellow beneficiaries, in my projects. But now it was impossible to dispute Bismarck: if I had acted alone, I would have achieved this on the first day. I would not repeat the mistake.

Poe! I had forgotten all about him. He had gone into the wall when the alien was working. I passed through the hole and into a new world. I called his name. He didn't respond, but the wall cavity was so huge that my voice couldn't begin to fill it. It was warm, quiet. One of the pipes to the sink wore condensation drops like heavy udders. This was perfect. Bismarck would have loved it.

I poked around for a while. It was on my way back up to the cabinet that I sighted the tip of Poe's antenna drooped over a clod of old plaster on the floor. I ran down to him—or rather, to his remains, badly decomposed. All along I had been thinking that he'd be obese by now. But of course, the moment Ira locked us out of the wall, he sealed Poe in *Fortunato!*

So the food stocks would be mine alone. I couldn't mourn for Poe; I had to bless my fortune. For the first time since the alien I was looking safely into the cabinet. I never really believed it would happen. Tupperware stood like mausolea, but there were many cardboard boxes, too. The pasta was mine, egg and spinach, all sizes and shapes. The cookies, the pancake mix, the rice, the kasha, the raisins, the chocolate pudding, the matzoh meal—mine, all mine!

The next evening I sat in the back of the cabinet, indifferent to the smell of Ira and Ruth cooking just a few feet away. I was eating so well I thought I might be in for a second geriatric molt. Ira saw the fallen bills on the second day of my stay. "This is silly," he said aloud to himself, as he took them out of the cabinet and put them into his pocket.

I was leading an ideal life. I was alone, but I was not lonely. The company of psychotic biblical roaches held no appeal for me. It was strange that pasta, which I had in abundance and could enjoy alone, would soon make me reconsider my position.

As I worked my way up the cavity of a piece of dried ziti, my rearquarters got a rousing rubbing. Though the chemicals had long since dispersed, I still carried the memory of the erection that G-string had raised and left unredressed in the motel. The ziti tingle turned irritating and uncomfortable as my mind was deluged with genital thoughts. I could not endure the idea that my last spermatophore, long in the chamber, would never be shot, that I would never again taste pheromones and experience the mad immersion of sex.

I needed sex; I needed company, too. It was not hard to admit.

I had resolved to return to the principles of natural selection. But I would not be doctrinaire. If Bismarck had still been out there scavenging, in ever greater danger for ever lesser gain, I doubt he would have felt compromised by the food and safety of my larder and fortress. Food and safety might restore the colony's sanity. What was to be gained by letting them die out there?

When I reached the living room doorway, everyone was gone. I was too late. Then I spotted a lone citizen in front of the fireplace. It was Columbo. I approached him with the good news about the cabinet.

He said, "You manipulated us, then you deserted us."

"I was on a long mission, and then I got caught in the motel."

"But here you are. A miracle."

"Look at me. I'm fat as a goose. I'm telling you the truth."

He looked warily at me. "I see you lost a leg."

"What happened to the others?"

He pointed an antenna straight up. "You're wasting your time." The mantel.

Couldn't anything happen at floor level anymore? I made my labored five-legged climb. Columbo seemed to be hoping I would fall, and I almost did as the texture changed from brick to mortar and back. When I reached the mantel I still didn't see the colony. I hoped they had regained enough sense to hide. I circled the glass candlesticks and the ceramic storm lantern, and even looked into its fuel well, with no luck. The arms of the heavy brass menorah—where the pursuit of Exodus might have sent them—were also empty.

Then I saw them—but not the starving animals who had shuffled so pathetically into the room. They were racing, romping, leaping around the chessboard. As I walked onto the board, they circled me, drowning out my words with chants.

Aaron, standing on the periphery, wagged his head. "They are set on mischief."

"What the hell are they doing?"

"The knight, the brass one. See how the citizens ring it?"

Now I saw a pattern to the chaos.

"In their eyes this is not a knight. As soon as Exodus disappeared it became their new god—the Golden Calf."

"Exodus instructed them to betray him?"

"No, my brother. Someone else did, long ago, and the memory incubated until now. It was you."

A citizen skidded across the board. We ducked behind the edge and he flew over our heads.

I said, "I was only telling a story. It was a joke. This is ridiculous."

"Yes, I see, just a joke." He turned to the board.

"I could have them tucked safely behind the cabinet in less than an hour."

"Beware," warned Bismarck's spirit. Save these lives, I said, that's all. I would not organize these citizens or influence their reproduction. But leave them to die? *That* would be a manipulation of our gene pool. With my five legs, I could not abandon citizens because of their defects.

Aaron did not respond. I would have to do the deed alone.

From the menorah I pulled a length of blackened wick, a staff—and made my way across the swarming board to the knight's square. "Who is on the Lord's side? Let him come unto me," I intoned.

Citizens screeched to a halt. It didn't seem to matter who played the prophet.

I said, "Ye have sinned a great sin; and now I will go up unto the Lord; peradventure I shall make atonement for your sin."

There was a silence as I walked slowly across the board, favoring my bad side as if I were shouldering under the weight of their wickedness. I crossed the mantel and disappeared behind the lamp.

"Sinners! They shall feel my wrath!" I boomed with the shuddering resonance of my new basso shell. I almost scared myself.

"The blinding light, the heat, hath confused them. Truly, they are righteous," I said in my normal voice.

"Righteousness doth not melt like butter in the noonday sun!" I thundered again.

I peeked around the lamp. The colony was frozen.

I lowered the volume and continued to plead, raising my voice on occasional words such as "penitent," "forgiveness," and "one more chance." Then I returned to the board. The citizens greeted me as if *I* were a golden calf.

"You have angered the Lord sorely with your idol; He is a jealous God."

Scores of citizens pushed the pawn to one side, and a horde assembled behind the bronze knight. With a roar of six hundred thousand they shoved it over the edge of the board and onto the floor. Ira would be tested by that one.

I said, "The Lord said Ye are a stiffnecked people."

"But we're not people."

"And we have no necks."

"Forget that one," I proclaimed. "The Lord has said to me: I beseech thee, shew me thy glory. And he said, I will make all goodness pass before thee, and I will proclaim the name of the Lord before thee; and will be gracious to whom I will be gracious, and will shew mercy on whom I will shew mercy."

The colony was rapt. It was time to make my play. "And the Lord said, Behold, there is a place by me, and thou shalt stand upon a kitchen cabinet. . ."

I braced myself for the backlash. But there was none. They bought it.

". . .And it shall come to pass, while my glory passeth by, that I will put thee in a clift of the cabinet, and will cover thee with my hand while I pass by. . ."

The herd stampeded over the edge of the mantel. They flowed through the living room and into the dining room. I had to discard my wick to keep up with the slowest of them.

I hadn't realized how completely I had lost track of time until I heard keys in the front door. We still had a few seconds, enough time to scatter around the dining room. But the colony kept moving as if nothing had happened, as if destiny placed them beyond earthly harm.

I still believed fervently in earthly harm. I pushed my way to the head of the flow. The leaders were approaching the kitchen doorway. "Stop! Stop! This is madness!" They ignored me and kept moving. Where was the influence I had had only minutes earlier? Then I saw Aaron near the back of the pack, rearing and pointing to himself.

I had to try. "And the Lord sayeth: go not unto the cabinet in the presence of thy mortal enemy: it dishonoreth me. Nay, go instead unto the baseboard, and here wait." Immediately they stopped and turned. Nimbly picking their way across the drifts of boric acid they filed into the baseboard opening.

After dinner I followed Ruth to the living room.

"Ira, look at this, the horse is on the floor."

He ran in. "The whole board has been pushed around. I told you. . ."

She cut him off. "Don't you dare. We've been through this."

"Then what the hell is going on in here? Some vandal breaks in and just messes up the chessboard?"

"Who's bronze, you or Lev?"

"Me."

"It was your horse. I think it wanted out."

"Very funny," said Ira. "And it's a knight, not a horse."

"Then he must have dismounted and made a run for it."

For the first time I could enjoy Ira's sulking, because I knew that in a few hours I would never have to witness it again.

I waited until they had washed, excreted, and were in bed breathing regularly before I returned to the baseboard with instructions for reaching the cabinet hole. "Praise the Lord!" I said as each citizen emerged.

The first was Augustine, whom I hadn't seen in so long I had taken him for dead. He would lead; converts are always more fanatical than lifers. The others came out quickly and followed him in perfect file. Augustine soon turned the corner into the kitchen, the colony moving like one great segmented insect. Our suffering would soon be over.

After the entire line had passed me I checked the baseboard one last time for laggards. Everyone was out. I leaped over the white drifts. I looked back and saluted. Farewell, bleak house! Where we go, behold, how good and pleasant it is for brethren to dwell together in unity. A little one shall become a thousand, and a small one a strong nation.

The others had disappeared into the kitchen. By the time I arrived, Augustine had started up the base cabinet, just where I had instructed, the others following in perfect order. I was pleased; but at the same time it bothered me that they didn't take the cabinet by storm. It was too calculating. I thought only ants attacked in queues.

It didn't matter. In the column were many friends, among them Barbarossa, Lifesaver, Underwriter's Lab, and Harris Tweed. They all looked a lot older now, their carapaces creased from malnutrition. I would fix that.

I lost sight of Augustine as he climbed onto the countertop. "Yo, Numbers," I heard from behind. "This be the place? Flow with milk and honey? Don't bullshit me now like you psycho brother with that stick."

"This be. Well, powdered milk and honey."

"All right muthafucka!" Sufur held out a leg for me to slap, then fell in, the last in line.

The underside of the wall cabinet, unfinished wood which had to be crossed upside down, was the most difficult part of the climb. Augustine started across it just as Sufur left the floor. Once the leaders reached the finished cabinet face, they re-gained speed. The entire colony was on their way. Guilty or not, I had made restitution.

It was time to join them. I would never again see this kitchen, except through the open cabinet doors. There were few things I'd miss. Just one, really—farewell to you, Bismarck, my truest friend. You will live on in me.

I stepped up off the vinyl. Goodbye to you, with your leg-busting patterns and noxious pine scent. We always knew it was fake. So long to you, boric acid; we were just looking. Food canisters, goodbye. We will do better. Farewell, cookbooks. We'll take ours au naturel. Goodbye to you, ammonia, and special regrets to Raid. You've given me some genuine thrills. Things won't be the same out back.

Ira, in parting, I'll say just this: I promise you that as you become older and balder, we will multiply to numbers you cannot imagine, filling the cavity behind the cabinet, all fifteen feet, floor to ceiling. One day we will meet again: The wall will crumble under our weight, and like a tidal wave we will engulf you and all your chattel. Expect no mercy, as you gave none.

AS AUGUSTINE squeezed into the cabinet, the line behind him slowed but stayed in perfect order. Now the good life was only a few steps away.

I was climbing the face of the base cabinet at five-legged speed, feeling a peace the likes of which I had never known before. Then I heard the distant *thwocking* of bamboo slippers; since American Woman, Ira never left bed without them. A nightmare about chessboard despoliation had probably woken him. Perhaps I had underestimated his loss to the colony. Who else could be so entertaining? On blue days, who would pick us up by making us feel so superior?

"Yo, Numbers. This be all right, outtasight," said Sufur. He was about a foot above me.

The toilet flushed. The sound of flip-flops went on too long for a return to the bedroom. Pacing? But it was getting louder. Maybe he couldn't wait—he was going to reset the chessboard now.

And louder still. He wasn't stopping in the living room. He was coming this way. God only knew what he wanted. He never snacked at night because it gave him bad dreams. He was probably going to check the door locks.

He passed that turn-off. He was approaching the kitchen. This was unimaginable. "Run!" I yelled. "Ira's coming."

Why didn't they do it? "Listen to me! Ira's coming! Jump! Run! Get off that cabinet!" The line would not break formation. To this day I wonder what might have happened if I had said, "Satan cometh. Jumpeth like the frog at the angry report!"

The flip-flops of death approached, with the entire colony displayed like sunbathers in a grade-D beach horror movie.

"Sufur! Jump! We'll go back up later."

"Just can't stop once my spark gets hot." He continued to climb.

I jumped from the cabinet and hobbled across the room toward the toe-kick. "Please!" I cried. But the lights came on. Destiny had arrived.

The slippers snapped explosively across the floor. The colony had no chance. Wait. They did have a chance. Ira wasn't wearing his glasses.

The mystery of the visit was then resolved. Ira pulled bent patriots from the pocket of his paisley robe. He opened the cabinet, rolled them up, and replaced them. Didn't he himself say it was silly to keep them there? I thought of ten different motives he might have. But I doubted he could seal the hole again, especially without his glasses.

After all, with hundreds of citizens marching less than a foot from his head, Ira had not seen one. Scores had to be through the hole by now, many more close behind them. But most were still climbing. Together they and Ira made a maddening scene of lethal slapstick, the hunted sleepwalking over the cross-hairs of the blind hunter's scope.

Ira rubbed his fingers. Dirt. Unwashed Ben was a vengeful old man, trying to stall Ira here. Ira bent over the sink to wash his hands. The line kept moving right above his head. I felt sick.

For the first time since we left the baseboard, I heard a *Blattella* other than Sufur speak. She was up on the underhang. "This is really doing it to my feet. I'm going back for a nap." It was Julia's daughter, Anise.

It wasn't easy to turn on that raw wood, and she took more than her sweet time. Clorox, who was right behind her, managed to shake her own trance—as she hadn't for my warning—long enough to avoid a collision. Junior did not. He smacked into Clorox's behind. Then Garlic cracked into Junior.

"Move over, will you? Look what you're doing to the line," said Clorox to Anise.

"It's a free country."

Citizens continued to rear-end each other, and a long pileup hung precariously from the cabinet bottom, right over Ira's balding head. Clorox took a jolt with every collision. "Get out of the way, you stupid GAP," she said to Anise. *Germanica*-American Princess.

"Go around."

Clorox grabbed her by the thorax and tore her loose from the wood. Please don't let go, I prayed, not yet, not until Ira leaves. She carried Anise off to the side of the underhang and stuck her back onto the wood, as calmly as if she were taking out the garbage.

Citizens quickly disengaged and the line resumed its disciplined motion. "Well, fuck you," Anise said. Nobody paid her any attention, which she couldn't stand. As she fluttered back toward the line, one of her legs caught on a splinter.

She was hooked. She stretched the leg so far I thought it would break off. But it was stronger than she was, and like a slingshot snapped her body back. She could not reach the wood again, and swung from the cabinet by the one leg, a little brown pendulum. "What a drag!" she said. The line kept moving past her. Ira continued to wash his hands.

And then the leg broke. She said, "Whoops," and landed in the middle of Ira's bald spot. He smacked himself with a soapy had. Direct hit. Anise was flattened, widened, guts extruding through every pore. Now she'd have her nap.

Had she stuck to his head, Anise could still have saved the colony. But she seemed to be eating out of his palm, where he immediately looked. "Jesus Christ!" he said, snapping his wrist. Still she stuck to him. He turned both taps up full force, and soon she was down the drain and on her way to ride the breakers.

Ira scrubbed his hands like a surgeon, then tore off several paper towels and made careful circuits of his pate. Bless your fastidiousness, Ira; every few seconds another citizen squeezed to safety.

Ira held the towels up nearly to the tip of his nose for examination. They must have been clean; there was no more rubbing. Then the cogitating began: Ira, how did that roach manage to land on your head?

He looked up, struggling to focus. He gasped and stepped back. I'm sure he had never seen anything like that line. I never had.

Stealthily he lowered himself to a squat, knees cracking and slippers slapping, and opened the base cabinet. He straightened slowly.

He removed the top, held the can before him, and, with one eye closed, took aim. The line continued to move at the same pace. I couldn't stand to watch, but I couldn't turn away. But Ira lowered the can. Was it conscience about engaging in genocide? No, he was just following orders: he had forgotten to shake the can.

He raised it again, and this time he fired. His first salvo missed everyone by two feet, but the second blanketed the citizens at the top of the wall cabinet. They screamed as the chemical flamed into their bodies. Convulsing, they fell from the heights into the sink and onto the countertop with horrifying, limb-severing crunches. Instinct—revived minutes too late—urged the victims to pull themselves off the countertop with legs, stumps, mouthparts. Some used their heads to push their detached parts to the floor, as if they could later reattach them—as if they had any chance to survive.

At least this black shower of limbs would warn off the citizens closer to the floor; they still had time to get away. But to my horror, the rest of the line kept moving up as if nothing had happened, ignoring the rain of disembodied antennae and legs that struck them, and the howls that probably had *Blattella* colonies on the fifth floor cowering. This was no crisis of organization. It was a lemming march.

Orderly as usual, Ira next swept the spray across the underhang. Scores of bodies rained into the sink. He turned on the water and washed them down the drain. And still the column continued to climb up the base cabinet.

Then the counter. A second bombing killed off many of the wounded lying there, causing a deathly diminuendo. But there was another horrible crescendo as spray struck citizens on the backsplash. I clasped my own shell as it began to vibrate. Ira jumped back so citizens pitching themselves over the edge wouldn't land on his exposed feet. But he was smiling. This man, this humanist who couldn't stand the idea of vivisecting the lowest rodent, anaesthetized, for medical purposes, took pleasure in our gratuitous slaughter.

Many died on impact with the floor, some virtually exploding; resilience was a casualty of the poison. A palp, someone's mouthpart, rolled all the way across the floor and under the toe-kick beside me. I kicked it back out. It sickened me.

Ira pushed the new casualties into the sink with a folded paper towel and washed them away, then bent over and took aim at the remaining survivors, on the base cabinet. I was too horrified to move. Spray deflecting off the wood caught me. I shut my spiracles as tight as I could, but the poison worked them like sharp gouges.

I had gotten just a taste. Poisoned bodies continued to plunge to the floor, landing on top of each other with mutilating force. No one could extricate himself from the howling, writhing mass.

I saw two citizens land clear of the pile. "Run!" I cried. Ira was so intent on the main kill that they could get to the stove. They made it halfway across the floor, then turned and started back. "No! This way!" I shouted. They circled and again headed for the stove, but turned back once more. Then I realized that they weren't headed anywhere, just running in chemically predestined circles, which became tighter and tighter, until they both spun in place. Then they toppled, legs still pumping, never to stand again. The male started to beat his wings, as grotesque a sexual farewell as the hanging human who springs an erection.

Suddenly a citizen came sprinting straight toward me. "Move yo ass!" Sufur! I always knew he was a survivor!

He was too obvious, the only citizen still moving in a straight line with any speed, and the flip-flops turned to follow him.

"Not here!" I cried, "Go over there."

"Move it, mutha. Here I come."

A long burst of spray caught Sufur square on the back. A fine mist reflected off him and engulfed me. It burned. My body started to contort, but, terrified that I would never be able to correct myself, I planted my legs and flexed, staying straight. The poison kept penetrating. When it reached my heart I was finished. How long would it take? I pictured parallel pits eating through me. But after a few minutes the pain slowed. The poison was exhausted. The torque on my body eased. The dose was too small. I would survive.

But Sufur wouldn't. With the most piercing scream of the night, he sprang straight up, more like a cricket than a cockroach, and landed on his side. He twisted so violently that the plates of his carapace began to snap and break apart, exposing his guts. I backed all the way under the toe-kick. When his eyes started to pop out, like caviar from the mouth of a squeamish debutante, I took off down the toe-kick.

I turned when I heard the cabinet open. Ira had killed his hundreds, but the last triumph was ours. Finger poised to annihilate those closest to eternal happiness, he would find that they had simply disappeared like brown smoke. With Ben blocking his view of the hole, he would be baffled. Even if he found it, he could do nothing but futilely spit poison through it.

Once again I was wrong. When the door opened all the way, Augustine and the others were still in the cabinet, in clear view. They were on the wrong shelf. They never found the hole.

Slowly Ira cleared the field, pushing boxes to the left, cans to the right, his breath loud and rasping. Then, with one interminable blast, he massacred them all. At last the spray can sputtered and burped, but it was too late for us. Screaming gave way to cries and whimpers and the sickening crack of more citizens on the countertop. The refrigerator fan went on.

Ira *thwacked* out of the room, and soon returned with the vacuum cleaner. I was grateful that its roar drowned out the death rattles of my colony. When he finished the cabinet and the counter, Ira turned to the floor. With the edge of the attachment, he chopped the pile of cadavers because it was too big and tightly knit to pick up. Bodies *pinged* as they ricocheted up the hose into the canister. I prayed the impact would kill the doomed survivors.

Ira made a last search for fugitives, then, smiling, unplugged the machine, turned off the light, and left the kitchen. The door of the hall closet closed. Soon I heard him telling war stories to Ruth. It revolted me that our deaths would bond them.

During my short stay in the well behind the cabinet, I thought I had been alone. Now I knew what alone really meant. What would I do? Stay here? Even if the hole was safe, I couldn't bear the thought of wading through the limbs that still littered the shelf. Should I move on and try to join another colony? But where? Who would tolerate a cripple, especially of my age? When scouts from other colonies found out what had happened, 3B would be annexed, and I would be exiled. I was scared. I didn't know what to do. I never wanted to be the last one, to live without my friends. I'm not that dedicated a survivor.

I had to get away from the kitchen. I decided on the dining room baseboard. It was eerie, but safe. It would do for now.

At the kitchen doorway I turned for a last look. The room was so calm that I had trouble believing what had just happened. Then I saw a form beneath the far toe-kick. Don't go back, I thought. But I couldn't stop myself.

The big citizen was terribly contorted, his head distended and somehow stuck between two of the abdominal tergites, like a neckless duck. I crept up the far side of the room so he couldn't see me.

Then I recognized him. Barbarossa! Who else was so big? A wise return, this. A chance to regain my last friend and then lose him. "Tell me, friend, what can I do for you?"

"Numbers?"

"Yes. How about getting your head loose."

"Paralyzed. . . Numbers, are you truly my friend?"

"Don't be ridiculous," I said, but he chilled me.

"Promise me."

I backed up. "I do."

"I believe you are honorable. There's a crack in the tergite behind my head. See it?"

I came closer. He stank of poison. I couldn't help looking back at the doorway. "Yes."

"One last favor. I swear I will never ask anything of you again. Tear it open."

Hadn't I already killed hundreds tonight? Suddenly I could see them all again, falling screaming from the countertop, so real that I backed out of their trajectory. And then I saw the silent, still silhouette of the ravaged Bismarck. This was carnage enough for a lifetime.

I wanted desperately to help Barbarossa, but I couldn't do this. I slipped away from him by a route he could not see. Then his voice froze me.

"Numbers, why have you forsaken me?"

That was it. I ran out of the kitchen and down the hall, and after that I don't know where I went. I remember only streaks of receding furniture. The legs of *Blattella* can be directly activated by external stimulus, without instruction from the brain; once my brain revived, it hadn't the slightest desire to contravene.

Some time later I found myself in the back of the hall closet, among groves of dust, musty old galoshes, mildewed widowed gloves, and other ageless debris. I felt better here. I hated the urgency that had polluted my life for months. I yearned to be part of a long, slow, predictable process again. I could die peacefully here.

I soon fell into the uneasy half-sleep that blurs the boundary between dream and reality. Scratching noises, loud and frantic, dominated my dream. I couldn't see who was making them. I woke up, trembling. The noises awoke with me.

Barbarossa. He was alive! I had to go save him. . . No, these sounds were local. Someone was in here with me, trapped in a boot or a shoe. I searched desperately. I called out. I even listened at the sides of the suitcases. No one answered.

Then it came to me. This was also the utility closet; I had managed not to see the vacuum cleaner, which sat right beside me. The tortured survivors were impaled in thick coils of dirt, pinned by each other's broken bodies, suffocating in fine soot, trying impossibly to dig their way out of the bag.

My legs didn't wait for instructions. I flew from the closet, and this time I didn't stop.

WHEN THOU PRAYEST, enter into thy closet, and when thou hast shut thy door, pray to thy Father which is in secret; and thy Father which seeth in secret shall reward thee openly.

All my life I had resisted this voice within me, scoffed at it, mocked it. Now, in my hour of hopelessness, I realized that I had been a fool. What was I, if not poor in spirit, and meek? Had I listened I would have realized this was not shameful, and certainly no justification for months of futile war and a lifetime of skepticism. I could have walked in peace knowing that I would inherit the earth. Now my heart and mind cleared. I wanted only to rejoice, and be exceedingly glad.

I avoided the kitchen for the rest of the week. During Saturday's cleaning, the kitchen was purged of poison. After the vacuuming was done, Ruth changed the bag. Now I could do as Our Father asked, return to the closet for prayer. The vacuum cleaner beside me was an icon of the power of Caesar, but I finally knew where my true faith lay.

And I, the first *Blattella germanica* to learn to kneel, heard: Blessed are they which are persecuted for righteousness' sake: for theirs is the kingdom of heaven.

The kingdom of heaven. The phrase elicited lovely images. I could see myself there, rubbing antennae with my friends, joking, eating. How much nobler and richer was the kingdom of heaven than the future I had imagined, an endless, meaningless tour through the nitrogen cycle. How smug I had been, how Godless.

In the closet I prayed for the colony. Father forgave me, and showed me them in eternal, shoeless, sprayless, motelless peace. And it was good.

Late Saturday night I returned to the kitchen. In the cabinet I found Father's second reward: He had indeed kept Ben from blocking off the hole again. O Father! Thou art too generous! I reentered my kingdom on earth.

I lived behind the cabinet, not by pasta alone, but by every Word that I could remember from the mouth of God. Now that the roaches were gone, the household regimens were gradually relaxed, and my piety was met with a plenty which embarrassed me. I was careful not to offend Father by refusing his offerings.

For the first time I was truly calm, spiritually content. I lived well, secure in the knowledge that some day I would pass on to an even better life. Only one thing rankled: Ira's indifference. His life went on exactly as before. The ancient Hebrews immemorialized their vanquished in the first Testament; surely our martyrs deserved recognition.

Oh pride, wretched vice. What did it matter who knew, as long as Our Father did. I remembered the word: to love mine enemies, bless them that curse me, do good to them that hate me, and pray for them which despitefully use me and persecute me; that I may be the child of my Father which is in heaven. I went all the way back to the hall closet to repent. Father believed in love, prayer, and, I was discovering, physical fitness.

After dinner the following Tuesday, Ira went to the living room and took down the chessboard. "I can't put this off anymore."

Ruth stood behind him. "Before you set the pieces up all symmetrical and boring, let's try something different. Let's put light and dark pieces on both sides. I'm amazed the Supreme Court hasn't integrated this game yet."

"You want me to bus them over?"

She made her configuration. "You see, now there won't be so much fighting. This queen can talk to this horse—this knight—and he can ride over to the other queen and relay her messages, like the pony express. The queens can get together for lunch, maybe take in a show, and discuss how they manipulate their kings. These bishops can check out the queens. And these towers should all be zoned into the same area. That reduces congestion in the center of the board.

"Face it, Ira. The pieces are upset. You and Lev play them off against each other as if—I hate to say it—as if they're no more than pawns. Try having a friendly game."

Blessed are the peacemakers; for they shall see God.

The doorbell rang. Ira answered it and brought Oliver back to the living room. Ruth said, "Hello. How are you? Where's Elizabeth?"

"She's fine. Say, that's some game you've got going. How did you get your pawns into your own back row? And look at that—each king is checkmated about three different ways. How do you know when the game is over, when one of you dies?"

Ira said, "This is Ruth's work. Pacifist chess."

"Let me guess," said Oliver. "The object of the game is to get to the enemy king and give him a Peter, Paul, and Mary album."

"No, no," said Ruth. "There is no enemy. Everybody cooperates. Look at the pattern on the board—positively post-Impressionist. You never get that in battle."

Oliver sat down and said, "This looks like fun. Mind if I try a variation?"

Ira looked at his watch. "Sure, why not." He loved his neighbor as himself.

Oliver reset the board. "Think of the board as a ghetto."

"Oh, no," said Ira.

"This pawn is the lawyer. This king is the pusher and murderer. He is surrounded by the police, who arrested him when someone sang. The object it to get the lawyer through the police cordon and spring the murderer before the songbird gets out of town."

"Did you want something, or were you just bored?" said Ira.

"A flashlight."

"Where I come from that's called chutzpa," said Ira.

"You won't believe this. My wife thinks she might be with child. . ."

"Really!" Ruth clapped. "Mazel tov."

"Not yet, Ruth. She thinks so about once a month. Now she wants me to take a look up there to see if I can see anything. I just pretend."

Ruth and Ira exchanged glances of incredulity. "Of course," said Ira. "I'm flattered you chose my flashlight."

"Remember the night you said you were going for a flashlight and ended up molesting my wife? You know what blew out the kitchen lights? Cockroaches! That's right. There was a whole bunch of them in a socket, deep fried. You didn't put them up to it, did you?"

Anger welled in me. For the first time since my rebirth I could find no comfort in the Book.

"Let's get the flashlight. You better do your examination before she goes into labor," said Ira. He let Oliver out and returned to the chessboard.

"When were you molesting his wife, Ira? You forgot to tell me about that."

"You know me. Molestation is my middle name." He started to separate the pieces by color.

"Then tell me, Ira Molestation Fishblatt. What were you after? A kiss? A feel? The whole pie?"

"'The whole pie'? That's positively pornographic. What's with you today? He is referring to the night the lights went out and I tore my suit."

But Ira felt guilty; I could see it in his pate. Whosoever looketh on a woman to lust after her hath committed adultery with her already in his heart, if he getteth the whole pie or no.

"Oh," said Ruth. "Do you think it was roaches in the outlet?"

"If any animal is stupid enough to fry itself, it's the cockroach. It's got a brain about the size of the head of a pin."

Oh, Ira, whosoever shall say, Thou art a pinhead, shall be in danger of hellfire.

Ira reset the board. "Did you kiss her?" said Ruth. "I wouldn't blame you. She's awfully cute."

"You think so? Then you do it. Hey, there's a knight missing." Ira looked on the mantel, then on the floor in front of it. "Here it is, right in the corner," he said, bending down. Then he recoiled and his voice changed. "Oh, my God. This is disgusting." He trotted into the kitchen and returned with the ammonia and a paper towel.

"Did the horsie make chips?" Ruth said. He gingerly picked up the piece, one finger on the mane, thumb on the felt, and saturated it. "Careful! You're spraying me!" she said.

Grimacing, Ira wiped the piece clean. "Do you know what was on it? Roach guts. The body is still on the floor."

I looked down. It was Columbo. Yet again I had witnessed the last loss.

"If you think you're disgusted, think how the roach feels," said Ruth.

Oh, Father, we do Thy bidding and destroy idols that offend Thee. Why dost Thou charge us such a price?

Ira said, "You kill them and kill them and they keep coming back. It's like they generate spontaneously out of plaster. Would you mind scooping up that body?"

"I'd love to, but I've sworn not to touch your chess things."

"Great." He folded the paper towel several times, and with head averted pinched it up. Straight-armed, he walked toward the kitchen.

Watching Columbo carried off by a wrinkled-nosed, goose-stepping Legal Aid lawyer made something in me snap. I felt as if I were awaking from a long, tortured sleep. As I had on my very first day, I stepped out of the book—this time for good. What love could I ever have expected, however deep my piety and far-ranging my forgiveness, from a human god? As my first friend's remains crepitated between Ira's fingers, I thought of the steer that had been last night's dinner, the sheep who gave his skin to keep Ruth warm, even the alligator assigned to baby Rufus's corns. We were all just sacrificial fodder for this frail, cruel kind. How had I ever thought we could be more?

By an honest mistake I had wandered into the wrong flock, and now I had to leave. If you have honor, Father, close fairly with me. I have served you truly, if briefly. You say to us: ask, and it shall be given you. I ask.

FATHER DENIED me the first week, and the third, but I continued to believe in our covenant. After a month my zeal was greater than ever. And on the fifth Sabbath, Father delivered unto me, and I rejoiced. We were even.

It was Saturday morning. Ira was still getting dressed when the doorbell rang. As he danced into his pants, the polyethylene packet of cocaine he had bought from Rufus the previous night fell from his pocket. The moment Ruth followed him out of the room, I pushed it behind one of the bed legs. The impact of the fall opened one end of the zip-lock seal. Perfect.

The conversation in the living room concluded with Ira saying, "We'll go with you." As soon as the door closed I got to work.

I had gone my whole life without tasting a single grain of cocaine. Now I had a trove. From habit I tasted the powder first with my outer sensors, which don't ingest. I detected two substances, one like mother's milk, the other bitter, caustic. This had to be the cocaine. I was amazed that anyone would ingest it, let alone pay so dearly for it.

The grains of lactose and cocaine were different sizes and textures, so I could easily sort them. The lactose was smooth and luscious, melting on my tongue with little pops, inflaming a hunger in me that I could not restrain. It radiated through me, suffusing me with energy. The cocaine I was happy to set aside.

I was a believer again—lactose was my new god. A wise and perfect food, I couldn't imagine that my body would ever again tolerate anything else. I dove deeper into the bag. The powder felt like a hundred nymphs massaging my underside. The hundred dollars per gram that Ira was paying for my pleasure did nothing to diminish it.

My strength was prodigious. I could jump now, really spring. The refrigerator handle, the wall cabinets, the raisin bran box, anything was mine. Bring on the water bugs. Give me a hold of Ira's short hairs and I'd make him mine. My mouth parts continued to move, but I could no longer feel them. I licked my mandibles furiously, compulsively. My heart sped. I rocked back and forth. For the first time since I had bedded Ruth my wing muscles were twitching. How had I lived so long without this stuff?

Seen through the polyethylene pouch, the bedroom was clouded and distorted. Hadn't I spent most of my life similarly hooded, by the brand of cowardice and confusion Ira and his library had taught me? It was ironic that it had taken a man-made packet of man-refined sugar to make me see the truth—that I, the history of this apartment, was its future. Sure, Ira and Ruth visited a few hours every night, but that gave them no more claim than the shadows which visited each day. My petty rebelliousness had acknowledged Ira's false truth; from this day forward I denied it. I could no longer fear him.

One last time I climbed to the mantel, thrilled by my fabulous strength. On the stumps of the Sabbath candles I rubbed my forelegs until they wore long gloves of wax.

Stifflegged I made my way to the bathroom. Behind the tub, up on the window sill, sat a flock of cans and bottles—cleansers, detergents, and disinfectants, Ira's stock in trade. At the very back I found the Drano.

I had always liked this can, with it's red hemispheric high-security top that looked like a mosquito-tracking radar. Opening it required a hard downward thumb and simultaneous upward tug. Ruth struggled with it every time, spilling powder onto the shoulder of the can, where the raised perimeter held it.

I picked up a grain of sodium hydroxide with my wax-protected forelegs. It was quite a bit bigger than the grains in the packet. Would Ira be tipped off? No, I could always trust in his need to think nothing ill of Rufus.

The severe handicap of walking on three legs was more than offset by the power of lactose, as I carried the grain down the tiles and back to the bedroom. I put the grain in the bag and took another hit of the wonderful sugar. The room pulsed with excitement. Lightning shot from the closets.

Though I spent the afternoon in continuous transport, I hadn't accumulated much of a pile of sodium hydroxide when Ira and Ruth returned.

While they cooked and ate their fatty, greasy food I buried myself in lactose, to filter out nauseous gases and indigestible prattle. I wasn't about to let Ira provoke me now.

He tried hard. It was no accident that he perpetrated coitus tonight, when I was right beneath them. It might have been safe to resume my rounds, but I wasn't taking any chances with this mission. The bed groaned and squeaked, and they unleashed their most punishing vocabulary. "Oh God! . . . Don't stop, lover. . . Never! . . . This is so nice. . . I love you. . . I love you too. . ."

I calmly waited them out. When the snoring began I set out again. My circuit became an exact repetition; I counted every step, thrilled with my precision. The pile of drain opener in the plastic packet grew.

Shortly after sunup I retired under the bed. Feet descended to slippers, and Ira shuffled to the bathroom. When he returned I sensed that something was wrong. He had looked behind the tub. He knew.

He *thwocked* down the hall, and I knew he would return armed with poison. I would not run. He would have to come get me.

He returned with two mugs.

Sleepily, Ruth said, "Oh, thank you, sweetheart."

"I slept awful," said Ira. "My back is killing me."

"Poor baby. Did you take Tylenol?"

Finally they got up and dressed, and the stench of breakfast began. I burrowed deeper into the lactose, my body charging, antennae whipping up a mist of powder.

I didn't venture out until the front door slammed. By noon I had moved every particle of lye from the rim of the can to the bedroom.

Together the cocaine and sodium hydroxide made a puny packet. Despite all I had eaten, the biggest pile, by far, was lactose. I could not bear the idea of my ambrosia crusting on Ira's snotty schnoz hairs. I spent the remainder of the afternoon moving grains of lactose to the rubber coaster beneath the bed leg, where they would be safe from the vacuum cleaner. Then I mixed the cocaine and lye. Very puny indeed. But Ira would find Rufus an excuse.

I pulled the packet into the middle of the bedroom floor and returned to my niche to await the millennium.

IRA AND RUTH came home late in the afternoon. He approached the bedroom twice, but only on his way to piss. It wasn't until bedtime that he came in. One shoe grazed the packet as he watched himself undress in the mirror. Look down, schmuck! Step on it, and you're out a hundred big ones. He turned, the packet right between his shoes, and sat down on the bed. "I'll be damned." Shaking his head, he picked it up. A few toots before turning in, Ira? Rough day at Bloomie's? But he put the packet in the drawer of his night table.

The longer the wait, the sweeter. Take your time, Ira. I'll be here.

But it was not an easy week for me. I lived on the sugar, which left me constantly charged. I paced furiously and slept badly. I was enraged by the way Ira squandered his evenings.

Friday at last. This was the off Sabbath: no company, no purchase, no responsibilities. After dinner Ruth went to take a bath and wash her hair. While the water was running, Ira appeared in the bedroom. He took the packet.

The accoutrements were out when I reached the living room. Ira was pouring my treat onto the pocket mirror. Unconcerned, he chopped the different-sized grains into a uniform powder. The razor blade screeched against the glass as he pushed the powder into cemetery rows. He rolled up a bill.

Would he share the treat with Ruth? I had thought about this. Yes, she was less fastidious, more accepting, more of an animal than he was. But then, she should know her survival was her own concern. What did she care for me? Where was she when the colony was massacred? She was the spirit behind the renovation, and of course the Tupperware. If I had to get her to get him, so be it.

Ira did call her, but not loudly enough for her to hear. The pig. With a shrug he leaned over the mirror. The powder seemed to disappear into one of Andrew Jackson's ears and fly out the other, into Ira's big beak.

He shot upright so fast that his chair nearly tipped over. His left hand grabbed the bridge of his nose. He said hoarsely, "Wow!" Eyes shut tightly and teeth clenched in pain, he still managed to smile. What could the fool have been thinking? That Rufus had finally accepted him, given him a dose of the real ghetto stuff?

Smitten in one nostril, Ira now turned the other nostril too, and his septum began dissolving from both sides. He straightened again, wiping streams of tears from his cheeks. But over the hard, clenched teeth, his mottled lips still smiled. I was enraged! I wanted him to realize exactly what was happening, to know the terror he had so generously dispensed. I wanted to see him pinwheeling on the ground in agony and mortal fear. I wanted him to look up through his tears and know I was his conqueror.

I was confounded when Ira lowered his face once more, but if this was way to defy me, so be it. As he inhaled, the first drop of blood fell to the mirror, but his tears hid it from him. The second drop landed on his hand. He lifted it to his glasses, then tentatively touched his finger to a nostril.

Blood suspended there by surface tension ran down into his palm. His spectacled lemur eyes stared, terrified. Yes, Ira, this time the blood is yours.

He turned his head toward the bathroom and opened his mouth. Nothing came out. His facial muscles twitched wildly. Bowing his head, he tightened his grip on the bridge of his nose. His face and his pate were dark red. Veins bulged from his neck, and a little curly one rose on his temple.

Blood flowed down over his lips and chin and dripped onto his crisp white shirt, where crimson tracers grew fat and fuzzy. Ira pawed them, leaving a gory grid. Did he finally understand that he wouldn't have to worry about the laundry anymore?

Grasping the table, Ira rose like a drunk. His eyes now just running slits, he scanned the room. Blood on the mirror, blood on his shirt, blood on the white brocade of the chair. He looked at his bloody palm, his bloody quivering fingers. He picked up the mirror and shattered it against the wall. Powder dusted the carpet. "Nigger!" he cried.

"What?" called Ruth from the tub.

Ira took a step toward her. But the sodium hydroxide was boring toward his brain, and he got no closer. His left knee buckled. He spun and his head plunged for the floor, striking a chord of daring dissonance on the edge of the table. Over the muted bass of skull meeting metal was the percussive tenor of his popping nose cartilage, the high tinkling of postmodern knick-knacks on the tabletop, and the cymbal crash of his shattering glasses. *Exultate!*

His head bounced once, and he rolled and hit the floor face up, unconscious. New cataracts of blood from his right eye and the gash across his temple joined the ones from his nose, running to the carpet.

I heard a soft burbling. Sour, half-digested chicken and rice rose slowly but forcefully into his mouth and ran down his cheek. It would have been just like Ira to hedge, to turn the other cheek too. But he had an even more cowardly and profane act in mind. He coughed, forming bubbles which rose and popped, shooting two droplets from his mouth to his forehead. Already circumcised and bar mitzvahed, he now anointed himself with vomitus, in extreme unction.

The afterlife would offer him no forgiveness, and I would not give him even the temporary comfort of hoping for it. I climbed onto his forehead and swabbed away the bitter fluid. When the unclean spirit is gone out of a man, he walketh through dry places, seeking rest, and findeth none.

Spasms convulsed his chest. His hegemony over his body was gone as surely as if he had been sprayed. His seditious arms twitched goodbye when they could have gone to his mouth and saved him. The cough faded into his chest. His left eye was glassy, shocked, perplexed. The other eye, lacerated by the broken glasses, was crusted with blood and humors. Remember, Ira: if thy right eye offend thee, pluck it out, and cast it from thee, for it is profitable for thee that one of thy members should perish, and not that thy whole body should be cast into hell. But here's the rub, old man. Since you can't pluck it, you're going.

My legs ached, so I went back to the bedroom for a charge of lactose. Ruth was still in the tub, singing: "No handsome face could ever take the place of My Guy. . ."

I returned to the living room and took a path of crust up Ira's chin. A stench of lye-burnt flesh and vomit lay over his face. The skin around his lips was turning blue, a great improvement over his usual pasty, pinkish gray.

Over a dusky cheek I walked toward the glasses. The left eye was glassier still. Now perhaps Ira saw me, huge and hairy, dominating his vision as I dominated his destiny. I jumped up and down on the lens, hoping his optic nerve had survived long enough to take my image to hell. Or maybe I would keep him here, for roaches and worms and mites to turn into shit and progeny.

I stayed on the lens until all motion had stopped. Blood had crusted to brown ribbons all over his face. The air around his mouth and nose was foul but still. I walked down onto his neck and put my antennae to his carotid artery. Nothing. I was free. The apartment was mine. I climbed back to the lens, and caught a reflection of myself over Ira's dead eye. And I said to us both, "Thou shalt give life for life, eye for eye, tooth for tooth, hand for hand, foot for foot, burning for burning, wound for wound, stripe for stripe."

The bathroom door creaked. "Ira, honey, could you bring me my bag? It's on the kitchen counter. Thank you."

I rapelled down a nostril hair, took a bloody trail to the floor, and headed back for a lactose bracer.

"I need my purse, Ira. Please, honey, I'm wet. Do you mind? Ira?"

"WHO ANSWERED THE DOOR?"

"Sometimes I did, sometimes Ira did."

"Where did you take him?"

"We usually had company in the living room when he arrived, so he'd come in and say hello. Sometimes he sat down for a few minutes."

"And then?"

"Then Ira and Rufus went into the kitchen to do their business. They always did that alone."

"This was after dinner?"

"Yes."

"OK, we're going to have to cook something. Who was the company?"

"The Wainscotts, our neighbors. But they had nothing to do with it."

"You see, Ruth, this is the thing. Everything's got to be normal when he walks in so he don't get raised up and run for it. If he's used to seeing the Wainwrights he should see the Wainwrights. Are they cool? Could they act normal when Rufus comes in?"

Ruth paused. "No, I don't think they could, to tell you the truth." She wiped her eyes, which were red and swollen.

"Did you have anything special out that he could see? Candy dishes or anything?"

"There were pastries and coffee in the living room, but you can't see that from here. Otherwise, just the Sabbath candles."

"Excuse my ignorance, but is that a Sabbath candle, the one in the glass?"

"No, that's for the dead."

"You think we could move it out of sight, just for an hour or so?"

She put her hand to her mouth. "Yes, I think it would be all right."

"Do you know where Rufus carries his gun? Have you seen a bulge under his armpit, in his belt, around his ankle?"

"Well, he never takes off his coat."

"Tell me, is this the only door to the apartment, or is there a fire door or a big window you could escape through?"

"Just the front door."

He pulled out a portable radio. "Dracula to blood bank. Set up the table on the fourth floor. All business comes in the front."

The radio crackled with static. "Copy, Dracula. I'm on my way. Call if you get thirsty. Jefferson is going to wait for the Roto-Rooter man at the bank. 10-4."

His partner, who had been looking over the apartment, returned to the front hallway. "This is the only door."

"No shit, O'Connell. You think the lady don't know that?"

"Just cause she know it don't mean you know it, DiNunzio."

"Well, I know it."

"Now you know it twice." O'Connell returned to the living room.

"OK, Ruth. This is what we're going to do. First of all, I don't want you making no phone calls or standing by the windows till he gets here. Just for security."

"What do you think I'm going to do, detective, tip off the man who killed my lover?"

"Just standard procedure. You know. Now, when you answer the door you got to get him inside far enough so me or O'Connell can get between him and the door. We'll take it from there. And the most important thing is this, Ruth: get the hell out of there. I don't want you getting hurt."

"Just tell me what you want me to say."

"Tell him to come into the kitchen. Tell him Ira's been feeling a little sick, and you gotta see if he's OK in the bathroom. Call Ira's name, and then get down the hall and stay there. All right, let's try it. I'll be Rufus."

"I'll be Ruth," said Ruth. I felt a stab of sympathy. She was a noble woman. "Just one more thing, detective. What makes you think he'll come back here?"

"Nothing's for sure in this business, Ruth. But I seen it lots of time when perps think they're so smart they'll never get caught and we're so dumb we'll never catch them. Those are the ones we catch."

While they rehearsed, I went to the living room. O'Connell was playing with the chessboard, jumping the pieces as if they were checkers.

I heard Ruth open the refrigerator, and a few minutes later the oven door squeaked and slammed. DiNunzio joined O'Connell in the living room. He moved the memorial candle to the window ledge as they discussed the positions they'd take for the collar. Now they had to wait.

DiNunzio opened his gym bag and tossed a white vest to O'Connell. "Might as well put these mothers on."

"I love spending Friday nights waiting for an armed and dangerous. Saves me from going out and eating too much pussy. I'm on a diet," said DiNunzio.

"Where is that broad?"

"In the kitchen."

"Is there a phone in there?"

"No. Relax."

"Relax," said O'Connell. He pulled out his revolver and spun the cylinder, checking the chambers. "You get a look at the caboose on her? Boy, did she get smacked with the ugly stick. I'm telling you, this ain't no homicide, it's a suicide." He put the gun back.

"Dumbest Hymie I ever heard of doing himself like that. You see the report on the stiff?" DiNunzio made a grim face as he pulled out the radio. He identified himself. "Waiting for perp. Have adequate floor plan. 10–4."

"When chicks get that fat the skin folds up, and mold and shit grows in there. It's fucking disgusting."

"Nothing wrong with flesh," said DiNunzio. "You know what they say: more cushion for the pushing."

"You fucking dagos. Nothing's too big for you."

And so their conversation went for nearly an hour. The smell of roast chicken was powerful now; resourceful Ruth had spiced it more heavily than usual. I began to wonder whether Rufus would show. He'd probably been tipped off two weeks ago by his network; as he always said, he was a businessman.

But at his usual time of arrival, the radio hissed on. "Calling Dracula. Man fitting script entering building: black male, tall, thin, in long green leather coat. Following him in. 10–4."

Ruth trotted into the living room. "That's him!"

The detectives flew off the sofa. O'Connell threw the gym bag behind the sofa. DiNunzio said, "OK, Ruth, nice and calm, everything's normal. Ask him into the kitchen, and pretend to check on Ira in the bathroom. It's gonna be easy."

She wrung her hands. "Should I turn off the chicken?"

"Don't worry about the chicken, Ruth. Just think about what you're doing. We'll be right there with you." I followed her back to the kitchen. The detectives hid nearby.

The doorbell rang. She took a deep breath, then went to answer. "Hello, Rufus."

"What's doin?" The door closed behind him. "Somethin' wrong with your eyes?"

"Oh," she said, dabbing at them. "Ira got me with the bug spray. It was an accident. He's not himself; he's got the runs. Come on into the kitchen, and I'll see if I can get him out of the bathroom without a disaster."

Rufus went into the kitchen unsuspecting, hands in pockets, humming. Ruth walked too fast toward the bathroom, obviously upset, but Rufus wasn't watching her. DiNunzio crept up the hall in his Nikes and O'Connell blocked the other end. Simultaneously they showed their shields with their left hands, guns drawn and cocked in their right. "Police," said DiNunzio.

Rufus was stunned. "What the fuck. . ."

He was cuffed and led to the door. DiNunzio said, "The bartender from Reggie's is in the morgue. Another client of yours, ain't he? He went out just like Mr. Fishblatt. Want to talk about it?"

We had risen!

RUTH HAD BEEN brave. Through all the forensic work, the busy week of Shiva, the phone calls and letters, she had been dry-eyed and controlled. Now the incident was closed; there was no more to do, and her suppressed grief overwhelmed her. She wailed, tears spotting her skirt. When she quieted and I thought she was spent, she would suddenly burst out with even greater intensity.

Watching from the doorway, I found the scene so heartbreaking that I almost regretted what I had done. I wanted to retire to the silence and solitude of the wall. But then I looked around at the huge airy spaces of the rooms, the furniture, the windows. I had won the apartment, not just the inside of a wall. All this was mine.

Perhaps best of all, I had won Ruth, as the ancient Hebrews won the women of the cities they conquered. I would keep her, and treat her gently, sensitively, but firmly, as Ira never had and never could. She would learn to obey me. She would come to love me. But if she refused me, I would dispose of her. I had reinherited the earth.

I climbed up her back and onto her head as she continued to sob. I stroked her hair. "Don't you worry, darling," I whispered. "There, there."

Ghost of Chance
William S. Burroughs
1-85242-406-0

Minus Time
Catherine Bush
1-85242-408-7

Tricks
Renaud Camus
1-85242-414-1

Somewhere in Advance of Nowhere
Jayne Cortez
1-85242-422-2

Endf of the Story
Lydia Davis
1-85242-420-6

Break It Down
Lydia Davis
1-85242-421-4

Powerless
Tim Dlugos
1-85442-407-9

You Got to Burn to Shine
John Giorno
1-85242-321-8

Margery Kempe
Robert Glück
1-85242-334-X

Jack the Modernist
Robert Glück
1-85242-333-1

To the Friend Whho Did Not Save My Life
Hérve Guibert
1-85242-328-5

Slow Death
Stewart Home
1-85242-519-9

Rent Boy
Gary Indiana
1-85242-324-2

Gone Tomorrow
Gary Indiana
1-85242-336-6

Haruko/Love Poems
June Jordan
1-85242-323-4

Stripping
Pagan Kennedy
1-85242-322-6

Spinsters
Pagan Kennedy
1-85242-405-2

The Medicine Burns
Adam Klein
1-85242-403-6

House Rules
Heather Lewis
1-85242-413-3

Bombay Talkie
Ameena Meer
1-85242-325-0

Armed Response
Ann Rower
1-85242-415-X

Nearly Roadkill
Caitlin Sullivan and Kate Bomstein
1-85242-418-4

Haunted Houses
Lynne Tillman
1-85242-400-1

Answer Song
David Trinidad
1-85242-329-3

Bedside Manners

Luisa Valenzuela

1-85242-313-7

The Roaches Have No King

Daniel Weiss

1-85242-326-9

Dear Dead Person and Other Stories

Benjamin Weissman

1-85242-330-7

SERPENT'S TAIL